MW01148418

THE SIN KEEPER

JORDAN QUEST FBI THRILLER SERIES BOOK 2

GARY WINSTON BROWN

This is a work of fiction. Names, characters, places, and incidents – and their usage for storytelling purposes – are crafted for the singular purpose of fictional entertainment and no absolute truths shall be derived from the information contained within. Locales, businesses, companies, events, government institutions, law enforcement agencies and private or educational institutions are used for atmospheric, entertainment and fictional purposes only. Furthermore, any resemblance or reference to persons living or dead is used fictitiously for atmospheric, entertainment and fictional purposes.

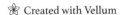 Created with Vellum

YOUR FREE BOOK IS WAITING

As a way of saying thank you for downloading this book (or box set), I'm offering a free book when you sign up for my spam-free newsletter. You'll also be the first to hear about upcoming releases, sales, and insider information.

JORDAN QUEST is the prequel novella to the Jordan Quest FBI thriller series and is available exclusively to newsletter subscribers.

Visit GaryWinstonBrown.com to sign up now and get your FREE book.

This book is dedicated to my beautiful wife, Fiona.
I'm lucky to have you in my life and in my corner.

ILYBBOBKS...ATS

"Men heap together the mistakes of their lives, and create a monster they call destiny."

— JOHN HOBBES

1

JORDAN QUEST WALKED through the ornately styled double doors and into the grand foyer of the Rosenfeld mansion. Of the two handcrafted Swarovski crystal inlays, one remained intact within its frame. The shattered fragments of its counterpart lay strewn across the expansive marble floor and twinkled like precious gems. The air felt thick, heavy, pungent, metallic, yet oddly aromatic; stale blood mixed with the smell of fresh cut roses. The flowers covered the main floor. Shadows darted into corners and escaped under tables, chased into hiding by the effusion of predawn light cascading down through the skylight of the domed cathedral ceiling. Jordan picked up one of the roses. The flower felt fresh, its petals velvet smooth to the touch, stem firm. Jordan walked around the unusual flower arrangement. She stood on the landing at the foot of the grand staircase and ran her fingers along the brass handrail, reading the latent psychic energy signature of the house:

One intruder... male... cat-quick from the entrance to the master bedroom. Two victims; one male, one female, middle-

aged. No time to react. Confusion in the acknowledgment of the intrusion, then sheer terror. He feels empowered, amped up, fueled from having achieved complete and total domination over them. She was an obstacle, her execution matter of fact, a single shot to the head, left temporal region. The male was the intended target. With him he took his time, fed on his total subjugation and incapacitating fear which the man confirmed with the sudden release of his bladder. Horror now, reflected in the man's eyes as he tries to rationalize the reality of his wife's instantaneous death. He advances quickly on the target, weapon pointed straight ahead, a pull of the trigger with every step. Thwup - one muffled gunshot to the left leg... thwup - one to the right shoulder... thwup - a third round, center mass... thwup - a fourth and final to the middle of the forehead. At the dead man's bedside now... not finished... not yet... not even close. Make the bastard suffer even more whether he can feel it or not. Take more, more, more. He draws a blade deep across his neck, ear to ear... near decapitation. So much blood. Quiet now... the silence is deafening.

There was something about the dead man's mouth...

Releasing her fingers from the railing, Jordan climbed the stairs. Special Agent Chris Hanover followed close behind.

"The place has been cleared," Hanover informed his partner. "Forensics was told to hold off until you completed your walk-through. Jesus, Jordan, you ever seen anything like this before? And what's with all the flowers?"

Jordan halted, raised her hand, made a fist. Hanover removed his sidearm from its holster. He placed his hand on his partner's shoulder and tapped it gently: a signal that he would follow her lead. An orange glow flickered at the top of the staircase past where the light from the grand dome could not penetrate, animating the hallway in a serpentine dance of shadow and light. Beyond the balcony the entrance to the west wing remained dark.

Jordan and Chris climbed the stairs. The hall, constructed of Sensacell glass, illuminated under the pressure of each step, and lit the way ahead. In the downstairs foyer the sunrise brought to life the floor-to-ceiling murals which graced the semi-circular walls of the grand entrance.

Movement in the corridor ahead... the rise and fall of a shadow, interrupted by the ebb and flow of dancing candlelight. The shape twisted and turned, then retreated quickly down the corridor.

Jordan drew her weapon and whispered to her partner. "I thought you were told the place had been cleared."

"I was," Hanover replied.

"Apparently not. You ready?"

"Yeah."

"Go."

The agents rushed along the balcony to the adjoining stone-floor corridor and cleared the corner, moving fast, staying quiet. Dozens of votives lined the long hallway. The light from their unsteady flames shuddered and blinked with the brush of air created by the passing agents. Ahead, the doors to the bedroom stood open. Jordan gestured to Chris to cover the right side of the hall as they approached the entrance. Together they breached the room.

The large waiting area of the master bedroom was a veritable showroom of fine art and antiquities. Matching Eileen Gray reading chairs flanked a beautiful handmade Chippendale desk. Ruby-red droplets glistened on the gleaming white surface of a diamond-accented Plume Blanche sofa and trailed evenly across the floor through the main entrance into the master bedroom. In the far corner of the room a glass display case featured priceless artifacts from the Ming dynasty, brilliantly adorned with natural pearl, sapphire, and turquoise gemstones. Two focal pieces were positioned prominently on a feature wall. The first was "Pont Neuf," an oil painting by the famed French artist, Renoir. The second was a page from Leonardo Da Vinci's manuscript of scientific writings, "Codex Leicester," mounted in a vacuum glass frame. Laser beam mounts installed in both the floor and ceiling indicated the artifacts were protected by a high-tech security system. Jordan recognized the pieces from FBI Criminal Investigation Field Alerts as artifacts suspected of being stolen by a fine art and collectibles theft-to-order ring. If the pieces in this room were real, and not excellent reproductions, their value would be in the hundreds of millions of dollars. Their presence here might also shed light on the motive for the murders.

Movement from inside the master bedroom now; a faint *thump-thump-thump* on the marble floor, followed by the sound of falling boxes. Jordan glanced at her partner. Chris had heard it too. He motioned with his weapon for them to move further into the bedroom.

The agents moved quickly through the open doors, Jordan covering the left side of the room, Hanover the right. On a blood-soaked California King bed lay the bodies of Itzhak Rosenfeld and his wife, Zahava. The woman lay across from her husband, her expression in death one of wide-eyed horror, accentuated by a bullet hole in the left side of her head. Her outstretched right hand, covered in rivers of dried blood, bone shards and fragments of brain matter, lay inches below the button to a panic alarm integrated into the headboard. Itzhak Rosenfeld had been attacked while reading. He sat slumped forward, mouth ajar, eyes open. Blood from a bullet hole in his forehead and a deep laceration to his neck ran down his left arm and pooled around a copy of *Medical Patent Law* which lay on the floor beside him. He had received three additional bullet wounds, one to his right shoulder, a second to his left leg, and a third to the middle of his chest, confirming Jordan's psychic reading taken from the first-floor handrail.

To the right of the deceased, a mirrored hallway led to a walk-in closet and immense dressing room. Its white marble floor was streaked with blood, as though the body of a third victim, yet to be discovered, had been dragged across it.

Hanover covered the right side of the corridor as the agents advanced toward the open room. Short of the threshold, motion sensors tripped the lighting system and brought the dressing room to life.

The luxuriously appointed room featured matching wardrobes, hers on the left, his on the right. Two Eames lounge chairs occupied the common area between them. Each respective wardrobe featured pull out racks for jackets and pants, an automated shoe carousel, numerous shelves, drawers to accommodate foldable clothing and accessories, and bullet resistant Armortex jewelry cases requiring key code access. The cabinet on Itzhak's side of the room showcased an extensive collection of luxury watches which included Patek Phillipe, Jaeger-LeCoultre, Vacheron and Ulysse Nardin. The second case, Zahava's, featured diamond bracelets, pendants, chokers, and necklaces from Van Cleef & Arpels, Graff, Bulgari and Mikimoto.

On Itzhak's side of the room four of five mirrored bifold doors were closed.

The bloody drag marks ended at the opening to the fifth.

Jordan trained her Glock on the door. Hanover threw it open.

The closet contained clothes as well as storage boxes.

Two of the boxes lay toppled over, their contents scattered across the floor. Switching on his flashlight, Hanover rested his service weapon atop his wrist and panned the tight beam over the discarded envelopes and papers.

From behind the boxes came an unsettling cry. The two agents stepped back and trained their weapons into the small room.

Two red eyes peered out from behind the fallen containers. A Golden Retriever pup stepped out of the shadows and into the light, its blonde coat matted with dried blood. The dog sat at Jordan's feet and whined pitifully, perhaps believing that it was about to meet the same terminal fate that had befallen its masters whom but a few short hours ago had been the center of its universe.

2

THERE IS COMFORT in the darkness. Shadows reach out from the corners of the room in which he hides, shape-shifting allies that serve to camouflage him from those he knows will be coming soon, duty-bound to capture or kill him. His actions within the last seventy-two hours have been unequivocally unacceptable, yet he is unaware that they are entirely out of his control.

Commander Ben Egan unscrewed and pocketed the silencer from the barrel of his SIG P226 MK-25 sidearm. The sound suppressor jingled against the shell casings he had retrieved from the master bedroom of the mansion he had visited last night. He removed the spent rounds and wrapped them in a swath of discarded cloth, returned them to his pocket, ejected and inspected the clip, and replenished the weapon to full capacity.

In the abandoned furniture factory in which he has taken refuge dozens of broken yellow and grey-stained windows hung precariously in rusted metal frames. Despite the passage of time, the odor of cleaning solvents, furniture polish and burnt machine oil from manufacturing equipment long since fallen into disrepair assaulted his senses. Spray-painted obscenities phosphoresced against the crumbling gray brick walls, cursing at him, then dripped down the wall, diluted by the pre-dawn light of a new day.

Here, in the farthest corner of the building, he has heaped together a rat's nest of a bed comprised of the discarded end-cuts of sofa fabric and industrial cotton batting. A sackcloth bag stuffed with cleaning rags and Styrofoam chips serves as a pillow, a tattered shipping blanket for covers. Stacks of wooden shipping pallets jut out from the wall in front of him, his hiding place, further framed by the north and west factory walls. This buttress does not serve to keep out would-be trespassers but rather provides the tactical advantage of a slat wall through which he can see yet remain hidden from view when they arrive in search of him, compromise his hideaway, and force him to stand his ground.

He found this place in the early hours of the morning after stealing an unlocked floral supply van in Thousand Oaks and leaving the Rosenfeld's with the gift of death in their lavish Hollywood Hills home. He doesn't know the reason why their death was deemed to be necessary, nor does he care. All he knows is that he was under orders to terminate them and that it was impossible for him to disregard the directive.

Filament-fastened to the projecting shelf of reality, Commander Egan closed his eyes and descended the silicon escarpment and complex micro-passageways of his computer-enhanced mind, reviewing the target termination requirements downloaded to his brain. All in order. Still, he is unable to shake the feeling that these kills were overtly personal.

His body is suddenly racked by an unfamiliar sensation: *pain*. He tries to convince himself that the feeling isn't real, merely an anomaly of his augmented central nervous system, but he cannot. The sensation is palpable, tactile. He is acutely aware that his mind is being accessed. He knows this because he has reached out in this same manner countless times in the course of his training, slipping undetected into the mind of his targets, both foreign and domestic: fanatical militants, corrupt government attaches, traitorous politicians, questionable business leaders... anyone his government believes could constitute even the slightest threat to national security... and extracts from them their most deeply guarded secrets, doing so without the need for psychoactive, sedative, narcoanalytic drug interrogation or torture, but rather by opening their mind to his. He then examines its contents as easily as one would retrieve a folder from an unlocked filing cabinet and records their secrets: identities of deep cover assets, high-value assassination targets, and classified field activity. Strategic support data and EYES ONLY intelligence reports flip through his mind like memory-testing flashcards. He records it all. When he is finished his target will be completely unaware that such an infiltration had ever taken place and will never have known their vulnerability. To them, they were simply recalling a memory.

Deep within his brain, psychological anti-tampering protocols have been established which he has been trained to initiate in the unlikely event of capture, though the bioaugmentation scientists at the Defense Advanced Research Projects Agency argued that such action would never become necessary. He recognizes the pain, another test, and struggles to recall his brain neural interface key; the *lock-down* code with which he has been provided, but he is incapable of accessing the word. He can sense the presence of the tester as he probes his mind. This one has been the deepest yet. It is evident to him the tester wants to tear him down, to break him. His head feels like it is on fire. If it were possible for him to feel pain in his brain this would be the equivalent of a psychological autopsy.

Never before has he experienced a test of such magnitude.

Once again, he struggles to recall the lock-down code and regain control of his faculties. His body has become incapacitated, feels as heavy as lead, and he knows he has no choice but to succumb to the test. He wonders if this is the end. They had warned him: *failure equals death.*

Should he die here and now, he knows his very existence will be disavowed. The specifics of the project for which he has been selected and in which he will play a pivotal role are known only to his handlers and the president of the United States. For these reasons he is viewed by his government as both a top-secret asset and an expendable risk to national security.

He always assumed that his death would come in the form of close quarter combat behind enemy lines. Never like this.

For the first time in his life he is aware of a complex and unsettling emotion: fear.

Finally, he recalls the code, *GENESIS*, and initiates the neural lockdown protocol. With the sudden cessation of the pain comes an incredible feeling of lightness and release.

He stared at the thin bracelet secured to his wrist. At the commencement of his training his handlers had informed him of its tremendous potential and that the extent of its powers would soon be revealed to him.

His ability to successfully defend against the intrusion into his mind signified the passing of the first phase of field testing.

Project Channeler was a go.

3

———

THE FRIGHTENED, BLOOD covered pup rolled on its back and pawed at Jordan's shoes.

Jordan ignored the dog and kept her gun trained on the open closet. Hanover swept his weapon and flashlight side to side and overhead in search of a suspect. Satisfied they were safe he holstered his gun.

"We're good," Chris said, "but look at this." He parted the clothes in Zahava's middle closet.

Jordan holstered her Glock and picked up the nervous puppy. The gold-embossed letters of her name, LUCY, were barely recognizable against the dog's blood-stained leather collar. Cradled in Jordan's arms, Lucy licked her face with her warm wet tongue. The pup let out a prolonged yawn, followed by *arooop!*

Hanover shone his flashlight on a red button flush-mounted into the back wall of the dead woman's closet.

"Panic room button?" Jordan asked.

Hanover nodded. "Probably. Homes like these usually have an escape room for use in the event of an emergency or home invasion. Considering the size of this place I'd bet there are more than one."

Chris pressed the button. With a whirring sound, the back wall of the closet clicked open, revealing a vault-like entrance door. Hanover spun the small wheel in the center of the door, heard the deadbolts release, then pushed it open and stepped inside. To his left, an orange keypad glowed. The room lights came on. Adjacent to the keypad a red plunger button with the words EMERGENCY: PRESS TO SEAL blinked rapidly.

"Hitting that button will close the door and put the room into lockdown," he said. "Nobody gets in after that."

"Too bad they never got the chance to use it," Jordan said. She stepped over the threshold and followed her partner into the room. Lucy's tail thumped softly against her leather jacket. The dog sniffed the air.

In keeping with the Rosenfeld's penchant for all things luxurious the panic room too was well appointed. A glass panel integrated into the wall provided an unobstructed view of the master bedroom.

"Two-way mirror," Jordan said. "Probably bullet- and fireproof. They'd be able to see everything that was going on in the bedroom from in here."

"And know when it was safe to leave," Hanover said. He pointed to an impressive bank of wall-mounted computer monitors. "They've got cameras covering every square inch of this place, inside and out. There's probably a hard drive we can access. We need to get a tech team in here asap. Our guy's probably on camera."

The safe room featured a king size bed, en suite bath with tub and shower, kitchenette, a well-stocked pantry and liquor cabinet, dozens of hardcover books, computer station and laptop, floor safe, four fully charged cellular phones and a satellite phone. A home defense arsenal consisting of two Desert Eagle 50 AE's, four Glock 19 semi-automatic handguns and four Mossberg 590 short barrel shotguns was mounted on the wall to the right of the mirror. Boxes of ammunition sat on shelves below the guns. Two bulletproof Kevlar vests and shoulder holsters hung on the wall beside the weapons.

"They could have spent weeks in here if they needed to," Jordan said.

Hanover removed one of the Desert Eagles from the display rack and examined it. "The Rosenfeld's knew their weapons," he said. "This baby could punch a hole through a bad guy and take part of the wall with it."

Jordan inspected the shotguns. "Fully-loaded," she said. "Personally, I'd pass on the handguns and go straight for the Moss."

"Yeah," Chris agreed. "Folks have a tendency to get outright pissed off at you when you open up on them with a Mossberg."

Jordan returned the weapon to the rack. "Why the hell would anyone see the need to have this kind of firepower on hand?"

"Beats me," Chris replied. "We should have a look in the pantry. Maybe we'll find a couple of surface-to-air missiles between the Skippy and the Folgers."

Lucy looked up and whined.

Hanover massaged the dog behind her ears. The anxious pup settled down, closed her eyes, and began to fall asleep in Jordan's arms.

"Looks like someone's found a new friend," he said.

Lucy began to snore softly. "Poor thing must be exhausted," Jordan said. She smoothed the matted fur out of the pup's eyes. The dog cradled deeper into Jordan's embrace, hid her head under her arm, let out a muffled sigh.

"We should make arrangements for the SPCA to pick her up after Forensics has processed her for trace evidence."

Jordan shook her head. "Lucy's been through enough for one day," she said. "The last thing she needs is to be left alone again. She can stay with me and the kids until we determine if a family member can take her."

"Fine by me," Hanover agreed.

"Let's get Lucy squared away, then try to figure out just what the hell happened here."

"Agreed."

AFTER HANDING the puppy over to Forensics, Jordan and Chris returned to the master bedroom. The flames from the votives that lined the staircase and hallway had burned out. The scent of melted candle wax hung heavy in the air. The Forensics team were busy photographing the room from every angle: the hand-painted murals, grand entrance and vestibule, and the glittering shards of crystal from the broken door pane which lay on the floor. One member of the team dusted the flower petals for prints. Another bagged and processed the items.

Jordan walked back along the glass hallway and looked over the balcony at the floral arrangement in the grand entrance below.

She suddenly called out to the agents below. "Stop!"

The forensics team stood up and stepped away from the scene they were in the midst of processing.

Hanover met Jordan at the handrail. "What the hell, Jordan?"

"Chris, look down," Jordan said. "Tell me what you see."

Hanover stared at the flowers spread out over the massive foyer. "I see roses. Lots and lots of friggin' roses." He raised his hands as if to say *and your point is?*

Jordan called down. "How many roses have you guys bagged and tagged?"

Forensics Specialist Steve Reynolds replied. "Ten so far. Why?"

"Do you remember exactly where you found them, Steve?"

"Sure."

"Put them back."

"Say what?"

"Every last one of them. Exactly where you found them."

"Seriously?"

"Sorry. It might be nothing, or it could be important."

"You're in charge, Jordan," Agent Reynolds replied. "Whatever you say."

Reynolds and his team returned the flowers to their previous locations on the marble floor. When he was finished, he gave Jordan the thumbs up.

"There," Jordan said to Chris. She pointed out the pattern on the floor. "Now do you see it?"

"Well, I'll be damned."

"They form a pattern, a number: 24."

"That can't be a coincidence," Chris said.

"Not a chance," Jordan replied. She called down to Agent Reynolds. "Steve, have one of your guys come up here and photograph this."

"On it," Reynolds replied.

The full light of morning now illuminated the master bedroom and the anteroom in which the Rosenfeld's displayed their collection of priceless antiquities and works of art. Lucy's bloody paw prints mapped the panicked course she had charted as she ran from room to room following the murder of her guardians. A blood trail smeared the floor from the coagulated puddle under which Itzhak's book lay to the walk-in closet where Lucy had been found.

Jordan stooped beside Itzhak's body and examined the blood pool with her flashlight. "Lucy lay down here," she said. "That's how she ended up covered in blood. At some point she got up and went into the closet."

"She must have caught our scent or heard us coming up the stairs, got spooked, then hid in the closet."

"You know what I don't get?" Jordan questioned. "If you're going to kill Mom and Dad, why not shoot the dog, too?"

"Maybe our killer's a pet lover," Chris replied. "People, no problem. Take 'em out like targets in a shooting gallery. But dogs, cats, dwarf bunnies... not happening."

"One thing's for certain," Jordan said. "This guy was a pro." She examined the headboard and the position of the dead woman's body. "The wife received a single shot a split second after she turned her head. The approximate angle of entry and exit places the shooter a good twenty feet away. Not an easy shot to make from that distance, especially in the dark. Maybe he used a laser sight or goggles."

"Or he consumes Vitamin A, bilberry, zinc and grape seed extract by the bucket," Chris said. "Great for improving night vision."

"And you know this how?"

"Dr. Oz. I never miss a show. The man totally rocks."

Jordan smiled.

"What about the handrail?" Chris asked. "Did you get a solid reading when you touched it?"

Jordan nodded. "Mr. Rosenfeld was the intended target.

This was personal. The UNSUB wanted it messy. Look at the kill: three body shots to incapacitate, a fourth to the head, then a knife to the throat."

"Mob hit maybe?" Hanover speculated.

"Could be. Whatever business the Rosenfeld's were into it's pretty evident they made a lot of money doing it."

"Maybe they owed more than they made... to the wrong kind of people."

"That's always a possibility."

Jordan took a pair of medical examination gloves out of her jacket pocket, snapped them on, removed her flashlight, then leaned over the corpse. She lifted the dead man's head. Rosenfeld's jaw fell slack.

She remembered her earlier vision: *something about the dead man's mouth.*

A plastic object had been inserted into his mouth. Jordan removed a pen from her lapel pocket and fished out the object. It fell into his lap. She glanced at Chris.

"Flash drive," he said.

4

DR. JASON MERRICK pulled off Pacific Coast Highway 1 at Aliso Creek behind a late model Winnebago which judging by the plume of smoke pouring from its exhaust pipe could clearly benefit from a forensic examination by a local mechanic. The vehicle, so laden with mountain bikes that its rear sports rack sagged perilously close to the ground, chugged its way into the designated area of the rest stop reserved for recreational vehicles. The multitude of stickers wallpapering its rear bumper eluded that some if not all of its occupants had '*Toured the Hoover Dam*' in Nevada, '*Conquered Pikes Peak*' in Colorado, and discovered that in Nebraska '*The best girls are from Omaha.*' Here in California, the bumper sticker advised that '*98% of Californians say, 'Oh shit!' before driving off the cliff into the Pacific, while the other 2% say 'hold my beer and watch this!*'

The door to the Winnebago opened. A group of twentysomethings exited the fifth wheel; three guys, three girls, college students he assumed, and walked across the parking lot in the direction of the restroom facilities. Merrick debated whether he should follow them and bring to their attention the abysmal state of the pollution-generating monstrosity. They would benefit from hearing his invaluable advice about the negative impact the machines acrid expulsion was having on the environment, and that their blatant disregard for global warming would probably catch up to and kill them one day in the form of a too-late diagnosis of stage-four squamous cell carcinoma which, perhaps, would be a fitting end for those demonstrating such total disregard for regularly scheduled engine maintenance and oft-neglected oil changes.

Merrick stepped out of the Chevy Suburban and inhaled the refreshing ocean air. The perfect blueness of the sky and the warmth of the sun on his face promised a perfect day.

West of the rest area, rising swells of the crystal blue Pacific were locked in fierce competition. The rolling waves gained momentum, crested, then raced up the bank of the shoreline, only to fall back and be absorbed by the sandy beach.

Merrick found himself overwhelmed with gratitude for the sun-kissed day and this his second chance at life. He even entertained a brief feeling of indebtedness to the venerable scientific minds who had come before him, although they had failed in their experiments where he had more than succeeded in his.

It felt good to be free of the lab. He felt relaxed, much more than he thought he would, and far better than he had for as long as he could remember. He attributed this emotional liberation to having finally reached the summit of his profession and now being unquestionably without peer. Training this mind to suppress his desire for revenge had proven to be a worthwhile discipline after all.

After leaving Dynamic Life Sciences, his first order of business had been to ditch his Porsche 911 in the parking lot of a local shopping mall. It was at the back of the mall where he had acquired the Suburban from a young home renovator. Despite the massive decal plastered on the side of the steel bin which read NO COMMERCIAL WASTE, Dan of *Dan's Home Improvements* had parked behind the Dumpster and was engaged in the illegal disposal of broken plasterboard, used paint cans, old light fixtures, a cracked yellow sink and matching Formica countertop, and the threadbare remains of a truly hideous orange and brown carpet.

Merrick had merely wished to voice his displeasure at the poor judgment the young contractor was exhibiting by improperly combining recyclables with corrosives and toxins (a threat to both the environment and human health in general) when the contractor, having taken offense to Merrick's intrusion, threatened to punch his lights out for sticking his nose in where it didn't belong, then encouraged him to be on his way by using the most impolite language. Merrick apologized profusely, agreed that he preferred his nose exactly where it was, then touched the metal band on his wrist and extended his hand. Taken aback, expecting further confrontation from the stranger and not receiving it, the contractor quickly cooled off and accepted Merrick's offer of contrition. He took Merrick's hand, and in doing so felt every nerve in his body come to life. First came the heat, as though his central nervous system was a furnace that had been cranked up as high as it could possibly go. He felt as if he was being fried alive, from the inside out. Just as quickly, his body temperature plummeted, as though he had been scooped out of a cauldron of boiling water and plunged deep into icy water.

Merrick stared into the contractor's eyes and noted the sudden physiological changes taking place within his body, in particular the rapid dilation and contraction of his pupils, coupled with his desire to speak yet being unable to utter a single word. Merrick let up on the strange energy force flooding throughout the man's body.

"Please... no more," Dan the Contractor said. His teeth chattered with such intensity Merrick thought he might actually grind them to dust as he spoke. "I... have... a family."

"So did I," Merrick replied. "Unfortunately, I really need your truck."

Merrick intensified the energy stream. The man's skin turned color, from pink to pale blue, then to ashen gray, and finally snow white. If the eyes were truly the window to the soul, Dan the Contractor's stare suggested that his life force had abandoned him. Merrick gripped his hand tighter and increased the cold energy, testing the limits of Project Channeler, then watched his body shatter into a thousand tiny fragments as easily as might a boulder that had been dipped in a vat of liquid nitrogen and struck with a sledgehammer.

Before closing the lift gate, Merrick removed from the truck a second roll of the grotesque carpet the contractor had not yet disposed of, unrolled it, kicked the man's frozen remains into it, then re-rolled the rug and tossed it into the Dumpster, along with the man's work boots and clothes. He pulled the magnetic business signs off the doors of the Suburban. After switching the license plates with those of his Porsche he left the mall and drove off in the direction of Laguna Beach.

Merrick checked his wristwatch. 10:50 A.M. His

colleagues would soon be arriving at the lab. They had worked all day yesterday and into the early hours of the morning at his request. He recommended they take advantage of a few extra hours of well-earned sleep to recharge their batteries and suggested they roll in around eleven instead of their usual eight o'clock start.

He, however, had arrived early. He opened the lab as usual, then coated the focus adjustment dials of the microscopes with a mother tincture of poison hemlock. Soon after his co-workers touched the equipment the poison would be absorbed through their skin and begin to circulate through their bloodstream. One by one they would start to exhibit symptoms of an unknown etiology: vomiting, convulsions, wheezing, delirium, lack of motor control, paralysis. Eventually they would collapse. Working in a top-secret military lab and unsure of what was happening to them Merrick knew their first instinct would be to suspect the lab had been compromised and that they had become the target of a chemical attack; terrorism perhaps. Panic would quickly ensue. One of them would hit a workstation alarm, immediately initiating Red Door protocol, after which no one would be permitted to enter or leave Dynamic Life Sciences or any of its labs until all emergency procedures had been followed. No action would be taken to help the men trapped in the lab – not even if they appeared to be dying - until the full extent of the threat had been determined. Only then would the lockdown be lifted, and the scientists permitted to receive medical attention... if they were still alive.

Whatever.

Merrick was confident he wouldn't be missed for the next couple of hours. Even if he had arrived for work, he wouldn't have been permitted access to the facility due to the lockdown.

He walked past the Winnebago and noted his reflection in the side window of the RV. Too much time spent working in labs over the years combined with too little time committed to exercise had left him overweight. He checked his profile in the tinted window, turning first to his left, then his right. Twenty pounds would have to go. Okay, maybe thirty. He promised himself that when his mission was complete, he would make a concerted effort to get back into shape. Such promises hadn't worked for him in the past. Perhaps this time would be different. The RV windows parabolic design and bronze tint did little to enhance the pallor of his skin. Rather than providing the illusion of a tanned and healthy glow his reflection still looked pale. Acne scars pock-marked his face like tiny craters, and his pudgy cheeks seemed even pudgier. His oversized head, about which he had been teased all his life, appeared chin-less, and dissolved into a short, wide neck. To better observe his appearance Merrick pushed his horn-rimmed glasses further up the bridge of his nose and smoothed his thinning hair into place. A lifetime of being short and rotund guaranteed he would forever remain the farthest thing from a chick magnet any woman could imagine. Before his late wife, Alma, the women who had been drawn to him were mostly Ph.D. candidates, attracted to him for his superior intellect. Merrick had established a name for himself in the field of synthetic biology. He was considered a scientific rock star and trailblazer due to his unparalleled advancements in the field of artificial neural networking and brain-computer interface communications known as neurocybernetics: merging the mind of man with biologically hosted computer technology. He had spent the last ten years working at Dynamic Life Sciences as a civilian military contractor. He had been provided with unlimited funding from the Defense Advanced Research Projects Agency to continue his breakthrough research into neuro-command telepathy, telekinesis, transmutation, and mind control. Human trials were now underway. Early results had shown Project Channeler to be an unprecedented success. Once weaponized, the technology would be of incalculable value to DARPA and he would be contractually obligated to surrender it to them. But that was something he had never intended to do.

Channeler would remain his and his alone.

He had already deployed it against them.

They just didn't know it yet.

This was how it had to be. There was no other way. Besides Alma, there had been only one other love in his life Merrick had treasured; his daughter, Paige, who had been ripped from their lives in the cruelest way a daughter could be wrenched away from two loving parents.

With Alma and Paige dead, Merrick was utterly alone at a time in his life when he should have been celebrating his personal and professional success surrounded by the family he so loved. Instead, he had become emotionally obliterated. Nothing mattered anymore, not even his esteemed reputation or his Top-Secret clearance. There were no rules left worth abiding by. No achievements worth a damn. No allegiances worth honoring.

All that remained was an unquenchable desire to find and destroy whoever had managed to pump the vitality out of him and leave in its place untenable bitterness and racking pain.

The white cotton Tommy Bahama shirt gaily flowered with pale yellow hibiscus and red ohia had proven to be an ideal choice to wear on this sunny Southern California day. The fit was comfortable and loose and nicely concealed the

Beretta pistol he had taken from dead Dan's glove box between his waistband and the small of his back. The store clerk had paired the shirt with stylish white slacks and a canvas belt, tan leather Rockport's, and a palm braid Fedora. All had been excellent choices. The cushioned soles of the shoes silenced Merrick's footfall as he walked past the RV. He'd left the Fedora on the front seat of the truck. The thought of burning the top of his head under the hot sun was preferable to the embarrassment of having to huff and puff his way along the beach chasing after the hat should a sudden gust of wind blow it off his head. He liked his new look so much that he wore the clothes out of the store. He bundled his stodgy old apparel into the shopping bag and tossed them in the trunk of the Suburban.

Merrick examined himself once more in the window of the RV. He had always been a physically weak man, preferring the development of his mind to that of his body. But strength (or even the Beretta for that matter) would not be required for him to find peace. He possessed two far deadlier assets, both of which he could bank on to obtain the justice he sought: the genius of his mind, and Project Channeler.

He trailed his fingers alongside the RV. The dusty vehicle shuddered under the energy of his touch. The mountain bikes shook and clattered against one another in the rack.

In the short time since he had arrived at Laguna Beach the parking lot had already reached its full capacity. The main entrance had been closed. Latecomers were being redirected to overflow lots across the street and down the road. Along the beach, volleyballs were being served high and spiked hard into the soft sand by well-tanned, rambunctious teens. Melanoma-conscious seniors lounged under blue canvas canopies, protected from the wrinkle-inducing UV rays of the sun. Some talked while others read or listened to music. Seagulls glided inches above the gently rolling Pacific in search of food that ventured fatally close to the surface of the water.

It seemed to Merrick that the police presence was unusually high for this relatively early hour of the day. Officers strolled along the beach and engaged the public in polite conversation. Down the beach from the volleyball game a well–muscled cop with movie-star good looks straddled his bicycle and leaned over the handlebars, chatting up three beautiful young women. The cop laughed and shifted his weight from side to side, impressively flexing his powerfully defined arms and legs. Merrick recognized the girls as the travelers in the atmosphere-defiling Winnebago.

Purchasing an ice cream cone from a vendor, Merrick walked along the beach and sat on a bench situated near the water's edge. From the shore to the horizon the glittering rays of the sun sparkled on the ocean like the camera flashes of celebrity–obsessed paparazzi.

Finishing the tasty treat, Merrick touched the metal band on his wrist. The energy field became visible. The band began to change color, first to blue, then yellow, finally rose-red. Activating the brain-neural interface supercharged his body. He submitted to its power, closed his eyes, and watched the blackness in front of them melt away. His mind no longer a blind and barren landscape, he observed with clarity the multidimensional images Channeler provided to him.

He paused before venturing further, testing the mindscape as a wild animal might call upon its trusted olfactory senses to reveal the presence of a hidden predator.

Merrick telepathically sought out the neuro-signature of his trial subject and observed his location in his mind.

A large building... a warehouse perhaps.

Banks of broken windows...

An obscenity-scarred wall...

The rank smell of burnt machine oil.

5

C HRIS HANOVER PARTED the bedroom curtains and looked down upon the gathering crowd. Outside the iron perimeter fence of the Rosenfeld estate police struggled to keep news crews at bay. Reporters attempted to out-flank one another to acquire the perfect backdrop for their live-to-air report of the ongoing murder investigation.

As the Forensics team photographed and videotaped the crime scene, Jordan showed them the secret panic room they had found hidden behind the bedroom wall.

She removed the flash drive from her pocket and handed it to Forensics Specialist Steve Reynolds. "I need to know what's on this right away," Jordan said. "Meet you in Mobile Command in ten minutes?"

"You got it J," Reynolds replied. He took the device and left the room.

"Judging by the number of flies buzzing around out there it looks like this has become a media shit storm," Hanover remarked as he watched additional teams of reporters converge on the scene.

A young agent named Hawkins handed him a report. "Sir, Command asked me to give you this. It's a workup on the victims."

"Thanks," Chris replied.

Hanover paced as he read the report aloud. "Itzhak Rosenfeld. Seventy-four years old. Israeli by birth. Emigrated to California with his wife, Zahava, in '86. Physician. Practiced here for twenty-five years. It seems the good doctor is... make that *was*... one of the world's preeminent plastic surgeons. His area of expertise was facial reconstruction and body defect surgery."

"I should have studied medicine instead of law," Jordan said. "A nose job here, tummy tuck there. Cha-ching."

"According to this, Rosenfeld's work as a surgeon represented only a fraction of how he earned his wealth."

"It gets better?" Jordan said. "Now you're just teasing me."

"A lot better," Chris replied. "It says here he was a prolific inventor of medical instruments and implants and pioneered many advanced surgical procedures. The man has over seven hundred patents to his name, plus copyrights and trademarks. Net worth is estimated at two billion."

"The book laying on the floor beside his bed deals with patent law."

"You think maybe he was killed out of professional jealousy?"

"Can't rule it out," Jordan replied. "Maybe somebody had two billion reasons to want him dead."

Hanover nodded and flipped to the next page of the report. "It seems the Rosenfeld's had established a number of non-profits, the most notable of which is *FreeSurge,* a humanitarian plastic and cosmetic surgery organization that performs operations on the poor, free of charge. Corrections to cleft palates and birth defects, repairs to the scars of war victims... that sort of thing. They'd raised millions over the years to fund the operational expenses of their charities."

"This doesn't make any sense," Jordan said. "How could two people who had done so much for so many end up like this?" She pointed to the corpses on the bed. "And what's with the arsenal in the safe room? I can see hiding a few handguns around the place, just in case. But all that weaponry? You and I don't even need that. And we deal with bad guys every day. And I can absolutely guarantee you there's no body armor hanging in my bedroom closet."

"Good thing," Chris replied. "You'd have a hard time finding something in your color. Besides, it's tough to match Kevlar with Vera Wang. You'd need a stylist."

"Seriously, Chris. That level of preparation is way over the top. The Rosenfeld's were afraid of something. Or someone."

"I agree. It doesn't add up."

"Anything in that report about Mrs. Rosenfeld?"

Hanover flipped the page. "Actually, it's *Judge* Zahava Rosenfeld, United States District Court for the Central District of California, Western Division, Los Angeles County. Very bright lady. Two degrees. The first an M.D. from Harvard, the second in law, from Yale. Judge Rosenfeld never practiced medicine, only law. Says here she was a fixture at charity fundraisers and Hollywood galas. You name it, the Rosenfeld's supported it."

"Kids?"

"None."

"What about family?"

"Dr. Rosenfeld's only brother died last year. Her Honor's parents died in Tel Aviv in 2001. Victims of a suicide bombing. No siblings." Hanover glanced at the bodies. "Did you see anything else when you touched the railing?"

"Just what I said before. Single-shooter, male... likely a pro. But something about him is off."

"Off?" Chris said. "You think? In my book anyone who kills like this fits the category of *off* rather nicely."

"I can't explain it any better than that."

"Your visions are always so clear, Jordan. What's different here?"

"The UNSUB's energy signature. I've never experienced one like it before. It fades in and out, kind of like a radio station signal that's not quite in range. Usually I see everything: the killer's face, surroundings, manner of dress, sights, and smells. Sometimes even the images of their victims will come through. But my reading on this killer is incomplete. As ridiculous as it sounds, it feels like I'm being... blocked."

"Any similarities to other cases?"

"You mean the El Segundo and Long Beach murders?"

"Yes."

Earlier in the week the agents had been called out to investigate two horrific killings that appeared to be related. The first victim, Michael Dowd, had been the owner of The Golden Rail, a famous strip club in El Segundo. Dowd had been enjoying a late-night swim when he was attacked. He had been found dead in his pool by his girlfriend, a dancer at the club, hands bound behind his back, feet tied to the side rails of the pool ladder, hanging upside down in the crimson water. He had been shot in the forehead. Hours later, police found his club manager, Julie Harper, dead in her Long Beach condominium. She was nude, hands and feet tied to the bed; legs spread eagle. A can of tire puncture sealant had been pushed into her mouth; its inflation tube shoved deep down her throat. The release trigger had been jammed open. The contents of the can had been permitted to free flow which flooded her airway with gluey orange foam and led to her immediate suffocation and death. The contents of a second can had been expelled into her vagina. She too had received a fatal gunshot wound to the head.

"Who the hell is this guy?" Chris said. "Four victims in one week and forensics hasn't turned up a shred of evidence. No fibers, prints, DNA... nothing. No one sees or hears a thing. And all we get on security cams is static. It's like the guy's a goddamn ghost. He pops in, does the deed, then *poof*... he's gone."

"Let me work the room again. Maybe I missed something."

"Even you can't see what isn't there, Jordan."

"I know. And for the record, he's pissing me off too."

Forensics had begun to process the secret room. Agent Ron Perkins, the teams lead investigator, walked out of the closet entrance carrying a notebook computer under each arm. Jordan stopped him.

"Ron," Jordan asked, "I understand Chef Hershoff was the first to arrive this morning."

"That's right," Perkins said. "Got here at four this morning, which for him is the norm. He opens the kitchen by five and has breakfast ready for the Rosenfeld's by six. The couple always kept to the same routine."

"He found the front door open when he arrived?"

Perkins nodded. "And the alarm off. When he stepped inside, he saw the roses laying on the floor and the glow from the votives upstairs. When he called out and didn't get a response, he knew something was wrong. He got scared, ran out of the house, and called 9-1-1. When LAPD arrived and saw the scene, they thought it might be our guy. They called us right away."

"Did your guys find anything when you processed Hershoff?"

"Just a few crystal shards stuck to the soles of his shoes which he picked up when he stepped through the front door. Besides that, he was clean."

"And no other staff were on duty at the time?

"None," Perkins said. According to Hershoff, the Rosen-feld's had strict rules when it came to their privacy. Unless they were hosting an event, no staff were to be on site after nine p.m. We allowed the maids, groundskeepers, and the Rosenfeld's personal driver through the barricade earlier. Needless to say, they're all pretty shook up. We're taking their statements in Mobile Command right now."

"So we have nothing to work with... again."

"Like Chris said, this guy's a ghost."

Agent Hawkins burst through the doorway, took a second to catch his breath, then spoke to Jordan and Chris. "Reynolds needs to see you in the MCU right away."

"He found something?" Jordan asked.

Hawkin's nodded. "The flash drive," he said. "You're not going to believe what's on it."

6

"**S**ON, STOP STARING at my credentials and open the goddamn gate!"

Colonel Quentin Hallier snatched his identification card out of the guard's hand and inched his car towards the too slow to open security gate. Clear of the barrier, he accelerated up the winding driveway of Dynamic Life Sciences as department heads quickly marshaled scientists and staff out of the building to designated EVACUATION stations.

Hallier screeched the car to a halt at the main entrance to the facility, stepped out of the vehicle, slammed the door, adjusted his tie, snapped his waistcoat taught and grumbled a slew of obscenities under his breath. Battle-proven and tasked with moving forward the most top-secret military science projects of the Defense Advanced Research Projects Agency, otherwise known as DARPA, Colonel Hallier was not accustomed to exchanging pleasantries. At six-foot-four, two-hundred-and-forty pounds he was an imposing presence who projected a *don't-even-think-of-screwing-with-me* bravado and a pot-boiling temper which seemed permanently set on simmer.

Hallier marched through the doorway and straight past Dr. Sook Han where he was met by a four-man armed security detail. "Talk to me, doctor," he said. "Tell me what you know."

Dr. Han hurried after the Colonel. The empty facility was quiet except for the echoing footfalls of the six men as they walked down the corridor toward the wing marked LABS.

"Shortly after eleven A.M. this morning," Han said, "a biohazard alarm was activated in the ANNBIC lab."

Hallier shot him a glance. "I don't speak *scientist* doctor. English please."

"Artificial Neural Network Brain Interface Communications lab, Colonel. We initiated Red Door protocol immediately. The suspected pathogen has been contained to the lab."

"Thus, the lockdown."

"Yes, sir."

"Casualties?"

"Two dead."

"Cause?"

"At first, we thought it might have been a contagion... some type of chemical attack the air-sniffing robots failed to detect – a nano spore, perhaps. North Korea has been working on that technology for years. But as it turned out it's some type of poison."

"So *not* airborne?"

"No, sir. The Biological and Infectious Agent Response Team is in the lab now. They sampled the air. It passed. But when they *fogged* the lab, they discovered yellow residue on the microscope dials. Some sort of clear liquid. We think a nerve agent was applied to the equipment. It turned color when it came in contact with the fogging chemical. I believe that as soon as the scientists touched the equipment the poison was transferred through their fingertips and into their bloodstream. Because it was invisible, they couldn't see it on the dials. It was just a matter of time before it attacked their central nervous system. The sample is being analyzed now to determine exactly what it is. Regardless, they didn't stand a chance."

"Jesus."

At the lab entrance, Dr. Han turned to Hallier. "Colonel, there's something I need to say."

"I'm listening."

"With the possible exception of the Centers for Disease Control and Prevention in Atlanta, DLS is the most secure research facility in the country and one of the best in the world. We have never had an incident occur here since we opened the doors fifteen years ago. This entire wing requires both retinal pattern biometric scanning and voice recognition to get through each door. In addition, there are three armed security checkpoints which staff must clear just to get to their lab. Yet despite all that security we end up going from zero occurrences to Red Door Protocol in minutes. Being breached once means we could get hit again. The next time it could be worse."

Hallier's temper was beginning to boil. "Worse than two dead?"

Han spoke calmly. "Sir, what if this was just a test? What if the true intention of this attack was to determine our level of vulnerability. Next time everyone in this facility could be dead."

A member of the security escort whose lapel nameplate read TAYLOR spoke. "Dr. Han, may I interject?"

Han nodded.

"Sir, the EVAC stations have submitted their head counts. All staff members are accounted for except one. Dr. Merrick hasn't reported into any of the marshaling areas."

"Are you sure?" Han asked.

"Positive." Sergeant Taylor opened a computer program on his tablet and showed it to Han and Hallier. "Every station on the DLS campus must report in during an emergency evacuation. A two-step process is followed. First, a biometric hand scan is taken of every employee the second they check into a station. Next, their medical status is assessed. See the names in green? Those are staff members who've checked-in and are fine. Names in yellow represent staff who are accounted for but are presenting with an acute medical issue. Could be a superficial wound, injured but conscious, that sort of thing. Names in blue are unconscious, unresponsive or require immediate transport to hospital by ambulance or LifeFlight. Names in black are VSA: vital signs absent. The deceased, Dr's Grant and Fullerton, are so listed. Names in red have not reported in or are yet unaccounted for. As you can see, only one staff member is red listed: Dr. Jason Merrick, the director of this lab."

Colonel Hallier turned to Han. "Was Merrick scheduled to be in today?"

"As far as I know," Han replied. "But as lab director and project lead, he's free to set his own hours."

Taylor referred back to the tablet. "The card key log indicates he swiped in a few minutes before eight this morning then out fifteen minutes later. There's no record of him returning to the campus, Colonel."

"Has he called in?"

"No, sir. Telephony reports no inbound calls logged from any of his contact numbers."

"What about Extranet login or computer activity?"

"Nothing."

"Is he being monitored?"

Taylor hesitated before answering. He glanced at Han.

"Don't worry about Dr. Han, Sergeant," Hallier said. "I need to know if Dr. Merrick is presently under surveillance. Is he the subject of an internal investigation?"

"No, sir. We have no open file on Dr. Merrick."

Han suddenly looked uncomfortable, perhaps wondering if *he* was being covertly monitored by DARPA agents.

The Colonel checked his watch and turned to Han. "Would it be out of the ordinary for Dr. Merrick not to have checked in by now?"

"Quite," Han replied. "Dr. Merrick is rarely away from his lab and has a reputation for expecting the same level of commitment from the scientists on his team. To my knowledge, he has not taken a vacation in years. Not since he lost his wife and daughter. Very sad."

Hallier looked through the narrow mesh window into the lab. Two members of the Biological and Infectious Agent Response Team were collecting blood and saliva samples from the floor where the research scientists had fallen and died while others sprayed, scrubbed, and carefully placed all exposed items into thick red disposal bags labeled BIOHAZARD.

"Is everything in the lab accounted for?" Hallier asked.

Neither Han nor Taylor responded.

Hallier raised his voice. "Has BIART inventoried the lab since the campus went into lockdown? Is anything is missing? Equipment... files?"

39

"No, Colonel," Han answered. "The lab hasn't been assessed yet." He pointed to a red light flashing above the door. "All lab entrances are computerized and tied into Central Station Monitoring. This door will remain locked until BIART stands down and Red Door protocol is cancelled."

"What about video surveillance?" Hallier asked.

"We record every square inch of the complex, except for the labs," Taylor answered.

"Why not the labs?"

"DARPA never saw the need for it because of our enhanced security equipment and guard stations," Han answered. "We also don't permit recording devices of any kind in the labs."

"That includes phones?" Hallier asked.

"Especially phones. Too much technology in one device. We prefer to eliminate the temptation for staff to take pictures, send texts or emails, or upload confidential information to the web. Besides, every lab entrance is equipped with an IntelliLock chamber. Once you step through the main entrance door to the lab the second door won't open if the system detects any electronic devices on your body or in the chamber itself. The only exceptions are Pacemakers and artificial limbs or a Level Five authorized override."

"You're telling me that being charged with treason for illegally disseminating secret government information isn't an effective enough deterrent?" Hallier asked.

"It's a Dark Web world out there, sir. Unfortunately, some people can still be bought." Han tapped his finger on a metal cabinet built into the wall outside the lab entrance which featured its own card key reader. "These are property storage boxes. All personal belongings must be locked in here before entering the lab."

"Can you open it, Sergeant?" Hallier asked.

"Yes sir," Taylor answered. "But the lab is still being processed. What if the contaminant made its way into the box? We could be exposed as soon as I open the door."

Hallier turned to Han. "Is that possible?"

"No," Han replied. "These units are triple sealed. There's no threat of exposure."

"Then open it," Hallier said.

Sergeant Taylor removed the master card key from his pocket and slid it through the reader. The access light on the metal box turned from amber to green. The cover panel clicked open.

The interior of the unit featured three separate key-locked compartments. The top compartment was labeled GRANT, the middle FULLERTON, the lowest MERRICK.

"You have the keys?" Hallier asked.

"Yes sir," Taylor replied.

"Open them."

Taylor opened each compartment. Despite Dr. Han's assurance that they were not at risk of being exposed to an unknown lethal contaminant he took a few steps back, nonetheless.

Dr. Grant's drawer contained the key fob to his Tesla, smartphone, watch and wallet.

Fullerton's drawer contained his smartphone and the key to his Harley.

Merrick's drawer included three items. The first was a crumpled photograph taken at the base of the Eiffel Tower while on a family vacation in Paris. Dr. Merrick stood beside his wife and daughter. The picture had been taken long before the day yet to come that would shatter his world forever.

Colonel Hallier removed the second item from the box: a thin metallic band.

"My God!" Han said. "That's the first-generation brain neural interface for Project Channeler. That technology is being developed specifically for DARPA. Under no circumstances is it to leave the lab."

The third item was an empty glass vial labeled LEEDA FIELD TRIAL. "And this?" Hallier asked.

"LEEDA," Dr. Han replied. "An injection technology developed to give our military an unprecedented advantage in covert warfare. If Merrick has misappropriated these technologies, the consequences could be unimaginable... even catastrophic."

Hallier turned over the photograph. On the back Merrick had scrawled three words:

'ALL WILL PAY'

THE COLONEL POCKETED the items and turned to Dr. Han and Sergeant Taylor.

"I'm ordering this facility to be placed on permanent lockdown. Until otherwise notified, Red Door protocol will remain in effect. Taylor, put your team on High Tactical Alert. Find Merrick. Have your people deep-sweep every square inch of this building and post guards at every entrance and exit. All Dynamic Life Sciences staff will be transported to Joint Forces Training Base Los Alamitos within the hour. We'll accommodate them until this matter is resolved. There is to be no discussion with staff about the reason for this action other than to say its protocol under these circumstances. Do I make myself clear?"

Taylor saluted. "Crystal, sir."

Han nodded. "I'll notify my people right away."

COLONEL HALLIER RETURNED to his car and placed a call. The connection was made but no greeting provided. He spoke:

"Pericles."

"Safe word?"

"Copernicus."

"State your message."

"Situation Report, Dynamic Life Sciences. Channeler and LEEDA projects compromised. Requesting ALPHA ONE priority."

Silence on the line.

The operator responded: "Pericles, you are green for emergency debriefing."

The call was immediately terminated.

7

O N THE QUIET cul-de-sac of multimillion dollar mansions where neighboring driveways proudly displayed fine automobiles from such luxury purveyors as Maserati, Aston Martin, Porsche, and Bentley, the Federal Bureau of Investigation's Mobile Command Unit looked conspicuously out of place.

Jordan and Chris climbed the metal stairs of the MCU and stepped inside. Several agents were busy conducting interviews with the Rosenfeld's staff. Concerned for the welfare of the house's personnel, Chef Hershoff had chosen to remain at the scene and assist the agents where needed. He was seated beside the house matron, Rosalia Cruz. Having arrived for what she had assumed would be another typical workday Rosalia was customarily attired in her black maid's dress with crisp white collar and cuffs, white apron, and black leather shoes. Hershoff held her hand and comforted her through her tears while the agent took her statement.

Seated in front of his computer at the opposite end of

the MCU, forensics lead investigator Steve Reynolds gestured to Jordan and Hanover to join him.

"Pull up a chair," Reynolds said as he drew a thick curtain along its ceiling track behind them. The sound-dampening material offered privacy and muted their conversation.

"I examined the flash drive you found on our victim," Reynolds said. He opened the drive. "It's not protected. No password or firewall. This file was not intended to hide information. The killer wanted us to have full access to it."

The drive contained a single file labeled "AWP." The document consisted of five alphanumeric lines:

DM 14PFnFlenmalGdqFNkdGkajnsDh6JnrFks
VT 29nRtHphyxnEnCGLbsMxfJhc
RI 12pFbGsfxkhFgLFxkElndgsKv7E
GA 36qHrLhdpfkDiTDHeiTfkduDn4Dqpr
PM 28eKbTdibfoRvQWTskYfrnkDd4Whb
HJ 26jTfdswrkIgBMFxoHftalDr7Puwm

"Any idea what it means?" Jordan asked.

"Not the foggiest."

"Could you lift any prints?" Chris asked.

"No joy," Reynolds replied. "The only contributions we're going to get from this will be confirmatory blood and saliva from Dr. Rosenfeld."

"Anything unique about the drive itself?"

Reynolds shook his head. "Just your run-of-the-mill generic flash drive. Retailers across the country sell thousands of these every day, not including online sales. What I can tell you is that the content was created two weeks ago and authored under the username "AWP." It's never been modified or revised."

The similarities between the murders in El Segundo and Long Beach paralleled the Rosenfeld killings. Was it possible that they were connected? So far Jordan and Chris were no further ahead than they had been earlier in the week. Their superiors were already looking for answers. The pressure to solve the case was on. Their newly formed partnership was already under the microscope.

Chris and Jordan thanked Agent Reynolds. "Let us know when you've figured out what it means," Jordan said. The agents turned to leave.

"Before you go, there's something you guys should know," Reynolds said.

"What's that?" Jordan asked.

"The breakage pattern of the front door's crystal inlay across the floor. It doesn't make sense."

"What do you mean?" Chris asked.

"Well, to put in simple terms, it's *wrong*. I've investigated dozens of home invasions over the years where shattered glass was found at the point of entry. Perpetrators break glass in several ways. Pro's usually tape it, break it, then peel it out of the frame. Amateurs just smash it using an object of opportunity, a piece of wood or a rock. But the one constant is *cast off*. There is a limit to the distance a piece of glass can travel when struck by force. The longest cast off I've ever documented was thirty-three feet from point of impact. A violent break was needed to achieve that distance. But here we found pieces of crystal lying against the baseboard on the far side of the Rosenfeld's vestibule. That's a distance of *eighty* feet from the point of impact. That's unheard of. The only logical means to achieve that distance of cast off is if the crystal insert had been framed with primer cord then detonated. We know that wasn't the case here because we checked. No evidence of an explosive compound was found on the insert, door frame, or the floor. Regardless, it was as if the glass had been simultaneously melted and blasted across the room."

"*Blasted?*" Chris said.

"Don't think I don't know how crazy that sounds," Reynolds said. "But like I said, I've been investigating crime scenes like this for a very long time. One more thing: The physical shape of the cast off was wrong too. Every piece we found in the vestibule, lobby, and against the walls was tiny and round, like marbles. Furthermore, the channel that secured the glass within the frame was completely smooth, no breaks in it whatsoever. It was like the crystal had been raised to its melting point and then blasted right out of the frame. Scientifically, I can't explain it."

"Thanks, Steve," Jordan said.

"You got it," Reynolds replied. He turned his attention back to the cryptic information on the computer screen.

Inside the Mobile Command Unit television monitors tuned to local stations reported on the tragedy that had befallen the citizens of the quiet street. The story was gaining traction, due in large part to the tony Hollywood Hills community in which the murders had occurred and the social and philanthropic prominence of the victims. News anchors shared the story with their viewers.

Jordan and Chris watched the replay of an interview in which FBI Special Agent and public relations spokesperson Janet Lynch fielded questions from reporters. Following the live update on-air news personalities conducted roundtable discussions and speculated to extremes on the events that had transpired in the early hours of the morning: Who had killed the Rosenfeld's? Why had they been murdered? What could have been the motivation for the killings? Were they targeted simply because they were among the world's super-rich, the one percent? One reporter went as far as to propose the erroneous and unsubstantiated theory that this was a case of *"murder-for-hire gone terribly wrong"* and that the murder of the Rosenfeld's might well be *"the first of more to come"* and *"the start of a killing spree the likes of which Hollywood has not seen since the Manson murders in 1969."* The media's desire to sensationalize the grisly murder details further disrespected the dead. A picture of the Rosenfeld home appeared beside an FBI booking photo of Charles Manson, the convicted leader of the murderous 'family' of the same name. Manson nor any of his deranged followers had anything to do with the death of the Rosenfeld's, of course. This was pure sensationalism and an outright debasement of journalistic integrity, wholly motivated by the network's desire to win the highest share of evening ratings. They had already determined that the viewing public could not possibly be satisfied with the minimal details being spoon fed to them by the FBI. They knew their audience salivated for more.

Chris listened to the lies being broadcast to the masses and offered a commentary of his own: "Assholes."

"That's putting it mildly," Jordan agreed.

The door to the Mobile Command Unit opened. A warm rush of incoming air brought with it the exquisite fragrance of frangipani from the dozens of red, yellow, white, and pink flowering trees which flanked the driveway leading up to the mansion. Forensic Specialist Mike Coventry entered the vehicle wearing a white Tyvek body suit which covered him from head to toe and strained to contain his generous belly. On his hands he wore latex gloves. A pair of disposable slippers covered his shoes. He pulled back the hood of the suit. Beads of sweat streamed from his brow. He looked less like a crime scene expert than a snowman who had discovered, too late, that the climate in Southern California was hot, not cold, and was about to expire into a puddle. In his arms he carried two large boxes filled with evidence collection bags.

"The first of many," Coventry said, acknowledging Jordan and Chris with a nod. He set the boxes down on a work surface beneath the television monitors. The agent removed the bags, wrote down a description of their contents, and assigned each an item number. To ensure against the threat of evidentiary loss or contamination he taped each of the envelopes closed, initialed and dated the lot, placed them inside a plastic container marked SEALED EVIDENCE - DO NOT TAMPER, then locked the bin with nylon zip ties. Coventry then locked the box in the EVIDENCE STORAGE cabinet under the table.

He nodded in the direction of the mansion. "We're still processing biologicals, ballistics and trace. Weapons and computers have been boxed. We'll run additional tests on them at the lab. Vic's should be ready for transport within the hour."

"Good work, Mike," Jordan said.

Coventry nodded, turned to leave. "Gotta get back. We've still got a couple of hours of work in there."

"Find anything useful?" Chris asked.

"As a matter of fact, yeah. You know the computer you found in the panic room? The password was written on the inside of the battery compartment. Brilliant, huh? Hawkins and I both thought that was a bonehead move for a smart guy like Rosenfeld. The doc had a couple of interesting files on there labeled Account 1 and Account 2. Both were password protected. But you'll never guess what the good doctor did."

"Used the same password for both files?" Jordan asked.

Coventry smiled and shot two fingers at her, gunslinger-style. "Exactly. And both files revealed he had a thing for the ladies."

"Meaning?" Jordan asked.

"They contain hundreds of photos. All women. Very risqué poses. The kind of pics you'd see on dating sites but with a lot less left to the imagination. No names, just numbers and letters under each picture. The files look like they had been ordered according to age. The girls in Account 1 are young, I'd say eighteen to twenty. The girls in Account 2 are twenty-plus."

"Has Hawkins packed up that computer yet?" Chris asked.

Coventry shrugged. "As far as I know he's still working on it. You know Hawk. One-part techno-geek, the other Sherlock Holmes. Give that guy a computer problem and he's like a dog on a bone. He won't let up until he's cracked it. Kid's smarter than all of us on our best day."

Jordan turned to Chris. "You thinking what I'm thinking?"

"Yeah," Hanover replied. "We need to see those files."

8

D IAMONDS DANCED IN the sunlight. Commander Ben Egan blinked the sleep out of his eyes. High above, dust particles floated past grime-baked windows on lazy air currents and glittered like twinkling stars, exposed by the penetrating rays of the midday sun, only to disappear into shadow the next.

The mind assault that had occurred hours ago had left him drained. When he awakened out of his deep slumber he bolted upright, straight-backed against the wall, his finger positioned on the trigger of his weapon.

Although his physiological and metabolic requirements were unlike those of ordinary men, rest was still a requirement, as too the need to eat. He had not consumed any food in the last seventy-two hours. Although the factory had served its purpose and proven to be an ideal hiding place, he would need to be on the move again very soon. He would steal what he needed to survive.

Though the specifics of his assignments were sent to him via Channeler's neural download, less important decisions such as when and how a target would be assassinated, the optimal points of ingress, egress and escape, and the most appropriate weaponry with which to carry out the termination were left to his discretion. Having successfully completed the Dowd, Harper, and Rosenfeld assignments he would receive the next target instruction set shortly, namely name and location. To receive any additional information he believed to be vital to the successful completion of the assignment he simply had to *think* his request. Confirmation data would be downloaded to his brain the second arrangements had been made.

Egan wasn't concerned about being tagged or identified by public security monitoring systems when he moved about in public. His biometric enhancements extended beyond his neural augmentation to the energy signature of his physical body. His aura - invisible to the naked eye – could become illuminated at will, making him appear as if he were an entity consisting of pure light energy, blurring the contours of his body to such a degree that he would be wholly unrecognizable by even the most sophisticated biometric detection systems.

Ben Egan had been required to give up everything in his life to become DARPA's most covert operative. The official cover story reported him as being killed in action during a black-ops mission in Kandahar; the sole victim of a rocket-propelled grenade. He accepted that lie to become the first scientifically augmented soldier in US military history; an opportunity that had proven impossible to resist.

As a career soldier, Commander Egan had learned to deal with the mental, emotional, and physical stress of evaluation testing. For most candidates, the grueling elimination protocols of the Project Channeler selection process had proved to be insurmountable. For Egan, they had been a walk in the park. As fellow members of Delta Force washed out of Channeler's Critical Evaluation Process he sailed through it, often to the disbelief of the medical team, his fellow soldiers, and his superiors. Ben Egan's ancestors had gifted him with a DNA of inconceivable genetic pedigree which had been recognized, harnessed, and refined early in his military career. During physical endurance evaluations it was suspected that his heart and lungs might be oversized; a theory later confirmed with the aid of magnetic resonance imaging. His heart could beat at a near impossible two-hundred-and-fifty times per minute and push an extraordinary volume of blood and oxygen throughout his body to feed his extremities. This seemingly inhuman advantage capitalized on muscle efficiency so greatly that it permitted him to achieve incredible feats of physical endurance with ease, such as the ability to traverse even the most inhospitable terrain at record breaking speed. His body was remarkably resistant to physical and cellular stress. He could not recall a time in his life when he had been ill; a fact substantiated by both his civilian and military medical histories. His high hypertrophy cell expression provided a significant advantage in physical strength. Even when faced with the duress of the battlefield he remained unnaturally calm. His body functioned at such a low metabolic rate that he could go for days without the need for food or sleep yet remaining quick-witted and mentally sharp. Quantitative sensory, cold pressor and pressure threshold testing confirmed his ability to withstand pain at levels exceeding five times those of the most elite-level soldier. He had proven himself to be devoid of fear and emotionally immune to even the most horrific conflicts encountered during his tenure with Delta Force. Ben Egan took immense pride in knowing that his God-given gifts, coupled with his ground-breaking neural interface augmen-

tation, made him virtually unstoppable. He had been transformed into the ideal soldier, the perfect killing machine.
His field trial handler, Dr. Jason Merrick, had warned him to
be prepared to experience minor annoyances such as
random physical or sensorial shocks - experiences that to
this point in his life had been utterly foreign to him. These
were to be considered normal responses to 'high range'
remote testing; part of the three-stage *Initiate-Measure-Eval-
uate* study being conducted by the scientists at Dynamic Life
Sciences in order to learn more about the field readiness of
the Channeler technology and his response to it. Being the
first of his kind, the scientists had even given him an
acronym - **GENESIS: GE**netic **N**eurally-**E**nhanced **S**ubver-
sive **I**ntelligence **S**upersoldier - and reminded him that the
successful completion of phase one field testing would
qualify him for advancement to Channeler's sister-study,
code named **LEEDA: L**ife **E**xtending **E**pidermal **D**efense
Augmentation. Controlled by the fight-or-flight response of
his sympathetic nervous system, LEEDA would be automat-
ically deployed when his brain confirmed a physical threat
was imminent. The epidermal cells of his skin would be
flooded with a compound DARPA scientists invented; a
derivative of spider silk, similar in structure to nano-cellu-
lose and Kevlar, yet organic and a thousand times stronger.
When released, his skin would be rendered virtually impenetrable by any known weapon. Post-assault, his cells would
instantly purge themselves of the chemical, reverse the
process, and return his skin to its normal state. The LEEDA
project would also slow his aging process to a rate significantly less than other humans, thereby extending his
usefulness as a military weapon for decades to come. The
promise of further enhancement to his already genetically
superior body and computerized mind with near super-

human abilities fed Egan's ego like methamphetamine to a drug addict. Channeler field testing would soon be complete. He was anxious to advance to the LEEDA project as quickly as possible.

He was pleased with his progress.

He hoped his superiors were as well.

The old furniture factory in which he had taken refuge was the largest of the dilapidated buildings occupying the abandoned business park; crypts of concrete and rusted metal left to die in an asphalt cemetery.

Decades earlier, before the sounding of the industrial era death knell bell which announced the end of their usefulness, businesses such as the old factory had thrived. Theirs was a time when pride of workmanship still mattered and a company's ability to supply its community with stable jobs at fair wages was as much a source of corporate pride as its requirement to turn a profit for its shareholders. However, years of steady economic decline soon favored price over quality, and the day finally arrived when the last of the company's chesterfields, dining tables, chairs, bookcases, and china cabinets were transported away in railcars on tracks that had served the companies within the abandoned park for decades, never to return. Doors had been closed; windows shuttered. For many of the former employees their small piece of the American Dream had decayed and died along with the building.

Egan rose to his feet from behind the cover of the shipping pallets and elicited a furious response from above. Startled out of their sleep, dozens of pigeons took flight from the steel rafters. The zealous expenditure of energy lasted only a few seconds before they soon circled back and resumed their resting place on the metal beams.

Needing a better understanding of the factory layout in

the event a quick escape should become necessary, Commander Egan climbed a rusty iron staircase to what had been the second-floor offices.

The first and largest office occupied half the north-east section of the building. Judging by its furnishings, he assumed it had been the production manager's office. A massive calendar, its pages yellow and brittle with age, corners curling outward from its wooden frame, was mounted on the largest wall of the room. Boxes for each day of the month were marked with notations referencing the production requirements for the coming weeks and months. The final notation, dated October 4th, 1962, read CLOSED.

Three filing trays on a wooden desk spoke to the last days in the life of the once grand plant. The first, labeled FORWARDING, overflowed with work orders identifying the items scheduled for manufacture and the various stations through which the raw materials would pass: wooden components to the kiln for drying, then on to the sanding, gluing, and varnishing departments; sofa spring assemblies to the fabrication shop; fabrics, cotton batting and leather to upholstering stations; completed pieces ready for final approval to the Inspector's benches. Detailed notes accompanied each of the work orders. Testifying to the pride the company had taken in its work, the forms bore the approval signatures of each station manager before the piece was permitted to move on to the next stage of the manufacturing process.

The second tray, marked COMPLETED, contained twenty such work orders, each stamped and dated, with authorized signatures and rail pick up dates scrawled on the bottom of the forms.

The third tray, labeled FIRST QUARTER 1963, was empty.

Like the factory walls on the first floor, this room too had been vandalized. Water-damaged blueprints, musty trade journals and accounting ledgers lay scattered about the room. Smashed out spun-steel fluorescent fixtures hung lopsided from the ceiling on broken metal chains. The cancer of decay that had metastasized throughout the building had claimed this room too, with terminal results. Painted floorboards had peeled, buckled, turned black with mold, and rotted away in places. The front legs of a wooden drafting table stood precariously close to a gaping wound in the middle of the floor. Egan stood beside the yawning maw and looked down upon the serpentine conveyor system that snaked its way through the factory. The floor sighed and moaned underfoot, then cried out as it surrendered to its diseased state and gave way, taking the doomed drafting table with it. Egan jumped back, aware that even his unique gifts might not permit him to recover from a twenty-foot fall resulting in impalement. He heard the old wooden table hit the floor below and smash into pieces.

The close call served as a reminder that securing the van was his immediate priority.

From the top of the staircase, Egan surveyed the production floor below. The massive steel door of the wood drying room had been left open. The faint effusion of pine, cedar, poplar, and maple still redolent in the old room created a perfumery of sorts: a pleasant aroma in stark contrast to the damp, musty air of the building. Along the west wall, exhaust tubes from the cutting, tooling, sanding, and varnishing rooms rose to the ceiling and connected to the central air exhaust and filtration systems. The rooms along the east wall were fewer in number and significantly larger. Judging by the discards of fabric and plastic wrap on the floor these areas had been dedicated to fabrication, upholstery, and shipping preparation. The southernmost section of the factory, once the staging area for the shipping of orders and receiving of raw materials, remained largely unencumbered.

Egan descended the iron staircase to the first floor and inspected the drying room. The cavernous chamber did little to mute the sounds of the old building. Ambient noises, faint pulses of life still left in the dying building, echoed off its walls: the occasional murmur from the unsettled pigeons perched high in the rafters; floors creaking under the shifting weight of gravity; the pop and click of metal in window frames as they expanded and contracted with the heat of the sun. Free at last from the geriatric grip of its decrepit metal frame, a pane of glass fell and shattered on the concrete factory floor.

When he had found the dilapidated factory in the pre-dawn hours, he had parked the flower delivery van in front of the drive-in doors of the shipping and receiving dock. Fortunately, the van had not been spotted by an overnight police patrol. Had that been the case the authorities would likely have run the plates, confirmed it was stolen, and entered the building to inspect the premises and determine if the thief were hiding inside.

Too risky. He needed to move the van inside the factory.

Egan closed his eyes and listened. He thought he could hear faint whispers coming from the kiln drying room. Ghosts of the old building perhaps.

He stepped out of the chamber and listened intently. Whispers became words. Words assembled into muted voices.

Clearer now, distinct.

One-hundred feet away, maybe less. Closing fast.

A commotion from the south end of the building now, outside the receiving doors.

Directions being issued.

No, not directions...

Orders.

The van had been had found. Which meant it was only a matter of minutes before the outside voices would come inside in search of him.

The safest place for him to be right now was where he had spent the night; hidden in the dark corner at the north end of the factory, behind the makeshift barricade of wooden shipping pallets.

Egan returned to the corner and peered through the stacked slats. The wall of the factory brightened as the back door opened and the shipping area filled with sunlight.

Six silhouettes made entry against the light.

Two men at first, then four more, spreading out quickly, moving fast.

He observed them and waited.

The strange metallic band on his wrist began to glow.

9

THE INTERCOM CRACKLED. "General, I have Colonel Hallier for you on COMSEC."

"Send it down the hall."

"Right away, sir."

"And call Dwight Hammond. Have him meet me in Briefing Room 1, ALPHA priority."

"Yes, sir."

Brigadier General Allan Ford picked up the EYES ONLY file folder from his desk and walked down the hall to the briefing room. The urgency with which Hallier's message had been relayed to him was disconcerting. He re-read the transcript subject line: *Situation alert. Level A1.*

The fact that the alert had come from Quentin Hallier bothered him. The Colonel was not the kind of man to sound an alarm without justification. There could be only one reason important enough for him to send the message using his ALPHA emergency identification: a problem had arisen which posed a threat to national security.

General Ford closed the briefing room door and opened the COMMUNICATION SECURITY video feed. Hallier's face filled the screen. Behind him, Dynamic Life Sciences security staff were busy escorting scientists and staff to buses destined for Joint Forces Training Base Los Alamitos.

Commander Dwight Hammond entered the room. Ford motioned to join him in front of the monitor.

"General, Commander," Hallier said.

Ford replied. "Why do I get the feeling you're about to ruin my perfectly good day, Quentin?"

"Sir, I've ordered Dynamic Life Sciences to be placed in lockdown. One of its scientists may no longer be operating within protocol."

"Who are we talking about?"

"Dr. Jason Merrick."

"Team leader on the Channeler and LEEDA projects?"

"Correct, sir. Confidence is high he may be responsible for an attack that occurred at the facility a few hours ago. Two scientists are dead, both members of his research team. Poisoned, according to DLS's Biohazard Response Team." Hallier removed the metal band and empty vial from his pocket. "He left these."

"The Challenger and LEEDA prototypes," Commander Hammond offered.

"Yes, along with this photograph." Hallier read the message on the back of the picture. "We have no idea what *All Will Pay* means or what he wants, but I'm assuming it's not good. We need to locate him immediately."

"Did Merrick kill those men?" Ford asked.

"That's how it's starting to look, sir."

"How soon can you get back to DARPA?"

"If it's all the same to you, General, I'd like to stay on site until the facility is secure and the staff is en route to JFTB Los Alamitos."

Ford nodded. "Very well."

"One more thing, General. We approved Merrick to go forward with human trials for Channeler and LEEDA."

"And?"

"Commander Egan is the control subject. If Merrick has other plans for Channeler and LEEDA, and he's turned Egan..."

"Egan shouldn't be a problem," Ford interrupted. "He's chipped. Locate him and bring him in."

"I'm afraid that's not possible sir. His bio-locator chip was removed when he was selected for Project Channeler."

"What about hemotracking?"

Hallier shook his head. "No, sir. For the same reason. Egan was given a transfusion. His blood's clean. He's totally free of nanoparticle GPS trackers."

"Are you trying to tell me our department's most valuable asset is... *lost*?"

"I can't answer that yet, General."

"Jesus Christ, Quentin! Either the horse has bolted the barn, or it hasn't. Which is it?"

Hallier paused. "Sir, I think we were set up. Merrick not only developed Channeler and LEEDA but also designed the selection criteria and project parameters for the test subjects. He had a hand in every part of the project."

"Your point, Colonel?"

"What if we missed something? What if Merrick had an end game in mind that no one saw coming? If Merrick outsmarted us and now has total control over Channeler and LEEDA, as well as Commander Egan, our citizens are in danger. No one except Merrick knows the full potential of this technology. In my opinion, the message is clear. Merrick plans to deploy Channeler and LEEDA for his own purposes. To what end we don't yet know."

"You need to find and secure Merrick and Egan and

reacquire Channeler and LEEDA, Colonel. Do you understand me?"

"Yes, sir."

"I'll scramble a black ops team. They'll be waiting for you when you arrive at JFTB Los Alamitos."

"Yes, sir."

General Ford slammed the file folder on the boardroom table. "You had complete oversight on this, Quentin. This was *your* project. I don't care if Merrick and Egan come back to us horizontally, vertically, or in a million godforsaken pieces. Consider both projects shut down."

Hallier's face was flush, neck rigid, mouth tightly drawn. "Copy that," he replied.

General Ford ended the transmission. The screen in the boardroom went black.

A computer-generated voice spoke: "COMSEC TERMINATED."

10

MARINA PUZANOVA WALKED out of the café Le Pain Quotidien in Moscow, dinner in hand; a to-go order of mushroom quiche with fresh green salad, cinnamon dolce latte, and a container of blueberry yogurt for dessert.

Her day was finishing the way it had started: hectic. Taras Verenich, her contact in Los Angeles, had left his second urgent message of the day. He had orders to fill from *well-financed buyers with particular demands* as he was prone to emphasize; powerful men and women who were accustomed to getting what they wanted when they asked for it and who were becoming impatient. Conversely, he had plenty of girls who were ready to fill Marina's European and Middle Eastern requests. In addition to being a sun-kissed paradise, Los Angeles had proven to be a well-stocked hunting ground. There were plenty of beautiful women who had no issue with bedding older men for big money. Taras' questions for Marina were always the same. How many girls did she need? Had the buyers been confirmed? And most annoyingly, how quickly would he be paid. Russian by birth but raised in the USA, now a hot shot immigration attorney with a bustling practice in L.A., Taras Verenich expressed and carried himself with the typical holier-than-thou attitude of every spoiled American Marina had ever known. Lately he had become a little too demanding for her liking. No matter. Hot shot immigration lawyer or not, he was still the smallest fish in a very big pond. She would remind him how easily he could be replaced. His behavior was typical of players new to The Company and getting their first taste of serious money. Sooner or later they all needed to be put in their place. And she was exactly the person to do it. She would also let him know that his attitude had not gone unnoticed. The message relayed to her by her superiors had been made clear: make sure Verenich knows The Company's demand for compliance is an order and not a request.

The evening was pleasant and warm. A gentle breeze blew up Novinskiy Boulevard. Marina brushed a wisp of blond hair away from her face. A block away, the gold-gilded parapets of the Kremlin took on a fiery glow in the waning daylight. As she stepped down the stairs of the café, her driver opened the back door of the shiny black town car. A sudden rush of warm air blew his jacket open and briefly exposed the Tokarev pistol secured in his shoulder holster. The driver scanned the street for any unusual movements that could be interpreted as a threat to Marina's safety. Satisfied that all was well, he fastened his jacket.

Marina's cell phone rang as she stepped into the car. She pressed a button on the center console. With a quiet hum, the soundproof privacy screen dividing the driver and passenger compartments raised and locked. The phone display read '035'. Marina stored her contacts by number only, having committed their corresponding client names to memory. She took the call.

"I missed you this morning," Konstantin said. A smile was evident in his gravelly voice.

"After what you put me through last night, I figured you'd had enough," Marina replied.

"Of you? Never. I left you a little treat. Did you find it?"

The tone of her voice was playful. "A treat?" Marina asked. She had learned long ago that it was in her best interest to ensure complete client satisfaction before, during, and after her outcalls. Besides, only those who could afford her ten-thousand dollar per night fee were given her private cell number. Her phone contained the names of dozens of such men and women.

"Check your purse," Konstantin said, "The inside pocket."

The compartment bulged. Marina unzipped her Palladino handbag and looked inside.

"What is this?" she said. She held the phone to her chest, lowered the privacy screen, mouthed the word *home* to her bodyguard and motioned for him to drive. The limousine pulled away from the curb as the screen rose and locked into place.

Konstantin laughed. "I suppose you'll just have to open it to find out!"

Men and their cocks, Marina thought. At least in Konstantin's case he was worth her time.

From her purse she removed a slim black box tied with a red satin ribbon, its cover embossed in silver with the letters "HW." Inside the box was the most beautiful watch she had ever seen. She gasped.

Konstantin heard her reaction. He laughed. "I take it you like it?"

"It's absolutely beautiful," she said. "I'm speechless."

"A small token of my appreciation, my love. Just promise

me you'll think of me when you wear it. I bought it in New York. It's Harry Winston. 18 karat yellow gold. Turn it over."

Marina looked at the back. It was numbered '1.'

"Only fifty of these exist in the world. You have number 1."

"You didn't need to do this, Konstantin."

"Yes, I did."

Marina felt the sincerity in his voice. It was the same sentiment men had bestowed upon her all her life.

"You are perfection, Marina," Konstantin said. "A work of art, just like the watch. And a masterpiece deserves a masterpiece."

"I'm flattered, Konstantin. Thank you."

"You're most welcome." The call waiting tone sounded on Konstantin's line. "I'm sorry, my love. I have to take this call. See you next week. Same time?"

"Of course."

"Enjoy your evening. And the watch. Good night."

"And you."

Marina ended the call and placed her phone on the passenger seat. She admired the watch for a few seconds then slipped it back into the box. She would have to remember to wear it when she met with Konstantin next week.

If only he knew how easy this is for me, she thought. Konstantin was no more important to her than 34 or 36 or any of the other numbered contacts in her phone.

And now, thanks to his call, her quiche was getting cold.

The smell of the food and the hot latte reminded her of how hungry she was. She was still thirty minutes from home. The latte couldn't wait. She opened the lid and inhaled its heavenly aroma.

On the seat, her the cell phone vibrated. The screen read

UNKNOWN CALLER. Perhaps one of her clients had shared her number with a friend, a practice strictly against Company policy. She also changed her number every sixty days. Marina debated whether to take the call or let it go to voicemail. She answered the phone.

"Hello?"

The line was open, but no one spoke.

"Who's calling please?"

The caller was silent. Seagulls cried in the background.

"I'm hanging up..."

"Her name was Paige," the caller said. He paused. "She was my daughter. And you killed her."

11

E VEN THOUGH THE key card tracking system indicated Jason Merrick had swiped out of Dynamic Life Sciences and left the campus shortly after 8:00 A.M., every nook and cranny of the facility needed to be searched. Sergeant Taylor rallied the members of his security team.

Hallier pointed to Taylor's computer tablet. "Can you access DLS personnel records with that?"

"Yes, sir," Taylor replied.

"How detailed are your reports?"

"Very."

"Send me everything you've got on Merrick."

"I'll email his file to you." Taylor tapped the tablet screen several times. "You should have it now, sir."

Hallier checked his phone. A copy of Merrick's personnel file was in his Inbox.

"Got it. Get back to me if your men turn up anything. Button this place up. When you're done, join the others at Los Alamitos."

"Yes, sir."

"Good work, son."

The Sergeant saluted. "Thank you, sir."

Hallier walked away from the security team and placed a call.

"Federal Bureau of Investigation, Los Angeles Field Office."

"This is Colonel Quentin Hallier with the Department of Defense Advanced Research Projects Agency. I need to speak with your Assistant Director in Charge immediately."

"I'm sorry sir, she's not available to speak…"

"I'm not asking, young lady," Hallier demanded. "Find her. Tell her this is a matter of national security."

"Right away, sir. Please hold."

HALLIER'S call was picked up seconds later. "This is Assistant Director Ann Ridgeway. How can I help you, Colonel?"

"Thank you for taking my call, Assistant Director. I have a missing persons situation that requires the immediate assistance of the Bureau."

"Shouldn't you be speaking to LAPD's Missing Persons Unit, Colonel?"

"Not under these circumstances. My subject is a civilian scientist with top secret clearance whose life could be in danger. It's possible he could be under the control of persons with an interest in extracting military secrets from him. Suffice it to say, we need to find him right away."

"When was he last seen?"

"Shortly after eight this morning."

The Assistant Director checked her watch. 1:10 P.M. "Colonel, he's been gone a little over five hours. Why are you reporting him missing so soon?"

Hallier knew Ridgeway was at a significant disadvantage in this discussion. He wasn't able to share with her the full story of the frightening events that had transpired within the last few hours at Dynamic Life Sciences and the potential danger Dr. Jason Merrick posed to the country. That information was Top Secret. She would have to be vetted, her security clearance raised by the Department of Defense before he could reveal the truth; that Merrick's sudden and unexplained disappearance, his actions, and probably his theft of the Channeler and LEEDA technologies, now placed the lives of every American citizen in danger. Even if he could reveal the information to her, she might find it too impossible to believe. But the threat was real, damn real, and he needed her support. Every second spent talking on the phone with her was time lost in the search for Merrick. God knows what plans he might already have executed and the catastrophic fallout those actions would bring. The message scrawled on the back of the family picture, *All Will Pay*, coupled with the murder of his colleagues, made one thing abundantly clear. Merrick was preparing to carry out a mission of his own with the most powerful military technology known to man at his disposal; a weapon so advanced that not even DARPA understood the full extent of its capabilities.

"I'm not at liberty to share the specifics of the situation with you at this time, Assistant Director. But suffice it to say this is a matter of the highest priority. I need your full and complete cooperation and I need it now. If it sounds like I'm telling you what to do it's because I am."

Being given an order by someone she had never spoken to before and who had no direct authority over her whatsoever did not sit well with Ann Ridgeway. "Colonel..."

Hallier didn't give her an opportunity to speak. He

continued. "I also need you to call LAPD and enlist their help in an observe-and-report capacity only. Give me your email address. I'll send you the targets file now."

Target? The Assistant Director took a few seconds to cool off before complying with Hallier's request.

"Thank you," the Colonel said. "The file is on its way. I'm coming to your office right now. Clear your schedule. Be ready for me when I arrive. Give me thirty minutes."

"Will anyone else be joining us, Colonel?" Director Ridgeway asked, perturbed by the demanding tone of the conversation. "CIA? NSA? The President?"

Hallier's reply brought with it a measure of honesty and foreboding that disturbed her. "For everyone's sake, let's hope it doesn't come to that."

EN ROUTE to the FBI Field Office, Hallier placed a call to DARPA. "This is Colonel Quentin Hallier. I need an emergency security approval."

"Level?" the voice asked

"Two."

"Contact?"

"Ridgeway, Ann. Assistant Director in Charge, Federal Bureau of Investigation, Los Angeles Field Office."

"Full or restricted permissions?"

"Restricted."

"Stand by."

After a few seconds, the caller spoke. "Your request has been approved, Colonel."

Hallier ended the call. The general's words played in his mind: *"This was your project. You had oversight on this, Quentin."*

Over the span of his military career, Hallier had

witnessed more than his share of the atrocities that man was capable of dispensing against his fellow man. But that was war, soldier against soldier, controlled circumstances for the most part.

This was different.

Though the why of it remained a mystery, Jason Merrick had given every indication that he was about to take the Channeler and LEEDA projects to a whole new level. Was it possible that the most technologically advanced military weapons in the world were now in the hands of a madman? If that was true, the consequences were unfathomable.

There were only two possible outcomes. The first, take Merrick and Egan into custody. The second was to kill them both. The safe recovery of Channeler and LEEDA was paramount. The lives of the two men would be a small sacrifice to pay to ensure the safety of the American people.

Hallier looked out his window as he traveled along the freeway. In the car beside him a young family laughed and carried on, living their lives as they should, free of worry and fear.

A little girl smiled and waved at him from the back seat of the car.

Hallier smiled, waved back.

If only they knew of the incredible danger in their midst.

The office of the FBI was less than twenty minutes away.

Perhaps in rallying their support this whole ugly mess could be put to rest within the next twenty-four hours.

Hallier slammed his foot down on the accelerator.

The government town car lurched ahead and rocketed along the interstate.

12

THE RUSSIAN MADAM was quiet. The unknown caller had gained access to her private line. Considering how frequently she changed her number this was not an easy task. Marina Puzanova listened. Wealthy and powerful men had been sharing their secrets with her all her life, usually after sex. From that she had learned three valuable lessons: say little, listen more, and make notes of the most intimate and pertinent details of the conversation. The latter could be used to extort vast fortunes from them, in exchange for her silence, at a later point in time, should the need arise. There was tension and hostility in his voice, which told her he was nervous, therefore not a professional. But why shouldn't he be nervous? Surely, he knew that in dealing with her he was dealing with The Company. Only a fool would be bold enough to reach out to her like this. Any man pitiful enough to attempt to entrap her in a telephone conversation, much less accuse her of murder, was indeed enjoying his last breath. He simply did not know it yet.

Marina opened a telephone conversation recording app

on her phone. She would extract as much information as she could from the caller. Later, she would share what she had learned with her superiors. The caller would be found and dealt with in the appropriate manner.

"I'm afraid you have me at a disadvantage," Marina said. "It seems you know me. But I have no idea who you are."

"Who I am is unimportant."

"Perhaps not to you."

"Yes, I know who you are," the caller said. "More accurately, I know *what* you are and what you did."

Fear of loss, Marina thought. Press him. Force him to get to the point.

"I'm sorry," Marina said. "I'm not prepared to pursue this discussion any further. Goodbye."

"Ten years ago!" the caller yelled. His voice had started strong but quickly weakened to a whisper. It broke with the final word.

It worked. It always did. Marina waited for the caller to speak. His breathing was heavy. In the background waves crashed, seagulls cried.

Get him talking.

"Why are you calling me?" Marina asked. "I've made it clear that I don't know you."

The caller's words were poison dipped. "You will come to know me very soon," the man said. "I'm going to take everything and everyone away from you, starting with your business."

Marina was not easily rattled, but the pain and conviction in his voice managed to silence her.

"Your operation is over. Done."

"Operation?" Marina said. "What you are talking about? I don't have an oper--."

"I know about the girls, the transfer points in Los Angeles, Miami, Moscow, Riga, Minsk, Tokyo, Abu Dhabi. Your connection to Russian organized crime. The Company. All of it."

Marina turned off the recording app. She had heard enough. She settled back in her seat, made herself comfortable, sipped her latte.

"You know," Marina said, "in certain cultures there are lines a person is best advised never to cross. To do so is to upset the natural order of things. Russia is one such country. You must know the information

you just shared with me has now placed you well over that line."

"I'm going to take it all apart in ways you can't even begin to imagine."

Marina laughed. "I really don't think so."

"I'll start with your company..."

"Bold threats for one man."

"...and end with you."

"How entertaining."

The caller paused. "Tell me, is Ilya enjoying his studies at Cal State? He has a girlfriend now. Did you know that? Pretty little thing. They spend a lot of time together. Mostly in Marina del Ray and Santa Monica."

The smoothness of the latte did nothing to alleviate the dryness Marina suddenly felt in her throat. She wanted to speak but couldn't. Her son. *How did he know about Ilya?*

"I don't hear you laughing anymore."

"Poshel na khui!" Marina yelled. "Fuck you!"

The line went dead.

Marina stared at the phone.

13

THE "BIG THREE" had arrived at the murder house. CNN, FOX NEWS and MSNBC mobile broadcast satellite trucks lumbered into position and stopped outside the iron gates of the Rosenfeld mansion.

Jordan and Chris stepped out of the FBI Mobile Command Unit. A reporter from FOX called out from behind the barricade. Her cameraman focused his camera squarely on Chris.

"Agent," the woman yelled. "What progress has been made in the investigation so far? Do you have a suspect yet? How bad is the crime scene?"

Chris started to walk toward the reporter. Jordan grabbed him by the arm. "Don't," she said. "She's not worth it. None of them are."

Agent Janet Lynch stepped in front of the two agents. She smiled and addressed the journalists, "I'll be happy to give you a statement," she said, then turned and warned Chris. "Don't even think about talking to the press, Agent Hanover."

GARY WINSTON BROWN

"Maybe we *should* escort her inside," Chris said to Jordan as they walked away. "Show her what a murder scene looks like up close and personal. Give her the full backstage pass. But first I'm going to set the timer on my phone. Because once we get upstairs and she meets the Rosenfeld's I'll bet it won't be more than five seconds before she pukes her guts up."

"Rein it in, Chris," Jordan said. "We've got more important things to worry about right now than her."

"The flash drive and the computer."

"Precisely."

CHRIS AND JORDAN found Agent Hawkins sitting behind the Chippendale desk in the waiting room outside the entrance to the master bedroom.

"What have you got for us, genius?" Jordan asked.

Hawkins motioned for them to take a chair on either side of the desk and settle in beside him.

"Lots," he replied. "I've been trying to wrap my head around this for the last hour. But now I think I know what we have here. Let me start with the flash drive."

Hawkins plugged the drive into the computer. The file labeled "AWP" flashed onto the screen.

"I still don't know what *AWP* stands for yet," Hawkins continued, "but that's not important right now. *This* is what's important."

He opened the file. Five alphanumeric lines, the entire contents of the file, appeared on the screen.

"Look at first line: *DM 14PFnFlenmalGdqFNkdGkajnsD-h6JnrFks*. It starts with two letters, then a space, and is followed by an alphanumeric code. It was those first two letters that kept throwing me off."

78

"How's that?" Jordan asked.

"I thought they were part of the code. They're not. I believe they're *identifiers* for that particular string of code."

"Meaning? Chris asked.

"Each of the identifiers is separate from the rest of the code. Like this one, starting with 'DM.' Each varies in length. The shortest is twenty-four characters long, the longest thirty-four.

"And that tells you what?" Jordan asked.

"My guess? These are Bitcoin keys."

"Bit-*what*?" Chris said.

"Bitcoin keys are account numbers generally used to facilitate financial transactions on the Internet between electronic wallets," Hawkins explained. "Bitcoin is money, just like regular currency. It's a popular means of transferring funds from one account to another between criminal organizations on the Dark Web. Each of these character codes meets the criteria for a Bitcoin address. A second key is required to withdraw the money from the account. All Bitcoin transactions are encrypted."

"Can we open these accounts and see what's in them?" Chris asked.

"Not without knowing the private keys," Hawkins replied. "I think these are just the public account keys. My guess is that the identifier signifies who the account belongs to. But truthfully, VT, RI, GA, PM and HJ could mean just about anything."

"So, the question remains," Jordan said. "What reason would the killer have to put this drive in Dr. Rosenfeld's mouth?"

"Because he wants us to open those accounts," Chris suggested. "Maybe there's something going on in the good doctor's life that he didn't want the world to know about."

"Probably," Hawkins said. He removed the flash drive from the laptop, opened the main drive containing two files labeled Account 1 and Account 2, and resized them so that they appeared side-by-side on the computer screen.

"There are pictures of hundreds of girls in these files," he continued. "No names, just pictures and corresponding codes. I think I know what this might be."

"Me too," Chris said.

"A shopping list," Jordan said.

14

BEN EGAN WATCHED the silhouettes enter through the receiving door at the back of the factory.

The group yelled, screamed, and tested the factory walls for echo.

"I told you guys this place was cool!" one of the men yelled as he ran into the plant. He picked up an object from the floor and threw it. One of the windows shattered.

"Yeah," one of the others replied. "The Sons of Satan used this place as their clubhouse for a while." He football-kicked an empty paint can. The container sailed through the air nearly the entire length of the factory, bounced along the floor, and spun to a stop in front of the pallets behind which Egan was hiding.

"Those guys used to do all kinds of weird shit in here," still another called out. "Animal sacrifices, devil worship, all sorts of stuff. My uncle's a cop. He talked about them all the time. Said every last one of those guys was bat-shit crazy."

Not professionals, Egan thought. Teenagers. Local toughs. Wannabe thugs.

The burliest of the men and apparent leader of the group stepped out from the shadows and crossed the factory floor to where an old furniture inspection station stood.

He barked an order at one of the men. "Get over here. Grab an end. Move it over there."

Together they slid the heavy wooden table aside. Remnants of old cloth and cotton batting covered the floor where the table had been situated. The leader kicked away the refuse. "This is what we came for," he said.

A bright beam of sunlight poured in through a cluster of windows that somehow had remained relatively free of dirt and grime and placed a spotlight on the area where they stood. A five-point pentagram was etched into the concrete floor. A horned goat's head stared up at the men from the middle of the satanic symbol. The words 'ETERNALLY S.O.S' surrounded the pentagram.

"Holy shit, Colin! You knew this was here?"

"Yeah. My brother rode with Sons of Satan 'til he got sent upstate," the leader replied. "He told me about it. He and the guys used to have what they called 'coming of age' parties here." Colin talked about his brother's experiences with the motorcycle gang as though they had been his own.

The smallest kid in the group spoke up. "What's a coming-of-age party?"

Colin smirked at the kid then shook his head, as if to infer he was stupid for not understanding the term. "S.O.S would bring their new prospects here. They'd tell them there was going to be a huge party... strippers, booze, coke, weed...whatever they wanted. Everybody was gonna get laid and get wasted. Except that was never the plan. Instead, they'd get jumped in, right here, on this very spot."

"Jumped in?" the same kid asked.

"They'd get the crap beat out of them. Fuck them up a

little. Not so much that they couldn't walk or talk... nothing that bad. They'd make them swear their allegiance to the club... called it 'becoming eternally S.O.S.' Then they'd make a blood bond. The new prospects had to do something that bound them to the club for life."

"Like what?" the kid asked.

"They'd send out a full-patch member to pick up a hooker and bring her back here. The guys would take turns partying with her. Then sometime before daybreak..."

Colin walked over to the wooden fabrication station. He removed a black-handled knife from a leather scabbard that had been fastened to the underside of the table.

"...they'd have a blood sacrifice. They'd force the prospect to kill her with this dagger while the rest of them watched. A whole club full of witnesses... a *blood bond*."

Colin opened the drawer of the table and removed a cloth bag. He opened it and took out its contents: five black candles, several books of matches, a silver bell, and a black leather-bound book. He laid the items out on the table.

"What are you doing?" the kid asked.

"Shut up, Kevin," Colin said. He knelt, placed a candle on each point of the pentagram and lit the wicks.

Kevin protested. "I don't like this, Colin." The boy was scared. "Not one bit."

"I said shut up!" Colin yelled. He stood and motioned to the teen on his right. "Get the little shit out of my sight, Jacob."

Jacob grabbed Kevin by the collar and held him tight. Kevin tried to struggle free, but it was no use. He was no match for the much stronger Jacob.

Colin picked up the silver bell and rang it once. The clear tone resonated throughout the factory. He turned it counterclockwise to signify the commencement of the ritual.

"It's time," Colin said.

The teens gathered around the pentagram. Jacob locked Kevin's arm behind his back, held him tight.

"Where is she?" Colin asked.

"Waiting at the back door," Jacob said. "She said the place creeps her out."

Colin walked to the table, picked up the black book, slipped the dagger into his belt. He turned to Lenny, his second in command.

"Get her."

Lenny nodded. He turned and headed toward the receiving area at the back of the factory.

"*No!*" Kevin struggled to break free of Jacob, couldn't. Lenny clamped his hand tightly over his mouth, muffling his words as he tried to scream. "*Rnnn, Laurrrnnn! Rnnnnn!*"

From the back of the factory, Lauren thought she heard her brother's muffled cry. She called out. "Kevin? You okay?"

Kevin bit down hard. Jacob screamed and pulled back his hand. Kevin shoved him aside and yelled. "Lauren! Get out of here now! Run Lauren... Run... *RUN!*"

Kevin heard his sister scream.

"Lenny, you asshole," Lauren said. "Take your hands off me! Let... me... go!"

Lenny walked back toward the group, pulling Lauren by her hair, holding her at arm's length. Suddenly he stopped dead in his tracks.

Colin looked at him. "What's wrong with you? Bring her over here!"

Lenny didn't reply.

"Jesus, Lenny! I said..."

Lenny pointed past the group.

At the back of the factory a man stood in the shadows. He stepped into the light.

"Let the girl go," he called out.

Startled, the group turned in the direction of the stranger's voice.

"I said let her go. *Now*."

15

H ALLIER WAS GREETED in the lobby of the FBI's Los Angeles field office by Special Agent Brent Cobb. Cobb pressed the elevator call button for the seventeenth floor.

"ADC Ridgeway is waiting for you, Colonel," he said. "She asked me to provide you with any assistance you'll need."

"That won't be necessary," Hallier said.

"Sir?"

Hallier didn't reply.

The elevator whisked the men to the seventeenth floor. "On your left, Colonel," Cobb said as the men exited the elevator.

Assistant Director in Charge Ann Ridgeway was speaking to her administrative assistant when Agent Cobb and Hallier walked through the double glass entrance doors into her office.

"ADC Ridgeway," Agent Cobb introduced, "Colonel Hallier from DARPA."

"Good to meet you, Colonel." The Assistant Director smiled and shook his hand.

"Likewise," Hallier replied. "We're on the clock Agent Ridgeway. You ready?"

Apparently as arrogant in person as he had been on the phone, Ann Ridgeway forced a smile and reminded herself of the Bureau's commitment to foster healthy inter-agency cooperation.

"Of course, Colonel," she replied. "Please come in. And it's *Assistant Director* if you please."

Agent Cobb tried to follow them into Ridgeway's office. Hallier stopped him at the door.

"Sorry son," he said, "you'll have to wait outside. You're not cleared for this discussion."

Cobb looked to his boss for direction.

"It's all right, Agent Cobb," Ridgeway said. "I'll contact you if I need you."

"Yes, ma'am." The agent nodded and left the office.

The Assistant Director's office was furnished more like a home than a place of business with a large rosewood desk and plush high-back leather chair. The wall-to-wall book-case behind the desk contained FBI procedural manuals as well as framed photos of special events in her life: hamming it up with friends over drinks, a family picture with her husband and two kids, all of them dressed in white, and their three German Sheppard's. A framed basketball jersey signed by Los Angeles Lakers basketball star LeBron James hung on one wall. On the other, the FBI Medal of Valor.

"I see you're a Lakers fan," Hallier said, pointing at the jersey.

Ann Ridgeway seated herself in her chair. "My brother-in-law is the Lakers strength training coach. LeBron's a friend."

"I'm more of a golf man myself," Hallier said. He turned his attention to the framed medal. "I'm impressed," he said.

"Don't be," Ridgeway said. "Any number of agents should have received that medal that day. I keep it there to remind me never let my guard down again. And of how an otherwise average day can go to hell in a heartbeat."

"Mind if I ask what happened?"

"Three agents and I were assigned to a return-to-prison transfer detail for a convict, Anton Carpaccio."

"I know the name from the news," Hallier said. "Serial killer. Twelve victims, right?"

"Fourteen," Ridgeway corrected. "Carpaccio drew a shiv on the wrong guy in prison. Ended up on the business end of the blade and took nine stab wounds for his trouble. Unfortunately for the rest of humanity the bastard didn't die. The prison rushed him to Cedars-Sinai Hospital for emergency surgery. Two weeks later the docs declared him well enough to leave and the State called us in to facilitate return transport. When the orderlies were helping him out of his wheelchair Carpaccio doubled over. One of the agents stepped in to help him. Big mistake. It was a setup. Carpaccio grabbed him around the neck, then got control of his gun. He drew down on another agent, Bill Cooper. Coop was on my left. I knew Carpaccio was going to shoot him, which he did. I threw myself in front of the shot and knocked Coop out of the way. Carpaccio's round caught me in the shoulder when we fell. Another agent, Trevor John-ston, was standing beyond of the line of fire. He shot Carpaccio just as he turned on him. One round, a perfect shot, right between his eyes. Blew out the back of his head. Bad for Carpaccio, good for us. We all went home to our families that day. Around here we call that a win."

"You saved Agent Cooper's life," Hallier said.

"Not me. Agent Johnston did. He saved all our lives when he took that shot. The only reason they gave me the medal is because I caught a bullet covering Coop."

"How's the shoulder now?"

ADC Ridgeway pointed to the framed basketball jersey and smiled. "Let's just say LeBron doesn't have anything to worry about."

Hallier cracked a smile.

The Assistant Director sat back in her chair. "So, tell me Colonel. What's so important that DARPA needs the Bureau's help? I thought you guys always flew solo when it came to matters of national security."

"Normally we do," Hallier replied. "But there is someone I need to find fast, and I can't rally enough manpower to cover the ground as quickly as you can. I need your help to track down a missing scientist by the name of Dr. Jason Merrick."

"By missing do you mean abducted?"

Hallier shrugged. "We don't know the full circumstances related to Dr. Merrick's disappearance yet. But we have reason to believe he may be in possession of a technology that has the potential to harm many people."

"You think he might be trying to sell the technology to our enemies?"

"I'm afraid that's a possibility."

"Why come to us and not LAPD?" Ridgeway asked. "They could put an army of feet on the street for you in a matter of seconds."

"That's precisely what I don't want," the Colonel replied. "This has to be done quietly. I need professionals, not street cops. Your team will be under explicit instructions to observe and report - that's all. I want Dr. Merrick located as soon as possible and placed under surveillance until my men are ready to make their move. The decision to engage will be made by me and no one else."

"So you're asking for the Bureau's help, but you don't think we're capable of taking Merrick into custody on your behalf. Is that it? Seriously, Colonel, we're a little better trained than you're giving us credit for."

"No, you're not, Assistant Director," Hallier replied curtly. "Not for Merrick."

Ann Ridgeway looked perplexed. "You know the one thing that I hate more than anything else, Colonel? When people aren't straight with me. You need to come clean, right now. I'm fine with this being your operation, but these are *my* people. Exactly what is it you're not telling me? Just how much danger will my agents be in?"

Hallier didn't answer.

Undaunted, the Assistant Director pressed him for a reply.

"All right, Colonel," she said. "Let me put the question to you another way." Ann Ridgeway leaned forward and placed her elbows on her desk. "Exactly what is it about Merrick that has DARPA's sphincter registering a ten-out-of-ten on the pucker scale?"

16

B LACK AND WHITES blocked off the store services lane at the back of the Corona Mews Shopping Mall. Chief Riley Jenkins had been called to the crime scene when it was confirmed that part of a human thumb had been found beside a Dumpster at the back of the mall. Deputy Jack Poole met him as he arrived and stepped out of his Jeep. The Chief was already in a sour mood. He had spent the last sixteen hours interrogating a suspect about a murder in a municipality that hadn't seen the commission of a violent crime in the last ten years. The experience had left him feeling drained and more than a little touchy.

"What've we got?" Jenkins asked. Poole met him at the Jeep and ducked under the black and yellow crime scene tape. Corona County coroner, Dr. Earl Kent, was kneeling on the ground at the foot of the garbage bin collecting samples from the ground and carefully placing them in plastic specimen jars.

"A couple of kids out for a bike ride found it while Dumpster diving," Poole replied. "Freaked 'em out when they saw it was real. They rode home and told their parents, who called us. We had already dispatched a unit to check out a complaint from a resident who backs onto the laneway. Guy reported a stench coming from the back of the mall. Said it smelled like rotten meat. Two of our guys puked their guts up as soon as they got here. Can't say I blame 'em either. It stinks to high heaven over there."

"What's that under your nose, Jack?" Chief Jenkins asked. He reached out his finger and touched a shiny layer of gel under Poole's nostrils.

Poole drew his head back, brushed away the Chief's hand. "Mentholatum," he muttered.

"Seriously... you?"

"Yep."

"And I thought you were a seasoned veteran."

Poole smirked. "You don't see me over there decorating the pavement with my lunch and messing up a perfectly good crime scene, do you? No. Why? Experience, my friend. Remember what happened last year with Stinky Steve?"

"The floater we hauled out of Royce Lake."

"Exactly. That dude was riper than my brother-in-law's farts. And believe me, that man can clear a room. I swear he stores up his crap for weeks. After Stinky Steve, me and my Mentholatum go everywhere together."

"I'll bet your wife loves that."

"She takes after her brother," Poole said. "Lucky me." He removed the small container of Mentholatum from his trouser pocket and offered it to the Chief. "Want some?"

Jenkins waved him off. "I'm good."

"Suit yourself," Poole said. He applied more of the menthol-scented gel under his nostrils. "Don't say I didn't warn ya."

Dr. Earl Kent scooped a specimen of gooey paste off the

asphalt at the foot of the Dumpster and spread it inside a sample jar. He stood as Chief Jenkins and Deputy Poole approached.

"Thumb's definitely human, Chief" Dr. Kent confirmed. "Distal phalanx. Part of the joint is still intact with some partial ridge detail remaining. Not much, but I've preserved it."

"Good," Jenkins replied. "Run the print. Let's see if we get a hit."

The medical examiner nodded and gestured toward the bin. "You need to look at this."

The men walked over to a section of carpet that lay open on the ground beside the garbage container. A thick opaque mass had congealed on the filthy floor covering, the result of its direct exposure to the afternoon sun.

"We pulled it out of the bin and unrolled it," Dr. Kent said. "Some of it leaked out. The whole container reeks."

"Leaked out?" Jenkins asked.

The coroner nodded. "They're liquefied remains, Chief. So far, the tip of the thumb is the only physical part of the body we've been able to find. Which is to say these remains might not comprise the whole body. After all, the thumb was found beside the Dumpster, not in it. This might just be the disposal site and not our primary crime scene."

"Jesus." Chief Jenkins removed his microphone from its shoulder clip. "4512 to Command," he said.

"Go ahead, 4512."

"Dispatch a K-9 to my location, 10-18. Tell them to meet me on scene."

"4512. K-9, 10-18, your location. Copy that."

"4512."

With the urgent assistance for a canine tracking dog requested, the Chief continued his discussion with Dr. Kent.

"What the hell could have caused this, doc?"

Kent shrugged. "If I were to speculate, I'd say alkaline hydrolysis, also called 'green death.' Funeral homes and crematoriums offer it these days as an alternative to traditional burial or cremation. The body is liquefied in a chemical bath at high temperature and then separated from ash and bone in a drying process. The dry remains are left. The liquid is disposed of off–site."

"Any funeral homes around here doing that?"

"None that I'm aware of. And if there were, state law would require them to use a pick-up service to properly dispose of the liquid waste."

"What if someone wanted to do it themselves... to dispose of a body this way. Could they?"

"I suppose so," Dr. Kent replied. "They'd need a pressure vessel large enough to accommodate a body and could handle a mixture of water and lye at a temperature just shy of boiling. But yes, it could be done."

"You thinking body dump, Chief?" Poole speculated. "Mexicans, maybe? Sinaloa cartel getting creative?"

"Could be," Jenkins answered.

An officer who had been sifting through the contents of the Dumpster called out. "Got something here, Chief."

The officer stood on a ladder that had been placed into the garbage bin to facilitate ease of entry and exit from the container. In his hands he held two magnetic car signs. Each read, *Dan's Home Improvements*. The phone number on the sign was local.

"Pass me a couple of evidence bags," the officer said. "There's more stuff down here the doc should take a look at."

Chief Jenkins removed his cell phone and dialed the number on the sign.

From somewhere within the disposal bin a phone rang. The officer poked around, found it. "Got it," he said. He passed the ringing phone to Jenkins. The Chief hit the speaker button just before the call went to voicemail. The announcement began to play: *'You've reached Dan Labrada at Dan's Home Improvements. Sorry I can't take your call at the present time...'*

"Son of a bitch," Chief Jenkins said.

He snatched the radio mic from his lapel: "4512 to Command," he snapped. "Where the hell is my K-9?"

17

HALLIER TOOK A SEAT. The Assistant Director was right. Her people would be in danger. She deserved to know the truth. To that end, an emergency security clearance had been approved to permit the Colonel to share sensitive military information with her in his search for Merrick.

"Ten years ago," Hallier began, "DARPA commenced a two-tier black book project with one simple objective: to create a human military asset that could be deployed at a moment's notice anywhere in the world in a battle-ready covert capacity. Dr. Jason Merrick was selected to lead the research team. We code-named the co-projects Channeler and LEEDA."

"Sounds like the plot of a Hollywood movie," Ridgeway said.

"Far from it," the Colonel replied. "Dr. Merrick was tasked to create organic and inorganic exploration technologies that would be capable of syncing with the human brain and which would permit psychic dimensional crossover. In truth, we've been able to do this for quite some time. But our objective for the Channeler and LEEDA projects was to take it to the next level."

"Exactly what do you mean by psychic exploration?"

"Mind travel. Also known as remote viewing."

"Dr. Merrick was able to accomplish this?"

"And more."

"My God."

Hallier continued. "The project succeeded beyond our wildest expectations. One of our best and brightest, a Commander by the name of Ben Egan, was selected to field test Channeler and push it to its limit. This morning, Merrick disappeared from DARPA's technological development think tank, Dynamic Life Sciences, under unusual circumstances." The Colonel removed the photograph of Merrick taken with his family in Paris and showed it to the Assistant Director. "I don't think for a second that he was abducted."

"Nice family shot," Ridgeway said. "But how is this relevant?"

"Read the back."

She turned over the picture. "All will pay," she said. "Merrick wrote this?"

"Yes."

"Sounds like a threat."

"We're proceeding under that assumption," Hallier said. He removed the Channeler prototype from his pocket and laid it on the desk. Ridgeway picked it up, examined it.

"What's this?"

"That is the result of nine years of research and investigation into man's ability to harness the secret capabilities of the human mind. It's the first prototype of Project Channeler. Merrick left it for us to find."

Ridgeway looked puzzled. "I don't understand. If you have the device in your possession what's the concern?"

"Like I said, that is the first prototype. We're now six generations beyond what you're holding in your hand. Merrick is in control of Channeler. And Commander Egan is missing as well."

"You think the Commander has turned?"

Hallier shook his head. "No," he replied. "I believe Egan is a just pawn in Merrick's game. But if Merrick has control of Channeler he's probably controlling Egan, too. The current version of Channeler imbues Egan with the power to do things we never thought humans could be capable of accomplishing, like physical energy transference, modulation, and telekinesis. We believe Merrick has achieved Channeler and LEEDA's penultimate goals: the ability to break down and rematerialize matter at the cellular level, at will, using nothing more than the power of the human mind."

"You're not saying what I *think* you're saying..."

"You would more commonly know it as teleportation."

The Assistant Director leaned back in her chair, speechless. Finally, she asked, "So this is real? We're actually able to do this?"

"Yes. And Channeler and LEEDA are just the tip of the iceberg, Assistant Director. I can't tell you where we plan to go from here. That's highly classified. Suffice it to say, we're just getting started."

"What about Commander Egan?" Ridgeway asked. "If Merrick is controlling Channeler, and Channeler is controlling the Commander, shouldn't we be looking for him too?"

"Yes," Hallier replied. "But finding Merrick is the key. Shut down Merrick and we shut down Egan and eliminate the threat in the process."

"And Project Channeler? What happens to it?"

"It's over. With Merrick, Egan and both technologies unaccounted for there is no telling what might happen. Both Merrick and the Commander might not be recoverable."

"Meaning?"

"Did you review the file I sent you on Merrick?"

"I did." Ann Ridgeway turned in her chair and retrieved the printout from her credenza.

Hallier continued. "Then you'll recall a reference to a personal tragedy the doctor endured many years ago. His daughter, Paige, was found dead. She had been murdered. The case was never solved. That incident broke him. Shortly afterward, Merrick's wife, Alma, was diagnosed with terminal cancer. Alma had always been a healthy and vibrant woman. The day that she received the news of her daughter's death she fell apart; probably lost her will to live. She refused to continue her cancer treatment. Merrick tried to encourage her to stay under care, but she wouldn't. It was only a matter of time before she was gone."

"And Dr. Merrick?"

"Took an extended leave. Closed himself off from the world. Had no contact with the lab whatsoever. Then one day he shows up. Throws himself back into his work. After that, progress on the Channeler and LEEDA projects picked up at an astonishing rate. Every month his team was announcing one new breakthrough or another. But despite all his success Merrick remained distant. He hardly engaged with his colleagues, just ran the projects. As one of them put it, he seemed continually preoccupied. He kept to himself. He was obsessed with working with the Commander and insisted on being his field handler. Even threatened to pull out of the project if we disagreed, so we let him have his way.

We weren't worried. He was under constant supervision, even though he never knew it. But somewhere along the way we dropped the ball. He found a way to steal Channeler and LEEDA for reasons we don't yet know."

"Do you think he plans to sell it?"

Hallier shook his head. "That's doubtful. Geniuses like Merrick are too personally invested in their work to part with it for mere financial gain. For them it is about receiving peer recognition in the scientific community. No, something more is going on here."

Ridgeway read the statement on the back of the picture again. "According to this, his intention seems pretty clear."

"I agree," Hallier said. "So, Assistant Director. Can I count on your help?"

ADC Ridgeway stood, extended her hand.

"I'll assemble a team right away. Let's go find your men, Colonel."

Hallier shook her hand. "Thank you. Your government appreciates your help." He turned to leave.

"One last thing, Colonel."

Hallier looked back at the Assistant Director. "Yes?"

"It's Ann."

Hallier smiled. "Quentin."

18

K-9 OFFICER KIP barked, wagged his tail, and jumped out of the back seat of the black and white Ford Explorer. Police Canine Supervisor Don Button attached Kip's search lead to his collar and made a fuss over his partner. He bounced the dogs training ball on the pavement, teased him and scratched his head. Kip knew it was time to go to work.

The dog sniffed the ground and followed a direct path to the Dumpster. Beside it, the open carpet that had been smeared with the foul-smelling matter had been bagged and tagged for forensic processing. Kip ran to the long plastic bag and lay down beside it, barking repeatedly, a confirmation to his partner that he had found precisely what he had been trained to find: human remains.

"Good boy, Kipper!" Officer Button said, "Such a good boy!" Button tossed Kip's hard rubber ball on the ground within catching distance of the dog. Kip pounced to his left, caught the ball mid-bounce, and began chewing contently on the rubber training toy.

"That confirms it," Chief Jenkins said to the coroner.

Dr. Kent patted the dog's head. "Yes, it does. I'll take the carpet to the morgue. We'll run a few tests. See what we come up with."

"You think this is Dan Labrada?" Jenkins asked.

"If his DNA is on file we'll know soon enough. Failing that, I'll have to send it to the State lab. I deal with natural causes: floaters, the occasional motor vehicle accident, death by misadventure, and so on. But this? This is... *soup*."

"Thanks for the visual, doc. Remind me not to have lunch with you anytime soon."

Dr. Kent knelt beside Kip. The German Shepherd rolled onto his back, soaked up the attention.

Officer Byers, who had been given the unfortunate job of scouring the disposal bin for evidence, threw his leg over the top of the Dumpster onto the ladder. He lost his balance, fell, and landed hard on the ground, twisting his ankle. He grabbed his foot. "Son of a bitch!" he yelled.

"You okay, Pat?" Jenkins asked.

Kip chuffed and rolled to his feet.

"Yeah, Chief. I'm good." Kip walked over to Byers and sniffed his foot.

Pat rubbed the dog's face. "Thanks, buddy. I'm okay."

Kip lay down beside Byers and started to bark.

"Either he smells dead guy on you," Officer Poole teased, "or you need to give serious thought to changing your deodorant, Pat."

"Funny," Byers replied, "This coming from the guy who discovered Stinky Steve. Or should I say, *wore* him for a few days?"

Poole crossed his arms. "That wasn't my fault, and you know it. He blew up."

"Damn straight he did. All over you."

Frustrated, Poole said, "Ask the doc. It could have

happened to you, the Chief... anyone who found that body was in for it. The guy had been cooking on the shore for a week."

"True, but you drew the short straw, Big Man. I heard he went up like a landmine. Boom!"

Deputy Poole looked at the coroner as if to say, 'a little help here, please?'

Dr. Kent took the hint. "The body breaks down," he explained, hoping to diffuse the goodhearted ribbing Officer Poole was taking. "Internal organs start to decay, gas is produced. Jack's right. Whoever was first to respond to the beached floater was likely going to experience what he did."

Poole smiled at Officer Byers. "There you go!" he said. "Doc just explained it perfectly."

"Sorry, Jack," Pat replied. "It must have been tough, buddy."

"It was," Poole said.

"...picking him out of your hair for a week."

Deputy Poole threw his hands in the air and walked away.

Chief Jenkins laughed. "You're a cruel man, Byers."

Byers smiled. "Hey, the Big Man's always riding me," he said. "I thought I'd have a little fun at his expense for a change." He grabbed the dog by the collar. "Hey, boy. How about helping me up?"

Kip pulled back and barked. Panting, he stared at his handler. Officer Button knew the meaning behind every sound his partner made as distinctly as he knew the sound of his own voice.

"He's alerting," Button said. "Move aside, Pat."

Byers rose gingerly to his feet as Officer Button leashed Kip. "Good boy, Kipper," he commanded. He teased the dog with the ball once more. "Ready?" Kip barked. "*Search!*"

The dog responded to the instruction and lunged forward, but only by a few feet. He pawed at the base of the Dumpster.

"Bin's empty, Don," Byers said. "Everything's been removed and tagged. Right down to the last scrap of paper."

"I don't think Kip's alerting to what's in the bin," Officer Button said. "He's alerting to what's under it."

Button threw the ball and released the dog from duty. He knelt and peered under the bin.

"Somebody hand me a pair of tweezers."

Dr. Kent opened his field bag and passed the implement to him.

"Got it," Button said as he slid his arm out from under the dumpster. A tiny metallic object was cinched between the pincers of the metal instrument. Dr. Kent offered an evidence bag. Button dropped the object into the plastic bag.

"Think that's what Kip was alerting to?" Button asked the coroner.

Dr. Kent inspected the item. "Dental implant. Titanium. Serialized. I'll have forensic odontology process it and run the number."

"Think it belonged to Labrada?" Officer Button asked.

"I hope so," Kent replied.

"You *hope* so?"

Dr. Kent nodded. "If it doesn't, we have an even bigger problem on our hands."

"Multiple victims," Chief Jenkins said.

"Exactly."

Kip threw his ball in the air, watched it bounce, crouched, waited for it to roll a good distance, then raced after it, caught it in his mouth and threw it in the air a second time. He stopped in front of the Chief's Jeep and watched the ball roll away. The dog barked twice, the second bark louder than the first, then lay on the ground.

"Looks like your partner's ready to call it a day," Byers said to Officer Button.

Kip barked three times. He looked over his shoulder in the direction of his handler.

Button stood and called out to his partner. "Kip, *Mark!*"

Kip barked.

"He's alerting again, Chief."

Chief Jenkins and Officer Byers walked to the dog. Button attached Kip's leash to his body harness.

"I don't see anything," Byers said.

"The first thing you need to know about Kip is that he's never wrong," Officer Button said. "He's on to something." Button praised the dog then gave him his search command. Kip walked under the barrier tape and out of the crime scene area, passing the Chief's Jeep and straining on his lead as he sniffed his way across the parking lot in the direction of the garage. He rounded the back of a black Porsche 911 and sat in front of its front bumper. The dog barked twice, then lay on the ground.

"This is it," Officer Button whispered. He grabbed Kip firmly by his collar and issued the dog a new command. "Kip... *Set!*"

The dog's gentle disposition changed immediately. The hackles raised on the back of his neck. He dropped low, tensed on his lead, growled.

"Dog's ready, Chief," Button said.

The officers readied their weapons and trained them on the front trunk of the Porsche.

"Break the window," the Chief demanded. "Pop the hood."

Officer Byers removed a collapsible baton from his duty

belt, snapped it open, smashed out the side window and opened the driver's door. He located the hood release under the dashboard and pulled the handle.

Kip strained, snarled, barked, and pulled. Officer Button maintained a firm grip on the dog's collar as he tore at the ground with his powerful front legs.

Poole raised the hood.

Empty.

"Clear!" the Chief called out. The officers holstered their weapons.

"Kip, *Steady*," Officer Button commanded. Kip relaxed and waited for his treat. Button rewarded the dog with his ball.

Byers looked at Officer Button. "What were you saying about Kip never being wrong?"

"He isn't. My guess is that he was tracking residue, probably from the killer's shoes."

The Chief nodded. "I agree. Jack, run the plates. Pat, go back to the primary and grab a couple of guys from forensics. Tell them to go over the car bumper to bumper."

"You got it, Chief." Officer Poole radioed in Jenkins request for a license plate search to Command.

Chief Jenkins removed a pair of latex gloves from his pocket, snapped them on and carefully lowered the driver's side sun visor. A plastic photo identification card with a metal belt clip fell onto the driver's seat. He picked it up.

"Employee access card," Jenkins said. "ID belongs to a Dr. Jason Merrick. Works at Dynamic Life Sciences."

"I know the place," Poole said. "Some kind of high-tech military research center. It's about ten minutes from here." Poole's radio crackled.

"Command, 3250."

Poole responded. "Go for 3250."

"Vehicle identification is a 2015 Chevy Suburban, silver, registered to a Daniel Raymond Labrada, Riverside, California. No warrants."

"3250. Copy."

Poole looked at Chief Jenkins and back at the Porsche. "That ain't no Suburban, Chief. Our guy switched plates."

Jenkins nodded. "Run the vehicle identification number on the Porsche and get its plates on the air. Make sure everyone knows they're looking for a Chevy Suburban and not a Porsche." Chief Jenkins placed the identification card in a plastic evidence bag and began to walk toward his Jeep. He called out to Poole.

"Manage the scene, Jack. Get in touch with me the minute you hear something on that Suburban."

"You got it, Chief. Where're you headed?"

"Dynamic Life Sciences." Jenkins replied. He held up the photo ID. "Dr. Merrick and I need to have a little chat."

19

L ENNY RELEASED HIS grip on the terrified girl. Lauren ran to her brother.

Ben Egan called out to Lauren and Kevin. "You two, over here."

Lauren picked up her pace as she ran. She had no idea who the stranger was or where he had come from, but at this moment she didn't care. There was confidence and strength in his voice, and she knew instinctively that he would protect them.

Kevin walked cautiously towards the stranger. Colin chased after him. Kevin heard him approaching from behind and tried to outrun the older boy. Too late, the leader caught up to him and put his arm around his neck. Kevin struggled under Colin's firm grip. The older boy drew the dagger from his back pocket and held it to his throat. Kevin felt the cold metal pressing against his skin. The razor edge of the blade cut him. A trickle of warm blood ran down his neck. He stopped resisting.

Colin maneuvered the boy in front of him. "Mister, I don't know who you are," he said, "but I'm telling you now, back off. I'll gut this little shit like a pig. Right here, right now."

"I don't think so," Ben Egan said.

Colin couldn't believe what he was hearing. "Are you out of your mind, asshole?" He laughed. "Fine by me, man. Huge mistake. Huge!"

The punk's body language changed. His shoulders tightened. He dropped his head, shuffled from side to side, and readied himself for the kill. Kevin moved with him, trying desperately to avoid the blade from cutting deeper. More blood ran down his neck. Kevin was more than just frightened now. He was terrified. He thought he might lose his water right then and there, maybe even soil his pants in front of the whole group. *As if that mattered*, he thought. In any second Colin would run the blade across his neck and cut him from ear to ear, maybe even cut his head clean off, and end his life. This was never supposed to have happened. The gang had told him the old factory was going to be a cool place to check out. They had insisted he bring his sister along. *Stupid!* Now, he had put both their lives in danger. Why the hell did he feel it was so important to impress Colin anyway? The older boy was nothing but trouble and had been all his life. His father had warned them to stay away from Colin Thackery and his delinquent family. He thought he could trust Lenny, that he was his friend. The two of them had played him for a fool. He had never felt so close to death before. Why should he? He was only seventeen years old. *Seventeen!* Too young to die, especially here, in a dirty abandoned factory on the outskirts of town. His body was becoming weak from fear. His legs felt like jelly, and he was sure they would be incapable of supporting him for very much longer. He couldn't fight because he couldn't move. Fear had left him physically incapacitated. He remembered hearing his grandmother whisper to his grandfather on his death bed: *make your peace with God*. So that's what he did. Kevin prayed that at the very least his body would be found. He was going to miss so much. His mother and father, family movie nights, the choice between watching a comedy or a thriller (usually settled by an all-out popcorn fight), his sister, Lauren, pain in the butt that she was, his classmates at school, even his obscenely fat doorstop of a cat, Moose.

"Remember, this is all on you, pal," Colin said to the stranger. Kevin felt Colin's grip tighten. Resignation overtook his body. He waited for the end to come.

Colin started to groan.

Then the strangest thing happened.

Kevin felt Colin release his chokehold. The blade of the knife no longer pressed against his throat. Colin's arm was extended in front of him now. It began to quiver, then shook so violently that the knife dropped out of his hand. The blade clanged on the concrete floor. There was a cry in Colin's voice, not one of upset, but of fear.

The man at the end of the factory spoke to Kevin. "Move away from him," he said. "Come here now. Get behind me."

Kevin ran to the stranger. He knew he had no good reason to trust him. For all he knew they had unwittingly stumbled into the hideout of a murderer who would kill them all sooner or later. Still, he ran. With his only two options being free of Colin or having the knife pressed to his throat the decision to run to the stranger seemed like the wisest choice.

When he was safely behind the stranger he turned and looked at Colin and his gang. The stranger was holding his hands out in front of him. On his wrist he wore a strange bracelet in which pulses of blue light throbbed. Kevin and

Lauren watched as the man raised his hands and opened his fingers. The light from the bracelet turned from blue to orange. Colin and his gang started to yell and scream and looked down at their feet. They tried to move their legs, couldn't. Their feet seemed glued to the floor. Lenny even tried to pull his feet out of his running shoes without success.

"What are you doing to us?" Colin cried out. "What *are* you?"

Ben Egan slowly raised his hands. The boys began to lift off the ground. They were now perhaps forty feet in the air, almost as high as the factory ceiling itself, screaming and flailing frantically. Droplets fell from Lenny as he felt his body press tightly against the roof of the factory. The pigeons that earlier had been frightened out of their sleep took flight once again among the steel girders and circled them madly, unsure what to make of the intruders in their midst. It was then that Kevin realized what the falling droplets were. The water was coming from Lenny. He had wet himself. Drops of urine splattered down upon the factory floor. One of the men had passed out from fear and hung limply in the air. The stranger dropped his hands to his side. The gang began to free fall, screaming as the ground rushed up to meet them. Lauren gasped and turned away, unable to bear witness to their imminent demise.

The stranger raised his hands quickly, faced his palms toward the ceiling, and halted their sudden descent. They hung in the air horizontally, facing the ground but unable to touch it, bodies frozen, unable to move. They were silent now. All of the fight had been drained out of them. Lenny peed again, then threw up.

Egan turned his palms to the floor and dropped his arms

to his side. The gang fell the last couple of feet onto the floor of the warehouse.

Kevin stood beside Ben Egan. He watched as the glow from the metal band around his wrist dissipated, turning from light blue to white, and finally back to its original metallic appearance.

"Holy shit on a stick!" Kevin said. "Did you see that Lauren? Did you?"

Egan looked at the boy. "Language, son," he said.

"Oh, sure, whatever you say, mister," Kevin said. "But... I mean... that was the coolest thing I've ever... how did you... holy sh--... I mean... *holy crap!*"

"Both of you wait here," Egan said.

Lauren began to walk after Ben Egan. Kevin grabbed his sister and pulled her back. "Seriously, Lauren?" Kevin said. "Didn't you just see him lift those guys off the ground? What part of *wait here* don't you understand? Duh!"

Egan walked across the factory to where the thugs lay sprawled on the floor. Colin looked at the ceremonial dagger laying a few feet in front of him, then up at Egan.

"You sure you want to do that?" Egan asked.

Colin's face was purple. He was seething with rage and embarrassment at being so completely and utterly dominated by the supernatural powers of the stranger. He lunged for the knife.

Egan waved his hand. The dagger lifted off the ground and streaked through the air with such velocity its blade penetrated deep into a wooden support column on the opposite side of the factory.

Egan looked at the gang as they gathered themselves up off the floor.

"Coming here was a mistake," he told them. "I can't let you leave."

Lenny pleaded with Egan. His pants were soaked in urine. A string of vomit hung from his chin. He wiped it away with his coat sleeve. "Look, man," he said. "It's all good. Just let us go. I swear to God no one's gonna talk."

"Shut up, Lenny!" Colin ordered.

Lenny continued. "We'll just walk outta here and leave you alone, mister. No problem. We don't want any trouble."

"It's a little late for that," Egan replied.

Colin looked over his shoulder at Lenny. "Shut up, you whiney little prick."

The band on Egan's wrist flashed bright blue. He waved his hand at Colin. Suddenly the punk was unable to speak. He grabbed his throat. The blood drained from his face. His lips began to turn blue.

"He's choking," Lenny yelled. He took a step toward Egan and raised his fist. "You're killing him, man! Let him go!"

Egan turned toward Lenny. Once more his feet became rooted to the factory floor. This time he didn't bother to struggle.

Egan walked up to Colin, grabbed his chin, pulled it up and stared into his eyes. The gang leader tried unsuccessfully to hold his gaze. Eyes watering, he struggled to catch his breath. Egan's eyes were cold, dark, and vacant, as though they were not the eyes of a human being capable of superhuman acts but those of a predator, a great white shark perhaps, well-practiced in circling its prey before moving in for the kill.

"I should kill you," Egan said, "Every one of you."

Colin's eyes began to close.

"You brought the girl here to kill her. Maybe rape her, too?"

Colin started to lose consciousness. His body fell slack.

Egan lowered his body to the floor and whispered in his ear. "That was it, wasn't it?"

Weakly, Colin nodded.

Egan stood up. He waved his hand.

The constriction around Colin's neck abated. He sucked in deep breaths of air. The color slowly began to return to his face. He gasped, choked, gasped again.

Egan looked down upon the pathetic bully huddled at his feet, curled in a fetal position. "There's something I want you to remember," he said.

Colin tended to the crushing pain in his throat. He looked up at Egan, breathed heavily.

"Ten seconds," Egan said. "Say it."

Colin swallowed. "Wh-what?"

"You heard me. *Say it*."

Colin forced out the words. "Ten... s-seconds."

"Good," Egan said. "Don't ever forget it. That's about as much time as you had left. Now get up." He pointed in the direction of the drying kiln and addressed the gang. "All of you," he said, "Over there. Move."

Colin slowly rose to his feet.

Egan stopped Colin as he walked past. "I'm not finished with you yet," he said. Egan pressed his finger against his chest. "Now you know what I'm capable of. If you ever threaten those kids again, I'll find you, no matter where you are. And when I do, I'm going to take back those ten seconds. Do we understand each other?"

Colin massaged his throat and nodded.

"Good," Egan said. "Now move your ass."

20

AGENT HAWKINS SCROLLED through the laptop computer file labeled 'Account 1'. The file contained one-hundred-and-twenty split frame pictures of young women, twelve per page. The left side was a glamor shot, the right a full body picture. Each of the women was provocatively dressed in tight fitting club wear, a bikini, or lingerie. The clothing choice had been carefully selected to accentuate both her beauty and physical attributes.

"Even looking past the makeup it's hard to tell the ages of the girls in this file," Hawkins commented. "I'd put the eldest in her early twenties. All appear to be American, an even mix of Caucasian, Hispanic, Asian and African American. Compare these to the pics in Account 2. Same ethnic mix, but older. Again, all stunning."

"Separate markets," Jordan speculated.

"For two types of buyers," Chris added.

Hawkins nodded. "Girls of this caliber would command a lot of money on the black market. This must be a big operation. The age range and quantity alone are impressive."

"A girl for every taste and budget," Chris said.

"Budget wouldn't even be a consideration," Hawkins replied. "These girls are top shelf all the way. A client would need to pay thousands of dollars to buy play time with these ladies."

Chris pointed to the number under each picture. "Looks like a file number. Can you search it?"

"Already tried," Hawkins said. "No luck. It's just a number, not a hyperlink." He paused. "Hmm... I wonder..."

"What are you thinking, Hawk?" Jordan asked.

"Hold on a second."

Hawkins opened the web browser and entered the first number from Account 1. *"Your search – 73962549174 – did not match any documents"* appeared on the screen.

"Well, it was worth a shot," Chris said.

"I'm not finished yet," Hawkins said. He opened the computers Favorites area and clicked on the History tab. "Let's see where Dr. Rosenfeld had been spending most of his time online." From the drop-down menu, he selected 'Most Recently Visited.'

Four websites appeared in the search. Hawkins clicked on each of the links. The first led to the doctor's own website, *Rosenfeld Advanced Surgical*. Hawkins spent a few minutes searching the site.

"Nothing out of the ordinary here," he said. "Overviews of Rosenfeld's product line... instructional videos... upcoming course and conference information... blah, blah, blah."

The second site was *FreeSurge International*, the Rosenfeld's global humanitarian aid organization. The site featured numerous pictures of Itzhak and Zahava with recipients of the services donated by the plastic surgery team; before and after pictures of children, living in impoverished war-torn countries, once without hope, now healed and all smiles. The cleft palate of a ten-year-old girl had been corrected. Her beautiful brown face beamed with pride and new-found confidence. The machete-hacked shoulder wound of a twelve-year-old boy was now healed and nearly invisible. The story below his picture told of how he had thrown his body over his infant sister to protect her against the guerilla forces who had invaded and plundered their small village and how by some miracle he had survived the attack. Now he wanted to become a surgeon when he grew up, just like the men and women of *FreeSurge* who had returned near-complete nerve function to his arm and given him a new lease on life.

The third site asked for the username and password to the members login area of the *American Society of Plastic Surgeons*.

The fourth website caught Hawkins attention: *Verenich Law*. He clicked on the link.

Verenich Law was based in San Diego, California. The firm's primary business was the provision of services for clients wishing to emigrate to America from Russia, Guatemala, Honduras, and Argentina. According to the ABOUT section of the website, the firm's principle, Taras Verenich, was born in Russia but had immigrated to America with his parents when he was just a boy. His personal story told of his family's struggle to survive the dark days of the Brezhnev regime, how they had lived on the street for a time, and the challenges of living day-to-day in a country once stricken with famine, poverty, and disease. He described his parent's distrust of their government, their lack of belief in the politics of the day and their desperate desire to move to America to give their son a better life. Verenich went on to state how much his parents had impressed upon him that whatever path he chose to follow in life he should always remember the importance of giving back and paying forward the blessings that had been bestowed upon them by way of their new beginning in America. He found the practice of law to be his calling and honored his parent's wish for him to help others by specializing in immigration law. Over the years, Verenich Law had assisted hundreds of new families to find a better life in the United States.

Hawkins read Verenich' bio and scrolled the site. "This doesn't make sense," he said.

"What doesn't?" Jordan asked.

"Why would this guy's website be one of Rosenfeld's most visited sites? I can understand the others because there is a logical medical connection to his work. But immigration law? I mean, just look at this site. It doesn't seem to warrant being one of Rosenfeld's most visited sites. It's your typical, cookie-cutter legal website. Standard Home and About pages, Client Testimonials, FAQ's, Contact page. Nothing about it says that Rosenfeld should have shown more than a passing interest in it. I don't get it."

"Maybe they're working together," Jordan asked. "Perhaps Verenich refers prospective patients from the countries he works with who are in need of FreeSurge's help."

"That's a possibility," Hawkins agreed. He scrolled each page of the website again. He sighed. "Something isn't passing the sniff test. I can't put my finger on it, but my gut is telling me that one and one don't add up to two here."

He returned to the Home page. Taras Verenich stood in the center of a group photo, surrounded by his support staff, flanked by the American flag on his left and state flag of California on his right. Hawkins scrolled down the page. Links to many articles written by the San Diego Union-

Tribune and San Jose Mercury-News promoted the good work of the lawyer and his team along with a KUSI San Diego News Channel video clip. By all accounts the firm enjoyed a solid reputation and had worked hard to promote a favorable public image within the community.

Hawkins scrolled down to the site map located at the bottom of the page. All the links were properly referenced. "Everything looks to be in order. But like I said, something just doesn't feel right. Shit!"

Frustrated, Hawkins poked the laptop's mouse pad with his finger. The cursor slid to the bottom of the screen and came to rest on the sites Notification of Copyright line. The last three words of the line read *All Rights Reserved.* The last letter of the word *Reserved* featured an underlined lower-case letter 'd.'

"Son of a gun," Hawkins said, smiling. "You were there all along. I almost missed you." He turned to Jordan and Chris. "See this? The *d* in Reserved?" He ran the cursor back and forth over the letter. He shook his head. "It's a hyper-link. Slick... very slick."

He clicked on the letter.

The screen turned black. In the middle, a cursor flashed.

He shifted in his chair, looked up at Jordan and Chris, then rubbed his hands together. "Here we go," he said.

Hawkins entered one of the numeric codes he had written down from the Account 1 file then pressed ENTER.

The picture of the girl from the file appeared onscreen. The three agents read her profile:

Name: Torina
Age: 19
Skin: White
Hair: Blond

Eyes: Blue
Weight: 110 lb
Height: 5' 4"
Piercing/tattoos: None
Languages: English, Spanish
Services: Full
Hourly: $700.00
Purchase: $800,000.00
Offer: Pending

"Gotcha," Hawkins said.

"Verenich is into prostitution," Jordan said.

"And human trafficking," Hawkins added.

"Which means Rosenfeld probably is too," Chris replied.

"It would certainly explain why someone sent a professional to kill him," Jordan said.

Hawkins pointed to the last line. "Verenich plans to sell this girl. An offer's been submitted."

Jordan instructed Agent Hawkins. "Run her picture through facial recognition and the National Crime Information Center. See if she's in the system. Great work, Hawk."

As Jordan and Chris stood to leave two orderlies from the Coroner's office exited the bedroom. The murder scene had been processed and cleared. The bodies of Itzhak and Zahava Rosenfeld, having now been officially released to the custody of the Los Angeles Coroner, rolled past them on steel gurneys.

"Think they were both involved?" Chris asked.

"That's what we're going to find out," Jordan said.

"I want to have a chat with Verenich."

"Me too," Jordan replied.

"Real bad."

"Ditto."

"I'm talking about a leave-your-gun-and-badge-in-the-car kind of chat."

"We still don't know exactly what Verenich' role is in all of this," Jordan said. "He may not be the key player."

"Maybe not. But there's a damn good chance he knows who is."

The agents watched the orderlies wheel the dead couple out of the room.

"Remember what I said earlier?" Jordan said.

"What's that?"

"That maybe I should have gone to med school instead of joining the Bureau."

"Yeah?"

Jordan rested her hand on her gun. "I take it back."

21

———

THE GANG'S FOOTFALLS reverberated off the concrete walls, metal ceiling and brittle glass panes of the old factory. The building sounded cavernous.

Once-tough Lenny began to cry. "It was just a joke, man. We only wanted to scare 'em. It was supposed to be a joke."

Colin looked over his shoulder as the group walked across the factory floor toward the wood drying kiln. "Shut up, Lenny," he said.

Egan shoved him from behind. The gang leader tripped but didn't fall.

"How'd you do that, freak?" Colin asked.

Egan didn't respond.

Colin pressed. "Let me guess. Somewhere there's a circus missing its main attraction."

Jacob turned to Lauren and Kevin. "It wasn't a joke, like Lenny said. It was Curt Thackery."

"Colin's brother?" Lauren replied. "But he's in prison."

Jacob nodded. "He told Colin that if he wanted in with the Sons of Satan, he'd have to make a blood sacrifice just like everybody else. Curt said he'd know when it was done 'cause he'd hear about it through the prison grapevine. He knows all about your family. You were targeted."

"Targeted?" Lauren asked. "What are you talking about?"

"Because of what your old man did to their family."

Kevin interjected. "Our family never had anything to do with the Thackery's, least of all our dad."

"Oh yes, he did," Jacob said. "Five years ago. The trial. Remember?"

"Yeah, I remember," Kevin said. "Some drug dealers sold meth to an undercover cop, then shot her."

"Your father was the jury foreman."

"So?"

"The drug dealers were members of the Sons of Satan and the guy who pulled the trigger was Colin's brother, Curt. Every one of those jurors, except your old man, is dead now. S.O.S took out a contract on them. The Bandidos bike club out of Santa Fe agreed to take out the jurors in exchange for S.O.S. giving them the manufacturing and distribution rights to their meth operation. They agreed. But by the time the cops caught wind of the hits it was too late. The Bandidos had fulfilled the contract. Eleven separate hits, all taking place the same night. They got everyone except your old man. You got lucky, that's all."

"Lucky?"

"Your parents were hosting a party that night. One of the hit men recognized Chief Kenton and called it off. Said their contract didn't involve taking out anyone but your father, least of all the Chief of Police. Besides, the Bandidos were given orders to make an example out of your dad."

"Why?"

"Because Curt knew your father hated him," Jacob said, "hated all the Thackery's. Your father lied when he accepted the position on that jury. The selection committee asked if he knew anything about the recent activities of a motorcycle gang operating in the state. He said he didn't. But everyone had heard about the shooting of the cop and the drug bust that went wrong, and that it was probably biker related. It was all over the news, for Christ's sake. He knew Curt was a member of S.O.S. and figured he was involved. He saw it as an opportunity to put him away for good. As it turned out, he was right."

Colin said coldly, "You're done, Jacob. When Curt hears about this, you're as good as dead."

Egan herded the group through the open door and into the wood drying room.

"Get in."

"Not happening, my friend," Colin said. Having readied himself for a second confrontation with the stranger, he spun around and attempted to drive a side kick into Egan's chest. Egan saw the attack coming and stepped back. As the kick brushed past, he caught the punk's foot in mid-flight and twisted it hard. Colin heard his ankle snap. He screamed and fell to the factory floor.

"My ankle!" he cried. "You broke my fucking ankle!"

Egan pointed to Jacob. "Get him up."

Jacob stepped forward, grabbed Colin by the arm and tried to help him to his feet. Colin knocked his hand away. "Get the fuck away from me, coward!"

"Get in the room," Egan said.

Colin hobbled across the threshold and into the large room with the rest of his gang.

"Move to the back."

From the darkness the men stared at Egan. They had come to the factory to kill the girl and her brother. Colin's plan had been to blood-bond them and seal their silence. As

Egan closed the heavy steel door, they rushed toward it. Too late, the lock bar found the latch. The muted screams of the men were barely audible outside the massive kiln.

"You can't leave them in there," Lauren protested. "They'll die!"

"She's right," Kevin said. "There's no air. They'll suffocate."

"No loss," Egan said. "The world will get over it."

"No!" Lauren pleaded. "They have families, people who still need them."

Egan double-checked the latch. It was secure. He turned to Lauren and her brother. "They came here with the intention of killing you both. You know that, right?"

"That doesn't mean that we have to kill *them*," Lauren said.

Egan stared at the siblings.

"Look, mister," Kevin said. "My sister and I appreciate your help. We really do. But we can't do this. You have to let them out of there. We won't tell anyone about this. Not our parents, the cops, nobody. You saved our lives, so we owe you. But please, let them go."

"The situation is a little more complicated than that," Egan said. "I shouldn't have intervened. All of you have seen things you shouldn't have. That was my fault."

Lauren stepped in front of her brother. "I don't know what you're doing here mister," she said, "but I do know that if you hadn't helped us when you did, we might not be alive right now. Let us help you. Whatever you need, we'll get it. Food, clothes, a place to stay, we'll take care of it. But you can't let them die in there. You just can't."

The beating on the drying room door had stopped. Silence prevailed. Perhaps the men inside were coming to terms with their fate.

"Oh, for Pete's sake," Egan conceded, having lost the staring contest with the teary-eyed girl. "All right. We'll compromise. Get behind me."

Lauren and Kevin ran behind Egan as he walked to the side wall of the kiln then watched as he spread his arms above his head and placed his palms against the wooden wall. The metal band on his wrist began to glow, the sections of the wall beneath his hands to smoke. Two explosions rocked the kiln room. Egan had blown holes in the upper part of the wooden wall. Screams came from inside the room. The banging on the steel door resumed.

"Whoa!" Kevin yelled. "How friggin' cool was that!"

Egan stepped back and turned to Lauren. "There. They can breathe now. Happy?"

Lauren crossed her arms and stared defiantly at Egan, as if the incredible feat of controlled telekinetic destruction she had just witnessed had done nothing to impress her. "It's a start," she said.

Egan smiled. "You're a stubborn young lady, aren't you?"

Lauren puffed her chest, stood straight and tall and replied confidently. "Yes. Yes, I am."

"You don't know the half of it," Kevin said. "Try living with her."

Egan listened at the wall of the wood kiln. Colin continued to yell at Jacob and Lenny, blaming them for getting him into their current predicament, threatening that 'none of this was over' and that all of them, as well as *the asshole* were yet to incur the wrath of his older brother, Curt, and the Sons of Satan. What Colin had neglected to share with his gang was that the only current member of the defunct motorcycle club was Curt himself, and that he would be safely locked away for many years to come. Lenny continued to weep.

"I have to leave," Egan said. "It's not safe for me here anymore." He gestured to the locked kiln door. "You two will be fine. Those jokers aren't going anywhere. Give me an hour, then go to the police." He looked at Kevin. "Tell them they tried to hurt your sister, but you got the better of them."

Lauren made a sour face. "Kevin? Going all Bruce Lee on those guys? Like anyone's going to believe that!"

"Colin mentioned your dad's friend is the Chief of Police," Egan replied.

"Yup," Lauren replied. "They're besties."

"Good. Then tell him. It'll be your word against Colin's. I'm sure he'll believe you over the brother of Curt Thackery."

"Where will you go?" Kevin asked.

Egan smiled. "Don't worry about me. I'll be fine." He fished the keys to the flower delivery van out of his pocket. To Kevin, he said, "Can you drive?"

"I've got my learners permit."

"Good enough. There's a van parked out back. Think you can drive it inside?"

"You bet!" Kevin said.

"Great." Egan tossed him the keys. "I'll get the door. Hurry."

Kevin caught the keys and ran to the back of the factory. "Gimme a minute," he yelled.

Egan walked to his former hiding place behind the wooden pallets with Lauren hot on his heels. He double-checked the area to ensure no indication of his presence in the factory would be detected.

"The receiving doors at the back are padlocked and rusted shut," Lauren said. "You're going to need to open it before Kevin can drive the van inside. Good luck with that."

Egan raised his hand. The bracelet began to glow. He smiled at the girl.

"Oh yeah," Lauren said. "I forgot. You're *Ironman*."

Egan smiled. "Something like that."

Kevin ran back toward them as they stepped out of the room.

"Mister!" he yelled.

"What's wrong?" Egan asked.

"Outside!" Kevin gasped, fighting to catch his breath. "Two police cars just pulled in. They've blocked in the van!"

22

 WAREHOUSE...
Screaming...
Pure energy, massive power, intensely focused...

"JORDAN, are you all right? Jordan? *JORDAN!* Hanover caught his partner as she fell into his arms. He helped her into a chair.

"I can feel him," Jordan said

"Feel who?" Chris asked.

"The killer."

Jordan sat forward and placed her head in her hands. Her mind and body had been weakened from the interaction. She ached. The connection with the killer had manifested itself physically as well as psychically. "My hands feel like they're on fire."

"Relax," Chris said. "You're fine. Take it easy for a second."

Jordan took a few deep breaths.

"Let me have a look," Chris said. "Open your hands for me."

Jordan gingerly opened her hands.

"*Jesus!*" Hanover called out. "I need a first aid kit over here now!"

Jordan assessed the damage. The assault had left her with first degree burns on both hands.

"You're going to be okay," Chris said. He held her hands in his. "I've got you."

"The intensity of his energy is off the charts," Jordan said. "I feel like I've been struck by lightning."

FROM THE COMFORT of his ocean side bench at Aliso Beach, Jason Merrick locked on to the commander's brain neural interface and connected with his subject.

He saw the warehouse, observed the activity in the building...

Saw Egan and the teenagers...

Heard the cries coming from inside the locked room...

Nuisances, he thought. Unnecessary distractions standing in the way of the completion of the mission.

He issued the kill order.

23

TARAS VERENICH ANSWERED his phone on the first ring: "Verenich Law."

"Who have you been talking to?"

"Marina?"

"Who the fuck have you been talking to?"

"Jesus, calm down. What are you talking about?"

"He knows everything! The girls, our routes... all of it! Do you have any idea what The Company will do to us if they even suspect that we have been compromised? They'll kill us both and do it in a way that won't be pretty. Do you want that to happen? *Do you?*"

Verenich paused. This was not the calm, cool, collected Marina that he knew. Nothing ever ruffled her feathers. Others were paid very well to do her ruffling for her.

"Tell me who called and what was said."

"I don't know who it was. But he knows everything about us. He said he's been watching my son. Which means he's in California. Which also means he's probably been watching you."

"I've been very careful, Marina."

"Apparently not careful enough!"

Taras stood from his desk and walked to his office window. He observed the two men seated in the now-familiar silver Mercedes on the upper deck of the parking lot across the street from his office. When they weren't there, they followed him from a distance as he went about his day.

He continued. "Marina, we both know The Company keeps its people under constant surveillance. There's no way I could have talked to or met with anyone without you or your superiors knowing about it. If I had, we wouldn't be having this conversation right now. I assure you that what-ever was said to you did not come from me. I'll help you, but you're going to have to trust me on that. Now, what is this about your son?"

Marina was quiet. She collected her thoughts. Anger had gotten the better of her, which was not her way.

"My son, Ilya, is studying at Cal State University. He's being watched."

"Then assign a shadow detail," Verenich said. "They'll watch over him, keep him safe."

"Impossible. The Company would find out if I did that. They would want to know why I felt it was necessary to place my son under protection. They'd suspect a problem; maybe even think I was making plans to get out or turn over on them. No, I can't do that." A hint of panic had returned to her voice.

"Then what are you going to do?"

"I've booked a flight to Los Angeles. I'm at the airport now. It leaves in thirty minutes. I need you to meet me at my hotel tomorrow at 1:00 P.M. I'll take care of this myself."

"Where will you be staying?"

"Downtown. The Ritz-Carlton."

Verenich confirmed. "Very well. I'll be there."

"Good. I'll email Ilya and let him know that I'll be in town for a few days."

"Would you like me to make any special preparations for your visit?"

"I'll need a weapon."

"That won't be a problem."

"I wouldn't expect it to be," Marina snapped. She hung up.

Taras slammed down the phone. "Bitch," he said.

24

THE MIRRORED GLASS walls of Dynamic Life Sciences reflected the fire of the afternoon sun. The fronds of the palm trees which flanked the main security gate danced in the gentle breeze and shone in the sunlight and gave the illusion that the tree might burst into flame at any second.

Chief Jenkins slowed the Jeep as the security guard stepped out of his booth and raised his hand. Although the parking lot was full not a single soul was in sight.

Jenkins eased the car to a stop as the guard walked to his door.

"Sorry, sir. We're closed," the guard said.

Jenkins checked his watch. "Seems a little early to be shutting down for the day. What's going on?"

"Evacuation drill," the guard replied. "Company requires us to do one every year in the event of an emergency. Keeps everyone on their toes."

"Makes sense," Jenkins said. "I guess you can never be too careful, especially given what you guys do here."

"*Sir?*"

"I mean, it's pretty high-tech stuff, right?"

The guard placed his arm on the roof of the Jeep. "Is there something that I can help you with Officer?"

"Actually," Jenkins said, "it's *Chief*. Corona Police." He tapped the department emblem on his car door. "Says so right here."

"So it does," the guard replied.

"Who's in charge here? I have a few questions."

The guard leaned closer and read the nameplate on Jenkins lapel. "Like I said, *Chief*. We're closed."

"It won't take long. Ten, fifteen minutes tops."

The guard folded his arms. "Exactly what part of evacuation drill don't you get?"

Jenkins took off his sunglasses and tossed them onto the passenger seat. "I need to speak with one of your employees."

"Then I suggest you come back tomorrow."

"See, that just doesn't work for me," Jenkins replied. "Here's why." He pointed down the road. "I have an active crime scene back there that's really fucked up. I'd share the details of it with you but I'm pretty sure you'd soil those crisply pressed pants of yours on the spot. Right now, I've only got two leads. One of them my guys are following up on as we speak. The second is what brought me here. So as much as I'm enjoying your company, I'm going to ask you for the second and final time. Who's in charge?"

The guard smiled, tipped his hat, then turned away from Chief Jenkins. "Have a good day, Officer." He headed back into the guardhouse.

Jenkins called out. "Does the name Dr. Jason Merrick mean anything to you?"

The guard stopped.

Jenkins opened his door and stepped out of the Jeep. "I want to talk to Merrick."

The guard walked back and faced him. "This is a military facility, sir. We're in lockdown. You need to leave. Now."

"Lockdown," Jenkins repeated. He stared at the guard. "You just told me this was an evacuation drill."

Caught in the lie, the guard did not respond. Jenkins pressed him. "It can only be one or the other," the Chief said. "Which is it? Lockdown or evac?"

The guard relaxed. "I can't help you."

"Can't or won't? And you still haven't answered my question."

"I could lose my job."

"Oh, there's no *could* about it," Jenkins said. "Interfere with my investigation for one more second and I'll guaran-damntee you'll lose your job."

Above the gate a camera panned, whined, and focused. The guard looked over his shoulder. The security team stationed inside the front desk had taken notice of the activity at the main entrance. A voice sounded through the guard's walkie-talkie.

"Main One, communications check."

The guard answered his radio. "Go for comms check, Main One."

The front desk security officer sounded concerned. "Everything okay down there, Noah?"

"Yeah, we're good," the guard replied. "Just a friendly visit from the local P.D."

Jenkins looked up at the camera and waved.

"Copy that. Give them our best."

"Will do."

The camera panned away from the gate.

"Nicely handled, Noah," Chief Jenkins said. "So..."

"We're in lockdown," Noah replied.

"Why?"

"We had a problem this morning. A poisoning or something like that. It happened in Dr. Merrick's lab. I arrived late for my shift, so I didn't get the full story. They shut the whole place down. I'm under strict orders to make sure no one enters or leaves."

"How bad was it?"

"Two dead. Research scientists. They worked with Dr. Merrick."

"Was Merrick hurt?"

"Don't know. We can't find him."

"What does that mean, you can't find him? You guys lose scientists around here on a regular basis?"

"I mean just what I said. As far as we can tell he's not in the facility. He's somewhere off campus."

"So no one's around?"

"Just security and the E.A. team."

"Where's the rest of the staff?"

"Everyone's been bussed to JFTB Los Alamitos as a precaution until Environmental Assessment and Hallier give the place the all clear."

"Who's Hallier?"

"Colonel Hallier. He's with DARPA. Dr. Merrick and his research team report to him."

"Hallier's with the Department of Defense?"

"Yeah." The guard was getting even more nervous. "Look, Chief, I've already told you too much and probably way more than I should have."

"You did the right thing, Noah."

"This can't come back to me, okay? If I'm ever asked, I'll confirm that we spoke. But we never had *this* conversation."

Jenkins offered his hand. The guard took it. "We're good. I appreciate your help, Noah."

"Sorry I couldn't help you find Dr. Merrick."

"It's all right. We'll track him down." Jenkins climbed into his Jeep and shifted the car into reverse. Noah walked back to his post.

"Hey, Noah," Jenkins called out. "Just one more question."

Noah turned around. "Yeah?"

"What kind of car does Merrick drive?"

"Porsche 911. Black."

Jenkins nodded. "Thanks." He spun the Jeep around and headed back down the road.

"Sweet Jesus," he said aloud. "What the hell is going on?"

25

MINUTES AFTER LEAVING the FBI field office, on his way to the Joint Forces Training Base Los Alamitos, Quentin Hallier's cell phone rang.

"Hallier."

"Colonel, this is Commander Rod Aikens, JFTB Los Alamitos. Just wanted to let you know your team is prepped and waiting for you per General Ford's request."

"And the DLS staff?"

"All tucked in, sir. We're taking good care of them."

"Good. I'm forty-five minutes out. I'll brief them on arrival."

"We're ready for you sir."

"Let our guests know they'll be going back to the lab as soon as DLS gives the all clear."

"Copy that, sir."

No sooner did Hallier end the call when his phone rang again. Ann Ridgeway was on the line.

"Good news, Quentin," the Assistant Director said. "We may have a lead on Dr. Merrick."

"Talk to me."

"We entered your information on Merrick into our system. It flagged a hit. An hour ago, Corona P.D. requested a VIN search on a black Porsche. The Vehicle Identification Number came back to Merrick."

"We need to talk to Corona Police. Find out what they have on Merrick."

"I thought you might want to do that, so I took the liberty of calling them. I caught their Chief, Riley Jenkins, just as he was leaving Dynamic Life Sciences. He was told they had shut the place down and asked me if I knew anything about it. I told him no."

"Why did Jenkins go to DLS?"

"Corona's dealing with a homicide, but he admitted they're not really sure what they've got on their hands. Their coroner confirmed finding liquefied human remains in a Dumpster at the back of the Corona Mews Shopping Mall. Their K9 tracked trace evidence from the Dumpster to a Porsche in the parking lot. They found Merrick's employee ID in the car. Jenkins went there looking for Merrick."

"Dammit!"

"It gets worse," Ridgeway replied. "When Corona ran the tag, it came back to a Chevy Suburban owned by a local contractor and not the Porsche. The guy's cell phone and personal effects were found in the Dumpster along with the remains."

"Merrick switched plates and killed him."

"Looks that way." The Assistant Director was quiet for a second. "Quentin," she said, "Could Merrick actually do that? Cause a body to liquefy?

"Channeler is a weapon, Ann," the Colonel replied. "One with many uses. Unfortunately, the only person who knows the full extent of its capabilities is Dr.

Merrick. But if I had to state with confidence whether or not I thought Merrick was behind this my answer would be yes."

"This is insane," the Assistant Director said. "How do we stop someone with that kind of ability? I've never dealt with a situation like this before. I have to admit that I'm a little worried about my people."

"I'll understand if you want to change your mind," Hallier replied. "You don't need to do anything you're not comfortable with. But you should know that I'm on my way to JFTB Los Alamitos right now to brief my assault team. The moment we locate Merrick, or Commander Egan, I'll deploy my people. Trust me, they'll give them the fight of their lives."

Ridgeway said, "We're not standing down, Colonel. I know if I came to you with a similar request you wouldn't say no."

"You're right."

"Then we'll support you all the way. I'll give you whatever resources you need."

"I appreciate that."

The Assistant Director paused. Hallier caught the hesitation. "If there's something else you want to say Ann, now's the time."

"It's a question, actually."

"Shoot."

"Has the Department of Defense ever used a psychic in an investigation?"

Hallier reflected on the dozens of reports he had received over the years referencing the advancements of Project Channeler and the multi-million-dollar budget DARPA had committed to researching the battlefield application of telepathic and brain-based speechless communication. "Yes," Hallier replied. "Projects Channeler and LEEDA are, in part, based on that principle."

"But those are man-made technologies. What if I told you that I knew someone who might be able to help? A person with very unique skills."

"I'd say you have my attention."

"Good. I'm talking about one of my agents. Her name is Jordan Quest. And she has an exceptional gift."

"And you think Agent Quest can help us find Merrick and Egan?

"I believe so."

"Then that's good enough for me. How soon can you get her in play?"

"Right away."

"Then set it up. But the clock is ticking on this, Ann. Agent Quest will need to be brought up to speed as quickly as possible. Can you both meet me at JFTB Los Alamitos in an hour?"

"Consider us on the way."

26

B EN EGAN PEERED through a slit in the frame of the back door. Outside the factory, two police cars had pulled into the receiving area at the back of the building and blocked in the van. Through breaks in the old concrete walls and rusty holes in the metal roll-up door, the flickering of the squad cars service lights cast a dizzying light show inside the factory. The older of the responding officers, a Sergeant as the triple bars on his shoulder lapel indicated, stood at the driver's window of the van. Egan watched him remove his flashlight from his service belt, test the beam against the palm of his hand, shine the light inside the vehicle, then speak to his partner. The young officer walked to the front of the van and spoke into his radio. Egan heard the crackling response to the junior officer's communication through the speaker of the police car:

"Dispatch, Three Bravo Twenty. Be advised subject vehicle is a white panel van, registered to Pacific Floral Supply in Thousand Oaks, reported stolen. Exercise caution."

The officers drew their guns. The Sergeant trained his weapon on the side door of the van. His partner covered

GARY WINSTON BROWN

him from a safe angle as the Sergeant tested the door handle.

Locked.

They circled the van, tried to gain access to the vehicle through the rear cargo and side doors, couldn't.

The Sergeant gestured to his partner to check the factory door. Egan stepped back into the shadows. The band on his wrist began to glow, deep blue. He found another crack in the door from which to covertly observe the police officers.

From behind him came a loud *BANG!*

Egan looked over his shoulder.

The hollow sound echoed off the walls of the factory. It was coming from inside the wooden kiln room.

BANG!... BANG!... BANG!

Outside, the young officer held up his hand, calling for quiet.

The Sergeant walked to the squad car and turned down the volume on the police radio to a whisper. He returned to his partner's side and listened.

Bang!... Bang!... Bang!... Bang!

Someone or something was inside the abandoned factory.

Standing on the other side of the receiving door within feet of Egan, the senior officer spoke into his radio. Egan heard the reply.

"Attention all units. Officers require assistance. American Heritage Furniture factory. Possible auto theft suspect on premises. Any available unit respond Code Two."

The police radio crackled. *"Dispatch, Two Delta Ten. Show us responding, Code 2."*

Another unit was on the way.

Maybe more.

144

Locating the stolen van at the back of the factory had given the Sergeant and his partner adequate reason to believe a suspect, possibly armed and dangerous, might be inside. They would wait until backup arrived before planning and executing their entry. Egan had no idea what level of response the police in this town were capable of. Perhaps a highly trained tactical team was on its way, capable of executing a breach of the factory with military precision. No matter. The local authorities could send in a small army if they wanted to. They still would not be a match for him.

His main concern was for Kevin and Lauren.

Who knows how the police in this town would respond when they came face to face with him. The kids could be injured or even killed when at last they stormed the factory. There was no way he was going to allow that to happen. Kevin and Lauren were innocents, drawn into circumstances not of their own making by a group of young psychopaths. Egan made a decision. He would protect himself, but also keep Kevin and Lauren out of harm's way at all cost.

He ran back through the factory. The teens had taken refuge behind the stacks of wooden pallets which had been his hideaway.

"You two need to get out of here, right now. In a few minutes, this place is going to be crawling with cops."

BANG!... BANG!... BANG!

The pounding on the steel kiln door continued, each crash louder than the last. The yelling escalated.

BANG!... HELP!... *BANG...BANG!!...* GET US OUT OF HERE!... *BANG!...* SOMEBODY!... *BANG!... BANG!... BANG!*

"No way," Kevin said. "We can talk to the cops. We'll tell them what you did for us. How you saved Lauren's life."

Egan put his hand on the young man's shoulder. "No, Kevin. You need to go. It's too dangerous. Take your sister and get out of here. Go straight to your dad's friend, Chief Kenton. Tell him your story. Just make sure you keep me out of it. Got it?"

"Yes, sir," Kevin replied. Lauren nodded.

"Good. Come with me."

Kevin and Lauren stepped out from behind the wooden barricade. Egan pointed to a row of fifty-gallon plastic drums which stood against the wall of the factory. The dagger he had caused to fly through the air was lodged in a wooden column beside the empty containers.

"There's a hole in the wall behind those containers. It's big enough for you to fit through." Egan looked around, found a piece of cloth on the floor, picked it up, handed it to Kevin.

He pointed. "See the knife?"

"Yeah," Kevin replied.

"Don't touch it. Wrap this cloth around the handle and pull it out of the column. Take it with you and give it to Kenton. It's got Colin's prints on it. Probably other finger-prints too. It's your proof of what went down here. Explain everything to Chief Kenton. He'll know what to do. Clear?"

"Clear."

"Good. Now go."

Kevin grabbed his sister's arm. Lauren resisted. She turned to Egan.

"Thank you," she said. She wrapped her arms around the Commander, held him tight.

Egan smiled. "You're welcome. Now get your asses out of here."

Kevin and Lauren ran to the wall. Lauren pushed the containers aside as Kevin wrestled the knife out of the column and wrapped it in the cloth. Egan watched the siblings scamper through the hole, free of the building.

Egan ran back to the receiving door at the far end of the factory and looked outside.

A third police car squealed to a stop in front of the van. Two officers jumped out of the vehicle, guns drawn. The Sergeant gestured. The men took up positions outside at opposite ends of the building.

Egan watched the Sergeant nod to his partner. He knew what was coming next.

Breach.

He walked to the middle of the factory floor, dropped to his knees, and waited.

The receiving door to the factory burst open. As the Sergeant's young partner rounded the corner, he saw Egan and heard the voices.

BANG!... GET US OUT OF HERE!... *BANG!... BANG!...* HELP!... *BANG!... BANG!... BANG!*

"In here!" the officer yelled. "He's in here!"

Egan slowly raised his arms, interlocked his fingers behind his head, and stared at the floor.

The rookie cop tried to suppress the anxiety in his voice. "Don't you move, mister!" he yelled. "Don't you dare fucking move!"

"Relax," Egan said.

The cop's hands trembled. *"What?"*

Egan repeated himself. He spoke calmly. "I said, relax. If you keep shaking like that someone's gonna get shot. My guess is that someone's going be me. And after the day I've had that would really piss me off. I strongly suggest you calm down and wait."

The young officer couldn't believe what he was hearing from a suspect he was holding at gunpoint. "Wait for what?"

"Backup."

The cop looked bewildered and even more scared than before.

Egan stared at the frightened officer. "Trust me, kid," he said. "I'm the last guy you want to try to take down by yourself."

27

THROUGH HER HANDS, *Jordan felt the intense heat building on the surface of the wooden wall under his touch, then watched it explode, hurtling splinters of wood and fiery embers into the darkness, leaving beneath his palms two near-perfect holes.*

Agent Hawkins ran back from the Rosenfeld's bathroom carrying two sopping wet towels. "Wrap her hands in these," he said to Chris. "The cold will reduce the swelling."

Hanover folded the wet towels around Jordan's hands. "What happened, Jordan?" he asked.

"It's called transference," Jordan replied. "When a connection is very strong, I can experience what the other person is experiencing. Sometimes it manifests itself physically, like this. It never lasts long. Ten minutes from now my hands will be fine."

"Ten minutes?" Hawkins said, referring to the angry red blisters. "Those are second-degree burns. They'll need at least a couple of weeks to heal."

Jordan shook her head. "That's what you'd think, Hawk. But it's not the case. I'll show you. Chris, take off the towel."

"But..."

Jordan insisted. "Really. It's okay."

Reluctantly, Chris unfolded the wet towels. The agents watched in disbelief as the blisters stopped weeping. Slowly, they began to reduce in size. The pinkness of her skin had started to return. Jordan wiggled her fingers.

"See?" she said, "Just temporary."

"I've never seen anything like that before in my life," Hawkins said.

"That makes two of us," Chris said. He reapplied the towel to her hand. "You must be a blast at parties. Kind of puts the whole watch-me-hang-a-spoon-off-my-nose trick to shame."

Jordan smiled. "It rarely occurs. But it happens."

"You called it *transference*," Hawkins said, mesmerized by the fantastic display of rapid healing he had just witnessed. "How does it work?"

"It's different every time. It depends on the other person and the strength of their psychic output."

"So you feel what they're feeling?"

"Yes. But not normally to this degree."

"What made this experience different?" Chris asked. "Why so severe a response?"

"Because I'd made a connection with him before. You might say we 'crossed wires.'"

"Are you talking about the energy signature you picked up from the railing downstairs? Our *suspect* did that to you?"

Jordan nodded. "Yes. But I don't think he knows that he did. It wasn't an attack. If that had been his intention, he could have done a lot more damage. I don't think he knows that I'm aware of him."

"Try to keep it that way," Chris said.

Jordan smiled. "No argument here."

"Can you hide from him?" Chris asked. "Tap into his energy signature but not allow him to tap into yours?"

"Possibly," Jordan answered. "Through remote viewing."

"How would that work?" Hawkins asked.

"Every energy signature is unique," Jordan explained, "the same way one cell phone differs from the next, yet millions of them are capable of sharing the airwaves simultaneously. If I can feel his frequency, there's a good chance that I can connect to it."

"And you'll be able to see what he's seeing?" Hawkins asked.

"That's right."

Chris removed the wet towels and inspected Jordan's hands. The blisters were gone. Her palms were smooth. No physical evidence of the burns remained.

Hawkins shook his head. "Incredible," he said. "If I hadn't seen this with my own eyes, I'd never have believed it. How will you know when it's safe to connect with him but not have this happen to you again?"

"I won't," Jordan answered. "But over the years I've learned to make one critical distinction."

"What's that?" Chris asked.

"Whether the energy signature is emanating from this side or the other."

"Other side?" Hawkins asked.

"Yes. The energy from those who have passed over affects me differently," Jordan explained. "Its effect is almost magnetic and feels cold and constricting, like a band tightening around my chest. Sometimes the dead can make it hard for me to breathe. It isn't that way with the living. Their energy strong, vital, animated."

"And this guy?" Chris asked. "Which side is he on?" He

looked at Hawkins and shook his head. "I can't believe I just asked that."

Jordan smiled. "Definitely on this side. He's very much alive."

"Great," Hawkins said. "Somehow I don't feel better knowing that."

Chris examined Jordan's hands once more. "How are you now?"

Her skin appeared normal. "Good to go," Jordan replied.

"Feel up to taking that drive to see Verenich?"

"Absolutely."

"I'm going to do a little more poking around and see what else I can come up with on these codes," Hawkins said. He stood, rounded the desk, and sat in front of the computer.

"Sounds good," Jordan said. "Call us when you have something."

"You got it," Hawkins replied.

Outside, a noise caught their attention. Jordan and Chris walked through the Rosenfeld's bedroom and looked out the window. The throng of reporters and news crews gathered at the front gate of the mansion were firing questions at Special Agent Lynch, demanding an update on the progress the Bureau was making inside the home.

"I want to take this guy down," Jordan said, "The harder, the better."

"Damn straight," Chris replied.

Jordan turned and looked at the blood-soaked bed. "Anyone capable of doing this doesn't deserve justice," she said.

"The game will play itself out Jordan, one way or the other," Chris replied. "And I have a pretty clear idea of how I want it to end for this guy. Especially after what he did to you."

"I can take care of myself, Chris," Jordan said firmly.

"I never said you couldn't. What I *am* saying is I've got your back. When he goes after you, he damn well better know he's going after me too."

"I'm tired of being two steps behind this guy," Jordan said. "It's time he found out what I'm capable of."

Chris looked at his partner. "Then show him."

Jordan nodded. "Come on. Let's get out of here."

28

PREOCCUPIED WITH THOUGHTS of his conversations with both FBI Assistant Director Ridgeway and the guard at Dynamic Life Sciences about Dr. Jason Merrick, Chief Riley Jenkins jumped in his seat when his cellphone rang. The Jeep jerked to the left. A loud vibration shook the vehicle as it caught the shoulder of the road. Jenkins corrected the Jeep and brought it back into the lane. The phone's display read JACK POOLE. He took the call.

"How goes the field trip, Chief?"

"Interesting to say the least. Tell me you've got something good for me, Jack."

"Looks that way. Doc Kent ran the thumbprint. LiveScan confirms it belongs to Labrada."

"How did Labrada end up with his fingerprints in AFIS?"

"Some guy broke into his truck five years ago trying to steal his tools," Poole said. "Labrada caught him in the act. Took a lead pipe to him. Beat him within an inch of his life. The guy ended up with a busted jaw, right parietal fracture, and a collapsed lung. Apparently, this wasn't Labrada's first time dealing with the cops. A restraining order had been issued against him six months earlier for knocking out his ex-wife's teeth. Sad... I kinda wish this guy was still alive."

"Why?"

"So I could beat the crap out of him myself."

"I didn't hear that, Deputy."

"Hey, in my book any guy who's pussy enough to lay a hand on a woman *needs* a good old-fashioned beat down. Probably best if it's calendar scheduled. Once a week would be good. You know, beer with the boys, burgers, fries, bowling, asshole beat down. Wednesdays would work for me."

"Sorry, Jack," Jenkins joked. "I missed all of that. Your radio must have cut out. You were saying something about Labrada?"

"Doc figures the pavement paste we found is probably all that's left of him."

"Any news on the implant Button found?"

"Yeah. It's serialized, all right. Doc put a *drop-whatever-the-fuck-you're-doing* call into Forensics. Told odontology to expect Byers. Pat's running it over to the lab as we speak. We should hear something soon."

"Good."

"What happened at Dynamic Life Sciences? You talk to this guy Merrick?"

"No such luck. The place is locked down. Merrick's AWOL."

"You gotta be shittin' me."

"I also got a call from the FBI."

"The Feds? What did they want?"

"They'd asked the DMV to flag Merrick's Porsche. Seems when we ran the plates, we tripped an alarm with them."

"Did they say why they were looking for Merrick?"

"No. They were more interested to know why *we* were."

"What'd you say?"

"That something seriously messed up is going on. And that we're still trying to put the pieces together. That's not all. The DoD is working with the FBI on this, too."

"Jesus. The feds *and* the Department of Defense? Who the hell is this Merrick guy, anyhow?"

"That's the question of the hour, Jack. And I've got a feeling we're going to know a lot more about him before the day is out."

"So what's the next step, Chief?" Poole asked. "What do you want us to do?"

"For now, sit tight. Keep the scene secure. Nobody crosses that tape without my say so. I don't care what kind of credentials they present. This happened on our turf, Jack. We're going to be kept in the loop whether they like it or not."

"Copy that."

The afternoon sun had started to set. Streaks of purple bruised the sky. "It's going to be dark in a couple of hours. Have the boy's tent and light the area. Make sure any evidence we haven't yet processed is protected. And set up privacy barriers around the perimeter. I don't want to see a reporter within a thousand feet of the scene."

"You got it," Poole replied.

"What's Labrada's current status, Jack? Does he have any family we can talk to?"

"Yeah," Poole replied. "His parole record indicates he remarried a couple of years ago. I'm guessin' wife number two never thought to have a background check done on him before she hooked up with this loser. But I digest."

Jenkins laughed. "The word is *digress*, Jack. Not digest."

Poole scoffed. "Thank you, Mr. Dictionary. Anyway, Labrada's got two kids. Wife lives in Norco."

"Send a unit to interview her," Jenkins ordered. "Find out when she last spoke to him. Ask her if it's okay if we take a look around. We need to turn this guy inside out. Call his cell phone provider. Ask them to provide us with a transcript of his calls, emails, texts, the works. Go back a year."

"You sure we need to go to all this trouble, Chief? An asshole like Labrada probably wouldn't be missed. Fifty bucks says when his wife finds out he's dead she'll do a happy dance right on the spot."

"I can't say I'd blame her if she did," Jenkins said. "But if there's a connection between Labrada and Merrick we need to know what it is. I don't want to come across another body like that again, and sure as hell not in Corona."

"No argument here."

"Thanks, Jack. Wait for me. I'll be there in fifteen."

Chief Jenkins ended the call.

Corona had always been a peaceful town. News of a crime this horrific would get out quickly. Jenkins knew he wouldn't be able to keep its gruesome details under wrap for much longer. It didn't take a genius to know that the Department of Defense and the FBI were already on their way. They would want to go over the Porsche and his crime scene with a fine-tooth comb and he would have no choice but to comply. They were looking for Merrick too. And by the sound of it their search was already well underway.

Suddenly the fifteen-minute drive back to the Corona Mews Shopping Center seemed too long.

Chief Jenkins turned on his service lights, fired up the siren and stepped on the gas.

He'd be there in ten.

29

THE VERY LAST thing Taras Verenich wanted was to be the subject of further scrutiny by The Company. He was already fed up with being under constant surveillance by the two-man detail parked in the lot across the street from his office.

Tomorrow's visit by Marina Puzanova couldn't have come at a worse time. She had mentioned nothing about informing her superiors about her trip. Which meant her arrival in Los Angeles would not go un-noticed. The operatives across the street or another surveillance team assigned by The Company would follow him tomorrow. They would recognize Marina immediately. Her presence in L.A. would be reported to The Company as a matter of operational protocol and raise a red flag in Moscow. Though a highly valued and respected asset to The Company she was still several promotions away from being permitted to travel freely around the world. Moscow was her base of operations, not Los Angeles. Questions would be asked. Her action would be viewed as reckless, possibly even a danger to others. Which could lead to deadly repercussions for them both. Though loyal to The Company, Verenich was not about to be dragged into someone else's mess, especially when it belonged to Marina Puzanova. He considered his options. He could try to get ahead of this and report Marina's scheduled visit to his superiors before she even left the country. But questions would arise from that: How long had he known about her plans to travel to America? Why did she reach out to him in the first place? Why did he not say anything sooner? Taras knew the penalty for an unsatisfactory answer could be a bullet to the head. The Company was a machine with a life force all its own. Its membership served a singular purpose - to further its existence, nothing more. No one was indispensable. Not even the great Marina Puzanova.

The reception area was full of new clients. In the boardroom, couples sat across from their assigned clerk and completed the documents necessary to facilitate the immigration of their family members from Russia to America. Business at Verenich Law was good. In fact, it was excellent. The Company had seen to that. They had paid for his ivy-league education and set him up in practice out of respect for the lifetime of service his late father had given to them. Taras had been the envy of his graduating class. Within weeks of passing the bar he was given the keys to his new office. The luxurious top-floor suite offered panoramic views of both the city of Los Angeles and the Pacific Ocean. One hundred percent of his clientele were funneled to him, all business owners or professionals who owed a debt to The Company and had agreed to repay it by acting as sponsors for the newcomers. The prospective immigrants all had one thing in common: they were young, female, breathtakingly beautiful and fully aware of the reason why they were coming to America – to pay off their family's debt by selling their body. But compared to their circumstances in their homeland, a job in America as a high-priced escort offered an opportunity for a better life; one of money, designer clothes, expensive cars, luxury homes, the intimate company of the rich and the protection of The Company. To Verenich' delight, the city of Moscow and its surrounding towns produced an endless supply of exceptional prospects. Taras made a point of personally assessing the talents of as many of the newcomers as possible before introducing them to their clientele.

The afternoon sun dappled on the waves of the steel blue Pacific. Verenich caught his reflection in the window. He adjusted his tie and flicked a speck of lint off the shoulder of his perfectly tailored Armani suit.

Elena, his personal assistant, tapped on his door.

Verenich watched a tour boat race across the water and slowly let out its safety line. A parasailer, tethered to the craft, climbed higher and higher into the clear, bright sky.

"Come in," he said.

Elena entered the office. Statuesque and poised, she was as beautiful as any of the escorts in The Company's employ. In her arms she carried a stack of file folders.

"The information you requested, Mr. Verenich."

Mr. Verenich. Taras never got tired of hearing the formal pronunciation of his name. "Place them on my desk," he replied.

"Yes, sir."

"I'll be out of the office tomorrow on a personal matter."

"Of course, sir. Do you wish to be contacted?"

"Only if it's an emergency. Otherwise just say I'm presently unreachable."

"Yes, sir." Elena turned to leave. Taras stopped her.

"Is Avel in the office?" he asked.

"I believe so."

"Tell him I need to see him right away."

"Yes, sir." Elena closed Taras' door as she left his office.

Avel knocked a minute later.

"Enter."

"You wanted to see me, Taras?" Avel asked.

"I need you to do something for me."

"Of course."

"I have a guest arriving tomorrow. She'll be in town for a few days. She's requested I make arrangements to assure her stay will be a safe one."

"Certainly," Avel replied. He knew exactly what Taras meant by a safe visit. "Does your guest have a preference?"

"Something small and light. Untraceable, of course."

"How soon do you need it?"

"Immediately. Have it delivered here."

Avel nodded. "I'll make a call." He left.

Verenich walked to his desk, opened his briefcase, tossed in the files, picked up the desk phone and placed a call.

"Dr. Granger speaking."

"It's me. We need to meet."

"When?"

"Tonight."

"That won't be possible. I've made plans."

"Un-make them."

"Why the urgency?"

"The reason isn't important. Meeting with me is."

Granger paused. Taras could hear her drumming her fingernails on the surface of her desk in the background.

"All right. Where?"

"Caridad's. Six o'clock. We're expecting a visitor."

"Who?"

"Six o'clock. Don't keep me waiting."

For as long as Ashley Granger had known him the lawyer had done little to hide his misogynistic attitude. Unless he wanted a woman, that was. In which case she knew of no one more charming and charismatic.

"I'll be there," she said. "By the way, have you been watching the news?"

"Should I be?"

"Rosenfeld is dead."

"*What?*"

"It happened this morning. What do you think we should --"?

Verenich hung up the phone.

Rosenfeld couldn't be dead, he thought. He raised the screen on his laptop and Googled '*Rosenfeld KTLA News.*' The video clip on the home page showed the elegant mansion and the driveway beyond its iron gate flanked by law enforcement vehicles. Verenich recognized the grand home. He clicked the PLAY button in the middle of the graphic. The report began:

"*It was to this palatial estate nestled high in the Hollywood Hills that police were called in the early hours of the morning, and where the deceased bodies of Dr. Itzhak Rosenfeld, a prominent local physician and entrepreneur, and his wife, Zahava, a retired Los Angeles court justice, were discovered. The affluent couple were well-known for their philanthropic efforts, both locally and internationally, having raised tens of millions of dollars for charity. Police are refusing to comment on the incident or to provide specific details about the cause of the couple's death and will say only that their investigation is on-going. But if the presence of the Federal Bureau of Investigation's Mobile Command Unit here at the scene is any indication, there is more to this story than authorities are letting on. Reporting live from the scene, I'm Mary Beth McDale, KTLA News."*

Verenich closed the computer cover, stood up from his desk, and walked to his office window.

Across the street, the occupants of the silver Mercedes maintained their post.

So, it was true. Rosenfeld was dead.

For him that meant only one thing.

The game had changed.

Taras Verenich suddenly felt very frightened.

And very, very exposed.

30

<hr />

BEN EGAN HEARD the sound of tires screeching to a halt as additional police units converged on the factory in response to Three Bravo Twenty's call for backup.

The responding officers rushed in through the back of the factory and surrounded him. He knelt in the middle of the floor, fingers interlaced behind his head, awaiting their instructions. The rookie cop who had been holding him at gunpoint stepped aside as two burly veterans moved in on him from behind and pushed him down, pinning him to the ground. Egan felt the strain on his neck as one of the cops pressed his face into the concrete floor while his partner buried his knee into his back. Handcuffed, now confident their suspect no longer posed a risk to their safety, the two officers pulled him to his feet.

BANG!... "GET US OUT OF HERE!"... *BANG!*... "CAN ANYBODY HEAR US?"... *BANG! BANG! BANG!*

Sergeant Brewer yelled at the rookie and pointed in the direction of the noise. "Palmer, open that door! Secure that room!"

"Yes, sir." The young officer was joined by the backup team. Guns drawn, they approached the wood drying kiln. "Police!" the rookie yelled. "Stand back from the door. Keep your hands in plain sight. *DO NOT MOVE!*"

A muffled voice yelled back from inside the locked room. "Whatever, man. Just get us the hell out of here!"

Palmer cranked back the steel door latch and heaved it open. The officers shone their flashlights into the dimly lit room and entered quickly, taking the gang members to the ground, handcuffing them. When the last man was secured one of the officers yelled, "*CLEAR!*" The team helped them to their feet and escorted them out of the room. Once convinced they were hostages and not a threat their hand-cuffs were removed.

Colin looked across the factory floor and saw Egan. "You!" he yelled. "Motherf--!" He started to run toward him.

Sergeant Brewer removed his baton from his duty belt, stepped in front of Colin and warned him. "Son, unless you want to go right back into those cuffs you better stop right there!"

"That prick tried to kill us!" Colin yelled.

"Actually, Sergeant," Egan said, "I didn't try to kill them. It was more like a good old-fashioned bitch-slapping."

Sergeant Brewer swung the baton around and pointed it at Egan. "I don't want to hear a damn word out of you. Not one. You hear me?"

Egan shrugged. "Just trying to help."

"Do I look like I need your help?" the Sergeant replied.

"No, sir. Absolutely not," Egan said. He raised his cuffed hands. "I'd say you and your men have everything well under control."

The Sergeant stared at his prisoner and shook his head.

"Son, for someone who's about to have the book thrown at him, you've got one hell of a mouth on you."

"I apologize, Sergeant," Egan replied. "It's just that there's somewhere I really need to be right now. Any chance we can speed this up?"

"Not very likely," Brewer said. He raised a finger. "Let's start with possession of stolen property..."

"Well," Egan said, "If you're going to make a list..."

The Sergeant raised a second finger. "Grand theft auto..."

"You can't be serious," Egan replied. "That old van? I'd hardly call it *grand*, plus it pulls to the left."

A third finger. "Unlawful trespass..."

"That's not entirely my fault. There aren't many places to stay around here. You know what this town really needs? A Motel 6."

"Breaking and entering..."

Egan shrugged. "Prevailing circumstances being what they are, I suppose I'll have to give you that one."

"And the cherry on top," Brewer said, pointing to the wood drying kiln. "Violation of Penal Code 236: False imprisonment, intentional and unlawful restraint, detention, confinement."

"I prefer to think of it as a 'time out,' Sergeant," Egan said. "They were very, very bad boys."

The arresting officers held Egan by his arms. Brewer motioned to them to walk him out of the factory.

"These gentlemen will escort you to your new accommodations," the Sergeant said. "I'll do my best to come up with a few more charges for you along the way."

"You are nothing if not thorough, Sergeant," Egan replied.

Brewer shook his head and dismissed him with a wave

of his hand. To the officers, he said, "Get this joker out of my sight."

The burly officers nodded. "You got it, Serge. Let's go, buddy."

Egan looked at the officer. "*Buddy*..." he replied. "We're friends now?"

"Move your ass, sunshine," the officer replied.

"Now you're just being disrespectful," Egan said.

The second officer scoffed. "As if a piece of crap like you is gonna get any respect from us."

"I can understand how you guys must feel," Egan said as they crossed the factory floor. "I was just hoping for a little small talk. So, how's the job going? The department treating you okay?"

"Shut up."

Egan glanced over his shoulder. Colin and his gang were giving their statements to Sergeant Brewer and Officer Palmer. Colin pointed his hands at the ground, raised them slowly to the ceiling, then dropped them quickly to his sides. Puzzled, Brewer looked at Egan, then back at Colin and the gang. He scratched his head. Whatever story he was being told it was evident he wasn't buying any of it.

"How's the comp plan?" Egan asked. "Let me guess. Minimum wage, plus all the donuts you can eat?"

The officers exchanged glances then lifted him off his feet. "Exactly what part of shut up don't you understand, asshole?"

Egan tried to walk, couldn't. His toes skimmed the floor. "I'm just trying to make conversation, boys."

"Screw you."

"What about the benefits package? Any good?"

The officers looked over their shoulders. Sergeant Brewer's back was turned to them. He was looking up at the ceiling, listening to Lenny's account of the story. The men seized their opportunity and drove their fists hard into Egan's kidneys. The force of the dual blows lifted him off the ground.

"Damn," Egan said. "Was that supposed to hurt?"

The officers didn't reply.

"Now, where were we?" Egan asked. "Oh, yeah. Benefits. You guys have decent long-term disability?"

Egan felt the officers tighten their grip on his arms. They were preparing to deliver a second, more powerful punch.

The band around his wrist began to glow.

The policemen suddenly experienced a rush of white-hot heat in their hands. "What the hell?" one of them yelled. They let go of Egan, stepped back, and watched as the handcuffs fell off the wrists of their prisoner and clatter on the factory floor.

Massaging his wrists, Egan turned and faced them. "I gave you guys every opportunity to play nice," he said. "You should have listened."

31

JORDAN AND CHRIS waited for LAPD to open the massive iron gate. The reporters outside the entrance to the Rosenfeld estate rushed the sedan, cameras and boom microphones pressed against the windows. As soon as they were clear of the entranceway Jordan accelerated.

Chris glanced back at the stately home as they rounded the cul-de-sac and headed for the main road. "Want a good deal on an estate?" he said. "There's nothing like a double-homicide to send a property's value straight to the basement."

Jordan smiled. "In this neighborhood? Not a chance. Just wait. With no family to inherit it there'll be a bidding war on the place by the end of the week."

"That's pretty sad," Chris said.

"No," Jordan replied. "That's L.A."

VERENICH LAW WAS LOCATED in a luxury office tower in downtown Los Angeles on West 7th Street, a twenty-minute drive from the Hollywood Hills home turned brutal murder scene. The firm occupied the penthouse floor. An ultra-modern stone reception desk anchored the space. Dozens of civic awards, letters of appreciation, plaques, photographs, autographed sports memorabilia, and military service honors were tastefully arranged in mirror-backed display cases. A glass dividing wall permitted an unencumbered view of the Pacific. In the boardroom, behind the see-through wall, a heated exchange between colleagues was taking place.

The agents approached the receptionist, whose name-plate on the corner of her desk identified her as Elena and presented their credentials. In the boardroom a man looked at the visitors, walked across the room, then touched a small panel on the divider. Instantly the glass transformed into a mirror-wall and reflected the reception area.

"May I help you?" Elena asked.

"My name is Special Agent Jordan Quest. This is Special Agent Chris Hanover," Jordan said. "We're with the FBI. We'd like to speak with Mr. Taras Verenich, please."

"Certainly." Elena pressed a button on the phone and spoke quietly. While they waited, Chris walked to the display cabinet and admired the impressive collection of gifts and awards.

The receptionist smiled. "Mr. Verenich will see you now. This way, please."

Elena escorted the agents down the hall to Verenich' office.

Taras rose from his desk, smiled, and shook their hands. "A visit from the FBI," he said. "I'm honored. How can my firm be of assistance to the Bureau?" He pointed to a small conference table in the corner of his office. "Please, make yourselves comfortable."

"Thank you, Mr. Verenich," Jordan said. "I hope this isn't too much of an intrusion."

"Not at all," the lawyer answered, "Just as long as you're not here to tell me that I'm in some sort of trouble!" Taras laughed. "Perhaps I should call *my* attorney?"

Jordan smiled. "No sir, that won't be necessary. We were hoping you might be able to help us with a case we're working on."

Verenich leaned forward and folded his hands together. "I'm happy to help in any way that I can. Ask away."

"Perhaps we could start by learning a little about your practice," Chris asked.

"Of course," the attorney said. "We specialize in immigration law. I own the practice and have for ten years now. There are seven associates whom I will admit do the majority of the work around here these days. Which permits the time to play a little golf now and then. I also employ three clerks who take care of the more mundane tasks, plus two administrators, and my right hand, Elena, whom you've already met, and without whom this place would most certainly fall to pieces." Taras laughed.

"Your clientele," Jordan asked. "Where are they coming from?"

"Russia, for the most part," Verenich answered. "But we also represent individuals from other countries such as Guatemala, Honduras and Argentina."

"And the emigration side of the practice?"

"College graduates, mostly. You know what today's young people are like. They're restless. They want to travel, see the world, experience different cultures. Fortunately for them, as long as their skills are in demand, they can work in any country of their choice. Japan and the United Arab Emirates are popular choices today."

"And what skills might those be?" Chris asked.

"Teaching. English mostly, plus math and science." Verenich hesitated. "But you asked me how I could help you with your case. Perhaps in the interest of time we can address that matter?"

"Of course," Jordan said. "We're interested in learning more about a particular individual."

"And whom might that be?" Verenich asked.

Judging by the abrupt change in the agent's body language it was apparent that the conversation was about to take a different turn, one Taras sensed he might not be entirely comfortable with. He suddenly felt as if he was being backed into a corner. He felt his face flush.

"Itzhak Rosenfeld," Jordan said.

Verenich shifted in his chair. "I'm sorry, Agent. Am I supposed to know this man?"

"Do you?" Chris asked.

Verenich ignored Hanover and directed his reply to Jordan. "Who is this Mr. Rosenfeld?"

"*Dr.* Rosenfeld," Chris corrected.

Verenich glanced at Chris. "Very well," he replied curtly, "Dr. Rosenfeld." To Jordan, he said, "I'm not familiar with him. Is he a client of my firm?"

"We were hoping you could tell us that," Jordan said.

Verenich stood. "I'll be happy to check into that for you."

"Thank you," Jordan said. "That would be greatly appreciated."

"As soon as you return with a warrant," Taras answered.

"And this was going so well," Chris said.

Verenich stood. "I'm sorry, Agents," he said. "I'm afraid I don't know your Dr. Rosenfeld. Unless you think it would be wise for me to make that call to my attorney, I'd like to suggest we draw this meeting to a close."

Jordan stood and shook Verenich' hand. The psychic connection was immediate and powerful: *Rosenfeld and Verenich... arguing... the lobby of the mansion...*

Chris recognized Jordan's reaction.

"Thank you, Mr. Verenich," Jordan said. "We appreciate your time. It was..."

"Stimulating," Chris finished.

"You're most welcome," Verenich said. He walked to his desk and pressed the reception call button on his phone. The click of high heels on granite was followed by muted footsteps on the carpeted hallway. Elena entered Taras' office.

"My secretary will see you out," Verenich said. "Enjoy the rest of your day."

The attorney waited for the agents to leave then picked up his phone. "Avel," he said. "Where is the package I ordered?"

AT THE FRONT DESK, Elena excused herself and wished the agents well. All incoming phone lines were lit up. She attended to the calls.

Chris whispered to Jordan. "You made a connection back there, didn't you?"

Jordan nodded. "He and Rosenfeld knew one another," she said. "No doubt about it."

The elevator call button rang. The doors parted. Chris stopped Jordan from entering the car. "Hold on a second," he said. He walked over to the glass awards cabinets.

"Take a look at this."

He pointed to an engraved plaque:

Presented to Verenich Law

In Appreciation of Your Financial Support
FreeSurge International

"I think we need to take Mr. Verenich up on his suggestion," Jordan said.

"You mean to apply for that warrant?" Chris replied.

"Precisely."

"You've got to give the guy credit," Chris said. "He's staying true to the stereotype."

"Meaning?"

"It's easy to tell if a lawyer is lying."

"How's that?"

"His lips are moving."

32

MERRICK EXPLORED THE souvenir stalls, casual shops, fashion boutiques and surf shacks along Laguna Beach. A group of seniors walked past, laden with purchases from the local vendors. On the ocean, a surfer executed a perfect aerial off the crest of an ill-tempered wave and flew through the air, only to be forced to bail into the churning backwash. On the beachfront basketball court, competitive tempers flared. What had started out as a friendly game of three-on-three had escalated into an all-out shoving match.

Merrick was confident that whatever matter Commander Egan was attending to in the factory was of minor concern and no cause for alarm. The mind-to-mind neural connection provided by Channeler was complete, and the assignment understood.

The boardwalk leading back to the Chevy Suburban was busy with pedestrian and bicycle traffic. Merrick watched a police cruiser enter the parking lot, cruise past the truck, stop, back up, idle and park. Two LAPD officers stepped out of the squad car. One of the cops spoke into his shoulder microphone as he walked to the front of the Suburban while his partner cupped his hands against the tinted window and peered inside. Merrick stepped off the pathway and stood behind a large palm tree, observing the officers. Their extreme interest in the Suburban told him his Porsche had been found. New transportation would be necessary. Having found the vehicle, they would probably assume there was a good chance that he was still in Laguna Beach. Merrick looked around. There were too many cops for his liking occupying the beach. This was not the place for a show-down with the authorities.

And there was still so much to be done.

The cop Merrick had earlier seen chatting up the young women on the beach now pedaled his bike toward the offi-cers who were investigating the stolen truck. One of the policemen pointed down the walkway in Merrick's direc-tion. The bike cop nodded and began riding along the path, scrutinizing the crowd. They were looking for him. They would have his DMV photo on their computers and phones. Which meant more police might soon arrive. He needed to leave the area as quickly as possible.

He walked back in the direction of the shops, cognizant of his pace, being careful not to draw unnecessary attention to himself. A crowd of exuberant gray-haired tourists stopped on the boardwalk to mingle and chat. Merrick eased his way into the group as the bike cop rode past. He turned as the cop looked in his direction, then watched him as he went on his way, exiting the path and heading down to the beach. A second cruiser had pulled into the parking lot and turned on its service lights. One of the officers exited the vehicle and walked the parking lot while his partner hustled down the beachfront steps to the path. It was apparent by their actions that they knew who they were looking for. The response to the morning's events at Dynamic Life Sciences had been swift, though it seemed odd to Merrick that DARPA would enlist the services of the LAPD to find him. He figured they would have preferred to handle the incident internally. If he were to have encountered anyone in the field, he assumed it would have been highly trained DARPA operatives, not the local police. In the greater scheme of things, it didn't matter. It would still be their mistake. Any effort to stop him would only result in sending good men to their death.

The afternoon traffic was light and moved along Pacific Coast Highway at a comfortable pace. Merrick jostled his way out of the group of seniors, strode toward the shops and stepped inside Ellie's Floral Boutique.

The wind chimes above the doorway of the flower shop jingled, announcing his entrance. From the back of the shop a voice called out. "Be right with you!"

Merrick peered between the intricate floral arrangements and looked out the front window. A third police car sped into the parking lot. Two officers jumped out of the vehicle and walked toward the Suburban. To Merrick, their actions were clear. A full-scale manhunt was now underway, and he was their person of interest.

Ellie walked out from the back of the shop. She was a stout Chinese woman in her mid-thirties. Her thick black hair was held neatly in place with two decorative chopsticks.

"Sorry to hold you up, hon," Ellie said. Her voice was devoid of even the slightest trace of an accent. "Something I can help you with?"

"I'm not quite sure," Merrick said. "Mind if I take a minute and look around?"

"Take as much time as you need," Ellie said. "Holler as soon as you're ready."

"I'll do that," Merrick replied. "Thank you."

"You're welcome, love," Ellie said. She disappeared into the back room.

In the parking lot, the police officers had organized themselves into two-man search teams. The first team was headed away from him, in the direction of the ice cream and fast-food vendors. The second was walking toward Ellie's, whose store happened to be the first of the retail shops along the esplanade.

Merrick activated Channeler. Blue light emanated from the device around his wrist and reflected in the window of the boutique. He raised his hand and focused the energy on the road.

Alerted to the sound of screeching brakes, crashing metal and breaking glass, the officers spun around and watched as a car left the road, took flight over the embankment, and headed toward the crowd, its engine roaring. The panicked look on the face of the young driver told them the car was not operating under his control, a jammed accelerator perhaps. The man was wrestling with the steering wheel to no avail. The car lurched to the left, then right, then left again, until finally it slammed into a concrete bench and rolled onto its side.

As the officers instinctively ran to the aid of the driver they suddenly stopped and watched in horror as a second vehicle left the road, following the first, then slammed into it and burst into flames.

Police and passersby ran to the cars to assist the screaming, trapped occupants.

Ellie walked out from the back room as Merrick opened the front door. She stepped out of the shop. Merrick heard her gasp, "My God!"

The commotion caused by the bizarre accident brought

the traffic to a standstill. Motorists stood outside of their vehicles, unsure what to make of the sudden catastrophe.

Ellie stood beside Merrick. Together they watched the incredible scene unfold.

In the distance could be heard the rising wail of sirens.

"Those poor people!" Ellie said.

Merrick nodded. "You have to be so careful on the road these days," he said. "Anything can happen."

33

"DID YOU SEE THAT?" Chris said as he climbed into the sedan and slammed the door. "The bastard lied right to our faces."

"Maybe we should go back," Jordan said. "Play good cop, bad cop. Press him harder. You be the bad cop."

"What do you mean? That *was* my bad cop."

"Seriously?"

"You're saying my bad cop isn't very convincing?"

"My son could have been more intimidating than you were. Besides, Verenich is right. We don't have anything on him that connects him directly to Rosenfeld. Which means we don't have grounds to request a warrant."

"Your son, huh?" Chris said. "Okay, here's a thought. We go back and you use some of your psychic stuff on him. Maybe put your fingertips on his temples and suck the salt out of his body until he starts to scream or dies, whichever comes first. I'm rather partial to the latter."

"I get the reference," Jordan said. "The original Star Trek series... big-ass, salt-sucking vampire. I saw that episode. Loved it."

"You don't even have to use your fingertip tentacles if you don't want to."

"I'm a psychic. I don't have tentacles. Nor can I suck the salt out of people."

"So you say."

"But if I did, and could, I can think of someone I'd use them on right now."

Chris smiled. "Okay, tentacles are out. How about using the FreeSurge plaque as our in?"

Jordan shook her head. "There are dozens of awards in those display cases. Any one of Verenich' associates could have put the plaque in the case without him even knowing about it."

"Still, it would be nice to put a little pressure on the worm. Watch him squirm on the hook."

"After our visit I'm sure he's doing quite a bit of squirming."

Jordan's phone rang. She answered the call through the car's speaker system. Agent Hawkins was on the line. "Tell me you've got something good for us, Hawk."

"I heard back from Cyber," Hawkins said. "The contents of the flash drive are account numbers just like I thought they were."

"Any ID on the account holders?" Chris asked.

"They're still working on it. As soon as I hear more, I'll get back to you. How's it going on your end?"

"Apparently I make a really crappy bad cop," Chris said.

"Huh?"

Jordan looked at Chris and shook her head. "Never mind, Hawk. Chris is just upset because I wouldn't suck the salt out of Verenich's body."

"You two need therapy," Hawkins replied.

Jordan's call waiting sounded. The display read RIDGEWAY.

"A.D.'s calling, Hawk," she said. "Gotta go."

"Later," Hawkins said. He hung up.

Jordan answered. "Assistant Director."

"Where are you now, Jordan?" Ann Ridgeway asked.

"Just leaving L.A., ma'am."

"I assume Agent Hanover is with you?"

"Yes. We're working the Rosenfeld murder in Hollywood. We're headed back to the scene now."

"Turn around. I need both of you to meet me in Corona as soon as possible. Highest priority."

Jordan glanced at Chris. What could be going down in Corona that was so important the Assistant Director would pull them away from an active murder investigation, much less one as high profile as the Rosenfeld case? Chris shrugged and pointed in the opposite direction as if to say, *let's go.*

"We're on our way."

"I'm sending the details to your phones now. As soon as possible, Agents." Ridgeway repeated. She hung up.

"What was that all about?" Chris asked. "Since when does Ridgeway get called out to the field?"

"Someone's putting pressure on her."

"So we're just supposed to drop the Rosenfeld case and let it get cold?"

"If the boss lady wants us in Corona, we go to Corona."

"Something's up."

"What a deductive mind you have."

"Very funny," Chris said.

"And to be clear, my abilities don't extend to being able to suck the salt out of bodies. Nor can I speak Klingon or shape-shift for that matter."

"Too bad. That would have been cool. But you *can* mind meld."

"Well, that's sort of true."

"So you know what that makes you, right?"

"I'm afraid to ask," Jordan said.

"Half-Vulcan."

"You're impossible."

Chris raised his hand and splayed his fingers into a V, Spock-style. "Live long and prosper, my friend."

"You can stop now."

He settled back in his seat and pointed ahead. "Set a course for the Corona zone. Ahead warp factor one."

"Don't make me hurt you, Hanover."

"My sodium's been a little high, lately. Think you can help with that?"

"Last warning."

34

NSURE WHAT TO make of the impossible act they had just witnessed, the officers rushed Egan. The Commander threw his arms open as the men attacked, sending them reeling across the factory floor in opposite directions from where he stood. Sergeant Brewer heard the commotion and turned around in time to witness his officers tumbling away from their prisoner. Having dispensed of his would-be assailants, Egan kicked the handcuffs aside and began walking towards Brewer and the gang. The Sergeant noticed the glowing band around his wrist.

Brewer stepped in front of the gang, drew his weapon, and trained it on Egan. "Stop right there!" he yelled.

Egan continued to advance.

"Don't make me shoot!" Brewer warned.

"See? I told you!" Colin yelled. "Just like that! That thing on his wrist. That's how he put us on the ceiling, man! The goddamn ceiling!"

Brewer widened his stance and gripped the gun tightly. "Last warning, son. Not one more step."

Egan raised his hand as Brewer fired. The peal of the gunshot repeated off the factory walls.

Brewer watched the slug fall to the ground in front of Egan. He fired again, a third time, a fourth. Each of the slugs fell harmlessly to the factory floor.

Egan walked up to the senior officer. The color had drained from the man's face. His arms were locked straight in front of him, weapon held tight, his hands shaking. The Sergeant stared at Egan in disbelief. He had fired four rounds at the man at point blank range with absolutely no effect.

"I'll take that, Sergeant," Egan said. He eased the gun out of his hands.

Colin and the others stepped back. Their previous experience with Egan's uncanny abilities had left them too afraid to consider challenging him a second time.

The old cop appeared to be in shock. "It's all right, Sergeant," Egan said. "You can relax. I'm not going to hurt you."

Sergeant Brewer heard Egan's voice and nodded but seemed unable to process his words. He turned his head and stared at Egan.

"You okay?" Egan asked.

Brewer nodded slowly.

"You're going to be fine," Egan said. "But I'm going to need you and your men to do me a favor."

Brewer nodded again. The look on his face was as though he had just learned that every impossible tale of science fiction that he had ever read about had suddenly been proven to be true and were not stories born of the imagination after all, but science *fact*.

The officers who had been dispatched to opposite sides of the factory floor slowly regained their senses and shuffled to their feet. He watched them raise their weapons and prepare to fire. Opening his arms, Egan cast a protective shield of energy around the sergeant, Colin, and his gang. The policemen kept firing until their clips were empty. Each round struck the invisible wall, then fell to the floor. The officers stared first at Egan, then each other.

"I warned you before," Egan said, "you should have played nice." He pointed his hand at the cops and opened his fingers. Channeler glowed. The weapons in the officer's hands suddenly became red-hot. Egan maintained the intense energy level for a few seconds, then released the men. The cops screamed, dropped their guns, and held their burned hands against their chest.

Egan made a fist and lifted the two officers several feet off the ground. They flailed helplessly in the air before he dropped them, hard.

"You," Egan said, pointing to the cop who had been the instigator of his beating. "Dipshit number one. Handcuff yourself to dipshit number two. And lose the utility belts. Drop them on the floor. Radios, weapons, car keys, everything. You too, Sergeant."

The officers refused to follow Egan's instructions.

Egan raised his hand. Channeler started to glow. "You're not gonna make me ask twice, are you? No one could be that stupid. Then again, I am talking to you two."

Reluctantly the officers removed their belts and handcuffed themselves to each another.

"Cuff keys too," Egan said, "Throw them on the ground."

The sergeant turned to Egan. There was fear was in his voice. "What are you going to do to us?"

"To you, Sergeant?" Egan replied. "Absolutely nothing. You're just doing your job. I know that. But you're in my way. And that's something I can't allow."

"Who... *what*... are you, son?" Brewer asked.

Egan put his hand on the veteran police officer's shoulder. "Sergeant, I'm afraid the answer to that question is way above your pay grade."

Egan turned to Colin Thackery and pointed in the direction of the kiln room. "Care to show them the way?"

"You have got to be friggin' kidding me!" Colin replied.

"Do I sound like I'm kidding? Get moving."

The officers followed Colin and his gang into the wood drying room.

Before closing the heavy kiln door, Egan spoke to Brewer. "Don't worry, Sergeant. You and the dipshits will be fine. Someone will come for you shortly. Right now, there's something important I need to take care of."

Brewer crossed the threshold and stepped into the room. He had regained his composure and sense of command. He looked at Egan, spoke curtly. "Assault on police... threatening the life of an officer of the law..."

"Still racking up those charges?" Egan said.

"You don't know what you've gotten yourself into, son."

Egan stared at the policeman. "Actually, Sergeant, I'm inclined to think that applies more to you than me. Now, please step back."

He closed the door to the wood drying room for the second time and secured the latch. Inside, the men were quiet.

Egan had to move fast. He was unsure if Sergeant Brewer had radioed for assistance while he was being dragged through the factory. He removed a police radio from one of the utility belts and clicked it on. Though unaware of the call signs of the units that had responded to the factory, he would be able to identify any chatter that sounded like it might have to do with calls relating to Brewer or his men.

After removing the weapons and spare ammunition clips from the officer's utility belts, he placed his hand over the pile of equipment and gear lying at his feet, activated Channeler, and liquefied the items.

Cal State University, Long Beach. That was the directive provided by Dr. Merrick in the neural interface transmission he received several minutes ago. The targets were there. He had to get to Long Beach as soon as possible.

First, the stolen van that had brought such undue attention to him had to be disposed of. It was still parked outside the factory, blocked in by the responding police cars.

Egan ran to the back of the factory and raised the drive-in door. Using Channeler, he levitated the van and the police cars off the ground. With the exception of one of the police units, he moved them inside the factory to the receiving area, lowered the door, sealed it shut, and started the engine of the remaining police car parked outside the factory.

Egan knew that a squad car being driven by a civilian might draw suspicion. Another police officer, not recognizing the driver, might pull him over and demand he identify himself. Egan opened the trunk of the unit and found what he was looking for. He removed the magnetic OUT OF SERVICE signs from the trunk and affixed them to the door panels, trunk and roof of the unit. Driving the car now wearing non-police attire shouldn't ring any alarms. He would be seen as a car jockey - a police mechanic, perhaps - transporting the vehicle to the service yard for repair.

Still, it wouldn't be long before dispatch realized they were unable to raise a radio response from not just one but three of their units. They would suspect the officers had encountered trouble at the factory. Additional units would be dispatched to the location, followed by an all-out search for the missing officers. Egan couldn't risk another encounter, especially if police agencies from neighboring jurisdictions were called in to help locate the missing units. He would have to get rid of the police car at the earliest possible opportunity and acquire a less conspicuous mode of transportation.

At the main road leading into the abandoned factory complex, Egan stopped for an ambulance as it screamed past, lights flashing and siren blaring, then raced after it. He stayed on the vehicles bumper as it tore through one inter-section after the next, down a series of side streets, and arrived at its final destination: Mercy Grace Hospital's Emergency entrance.

Egan parked on the street outside the hospital. The road ahead was divided. Straight ahead was the route the ambulance had taken. A sign on his left read, RESTRICTED PARKING - HOSPITAL STAFF AND AUTHORIZED VEHICLES ONLY BEYOND THIS POINT.

A motorcycle whizzed past and zipped into the Restricted Parking area. The rider raced the engine before backing into his designated space.

Egan had an idea. He stepped out of the car, removed the OUT OF SERVICE signs from the vehicle, and returned them to the trunk. He cruised up the roadway into the Restricted Parking area and watched the motorcyclist as he removed his helmet and locked his bike. The sign on his parking spot read DR. BRIAN HARVEY, M.D.

Egan backed the squad car into a space between another police cruiser and a vintage Aston Martin. Dr. Harvey rummaged through his backpack, pulled out his hospital ID, clipped it to his belt, then strolled up the walkway and entered the building through the doors marked STAFF ONLY.

Egan walked over to Dr. Harvey's motorcycle and placed his hand over the ignition switch of the Kawasaki Ninja. The engine came to life and thrummed impatiently. Egan slipped on the safety helmet, straddled the bike, eased it out of its parking space, then shifted it into gear and cruised out of the parking lot.

The young doctor would be on call for at least the next eight hours, probably twelve. In the meantime, he would never know that his motorcycle had been stolen.

The last place anyone would expect to find the missing police car would be in the reserved parking area of Mercy General Hospital, sitting alongside the other emergency vehicles.

Egan hit the main road and gunned the bike.

He was free of the factory.

Free of the police.

Free.

Cal State University awaited.

As did his targets.

35

THE UNMARKED SEDANS slowed as they approached the main entrance to the Corona Mews Shopping Centre. The occupants flashed Deputy Poole their ID: FBI and military. He spoke into his radio as he waved them through. "We got visitors, Chief."

Jenkins responded. "Copy that, Jack."

Ann Ridgeway waited as Jordan, Chris, and Colonel Hallier pulled into the parking lot adjacent to the privacy barrier and stepped out of their cars. Ridgeway introduced Jordan and Chris to Colonel Hallier. Together they walked through the alcove of the privacy blind and into the active crime scene.

ADC Ridgeway called out. "Chief Jenkins?"

Jenkins walked to the group. "Agent Ridgeway, I presume? Sorry we couldn't be meeting under better circumstances."

"I agree," Ridgeway replied. "These are my colleagues, Special Agents Jordan Quest and Chris Hallier, and Colonel Quentin Hallier with the Department of Defense."

"DARPA, specifically," Hallier said.

GARY WINSTON BROWN

"You're just the man I want to talk to, Colonel," Chief Jenkins said.

"How's that?" Hallier replied.

"You mind telling me what's going on at Dynamic Life Sciences? I was told you'd shut the place down."

Hallier came straight to the point. "Sorry, Chief. DLS isn't open for discussion. And, quite frankly, I don't have the time or the patience to play politics with you right now. Here's what's going to happen. You're going to hand over all the evidence your people have collected to these agents who are operating under my authority. This crime scene is now the jurisdiction of the Department of Defense. From this moment on neither you nor any member of your department is permitted to discuss any element of this case under penalty of violating the Defense Secrets Act. Do you understand, Chief Jenkins?"

"I'll tell you what I *understand,* Colonel," Jenkins replied. "That's not going to happen. This is *my* town, and I've got a situation here that poses a threat to the very people who pay me to keep them safe. If you think that I'm just going to let you waltz in here and tell my department to stand down..."

"Yes, Chief," Hallier interrupted. "That's precisely what you're going to do."

"You're out of your goddamn mind."

While the two men argued, Assistant Director Ridgeway motioned to Jordan. They stepped away from the group. She spoke quietly.

"Take a look around. Tell me what you find."

Jordan nodded. She turned to Chris. "Let's take a walk."

Jenkins raised his hand to the two agents. "You two can stop right there. No one goes anywhere until I get some answers."

"Go ahead, Agents," Hallier said. "Chief Jenkins and I will sort this out."

Jordan and Chris walked around the numbered evidence location markers. One of Jenkins officers was busy photographing the scene from different angles.

"I'll talk to him," Chris said. "Go do your thing."

Hanover identified himself to the officer and began questioning him about the day's events.

Jordan walked to the Dumpster and ran her fingers along its chipped surface.

Two men... one older, the other much younger... anger mixed with calm... immense energy. Jordan felt her body begin to tremble, come alive. *Massive extremes of expansion and contraction, alternating one second to the next...* as if the molecular bonds that held her body together no longer complied with the immutable laws of science. The sensation was as if every nerve ending had suddenly short-circuited, the life-maintaining synapse-to-synapse electrical conduction made impossible. *Death followed darkness.*

Drawn by a pungent smell not coming from inside the container, Jordan drew her hand away from the garbage bin. A large tarp, surrounded by numbered yellow tent markers, covered an area of the crime scene. Jordan knelt and placed her hand above it. The area smelled like rotting flesh. Her gift revealed that human remains had been rolled up into a section of carpet and thrown into the bin. The evidence under the tarp offered the same psychic reading as that from within the Dumpster. The victim had been transferred from there to here. The latent energy signature was male.

The reading, however, was confusing. Several energy forces fought for dominance over her psychic senses. The victim's signature was clear. But two additional signatures were also present and appeared to be layered, one atop the another. But this was impossible. Dead or alive, two energy signatures could not occupy the same body at the same time. However, this was the *world-between-worlds* where the laws of man did not apply. Jordan concentrated harder and drew a weak match to one of the two signatures. The sensation was close but not identical to the energy signature of the killer which she had felt in the Rosenfeld's bedroom. Similar, but not the same. Whoever murdered this victim shared a profound energetic connection to the Rosenfeld's killer. Jordan toyed with the hypothesis that there might be two killers, twins perhaps, identical, or fraternal, then quickly dismissed that theory. She had assisted the police with cases involving twin serial killers in the past. She knew what genetically shared psychic signatures felt like. That was not the case here.

The Assistant Director called out and motioned for her and Chris to join her as Chief Jenkins stepped outside the barrier. Chris thanked the officer for his time and joined his partner.

"Anything?" Ridgeway asked.

"I felt the presence of the Rosenfeld's killer here," Jordan said. "But he didn't kill Chief Jenkins victim. Someone else did. The energy signature of Jenkins UNSUB is very close, but not the same. There's a connection between them. But I don't know what it is."

Chris added. "Also, the manner of death is entirely different. Our guy shot the Rosenfeld's - very precise, very professional. Plus, he made a big deal about setting up the crime scene, from leaving flowers everywhere to concealing a flash drive in Rosenfeld's mouth." He pointed to the officer standing behind him. Ridgeway watched the man lift a corner of the tarp and examine the ground beneath it. "That cop says the remains of their guy looked like it'd been put through a juicer. All that was left were bits and pieces."

Jordan, Chris, and Ridgeway exited the crime scene and walked into the parking lot. Jenkins and Hallier stood beside the black Porsche. They continued to argue.

"Looks like Jenkins isn't taking the news about having to hand over his investigation to the Department of Defense very well," Ridgeway said. "I'll inform Colonel Hallier about what you read at the scene. This is his show now. There are unusual circumstances surrounding this case that you'll both need to be read in on. But they're matters of national security. And that information has to come from Colonel Hallier, not me."

"Understood, ma'am," Jordan said.

"Good."

Ridgeway looked at the two men. The confrontation between Chief Jenkins and Colonel Hallier was getting heated. "Someone needs to send those two to their respective corners before we end up with another homicide on our hands. Better give me a minute."

Chief Jenkins was irate. He walked away from the Colonel, stormed past Jordan, Chris, and Ridgeway, said nothing, barked something into his radio about 'standing down until scientists from the Department of Defense arrive' and marched around the barrier into the crime scene.

Hallier joined the agents.

"Everything all right?" ADC Ridgeway asked the Colonel.

Hallier rolled his eyes. "Don't worry about the Chief. He'll be fine. He's just trying to see how high up the tree he can piss." He changed the subject. "The Assistant Director informs me you have a very unique talent, Agent Quest."

"Yes, sir," Jordan replied.

Hallier pointed to the Porsche. "See that car? It belongs to one of the men we're looking for, Dr. Jason Merrick. I think he may be responsible for killing Jenkins' victim. I need to find Merrick and another man who may be with him, Commander Ben Egan. Think you can help me with that?"

"Of course, Colonel."

"All right, then. Let's get to it."

36

HOW HAD THE FBI connected him to Rosenfeld?

Taras Verenich' efforts to subdue his rising panic was proving to be an exercise in futility. His palms were soaked with sweat. His heart pounded with such ferocity he feared he might go into cardiac arrest at any second.

He had to get out of Los Angeles, fast. He was suddenly on the radar of the FBI. Which meant something had gone terribly wrong. The agents had asked if he knew Itzhak Rosenfeld. If they were asking questions about his connection to the philanthropist what else did they know? Had The Company been compromised? Were preparations already underway to make changes in the American operation? Marina was on her way from Russia at this very moment. The purpose of her trip was two-fold: to meet with him, and to deal with the mysterious stranger who had threatened to harm both her and her son. But was her visit just a ruse? Perhaps she had been instructed to come to America for the express purpose of killing him and to tie up any loose ends which The Company had deemed to be necessary. Had *he* become a loose end?

Taras pressed a button under his desk. A framed Norman Rockwell painting located above his credenza slid up the wall on a hidden track, exposing a wall safe. Verenich punched in the electronic combination. The door clicked open.

Taras placed his briefcase on his desk, opened the latches, then turned his attention to the safe.

He removed several passports, excellent quality fakes he had commissioned shortly after he joined The Company. He tossed them into the case along with a notebook labeled CONTINGENCY. The details of every meeting and telephone call he had ever had with Marina was recorded in the book. It was his book of secrets about The Company; an insurance policy he could sell to the highest bidder, if and when taking such action should become necessary. His every instinct was telling him now was the time to cash out. He grabbed several bundles of cash and a burner phone from the safe, threw the items in the briefcase, locked it, placed the case under his desk and pressed the button beneath his desk again. The painting returned to its home position on the wall.

Taras picked up the phone and buzzed Avel.

"Yes, Mr. Verenich?"

"The package?" he said. "Do you have it?"

"Yes sir."

"Bring it to my office."

"Right away, sir."

Avel stepped into Taras' office carrying a small box under his arm. He closed the office door and handed the parcel to the lawyer.

"How much?" Taras asked.

"A grand, plus another two-hundred for the extras."

Taras opened the box and inspected the order: a fully loaded Colt semi-automatic 9mm handgun, four pre-loaded clips and six boxes of ammunition.

"Satisfactory?" Avel asked.

Taras nodded. He returned the items to the box. "One more thing."

"Of course."

"The Ferrari is parked in the underground. You know my detailer?"

"Coventry's?"

"Yes. I'll be out for a while. Run it over there. Tell them I want the works. Interior and exterior cleaning, vacuum, wet gloss polish. I'll pick it up later."

"Certainly."

"And use the west exit when you leave the building, not the east."

Avel laughed. "What difference does it matter which exit I --?"

Taras snapped at him. "The *west* exit, Avel."

Avel nodded. "Of course, sir. The west exit. My apologies."

Taras handed him the ignition fob to his Ferrari 488. "You better get moving. I'm already running late."

"Right away, sir," Avel said. He left the room.

Taras removed the gun from the box, slipped on his blazer, shoved the weapon into his waistband and placed a clip in each coat pocket. He walked across his office, stood out of sight beside the window, peered through the blinds at the street below, and waited.

A minute later, Avel exited the underground parking lot from the west side of the building, as instructed. Taras listened to the whine of the Ferrari as Avel slowed at the exit, then heard it scream to life as he sped up the road, racing through the amber traffic light. Across the street, the surveillance team witnessed the Ferrari leave the building and speed up the road. The Mercedes squealed out of its parking space, raced down the ramp to the first level, tore out of the parking structure, then braked hard at the red light. When the traffic light turned green the sedan raced up the road in pursuit of the sports car.

Taras waited until the car was out of sight. He walked to his desk, picked up the phone, and placed a call.

"Elite Air."

"I need to book a jet."

"Your account number, please?"

"TA-24-1667."

A pause, then, "Thank you, Mr. Antipov. When and where, sir?"

Taras almost corrected the Elite Air service rep when he addressed him by his false surname, *Antipov.*

"Tonight. Los Angeles to Costa Rica. Direct."

"Number in your party?"

"Just me."

"Very good, sir. You're confirmed for 9:00 P.M. departure. Would you like your ticket emailed to you?"

"I'll pick it up at the counter."

"Thank you, Mr. Antipov," the rep said. "We'll see you soon. Thank you for choosing Elite--"

Verenich hung up the phone, reached under his desk, grabbed the briefcase.

He would leave the country tonight following his meeting with Ashley Granger and get out before everything hit the fan. If Marina Puzanova was being sent from Russia to kill him he'd make sure she never got the chance. If the purpose of her visit was legitimate, to find and eliminate the threat to her son, then she would have to fend for herself. One way or the other, Taras was determined to stay one step ahead of The Company and the FBI. And stay alive.

"I'm out for the evening, Elena," Taras said as he walked past his receptionist and pressed the elevator call button.

"Yes, sir."

The doors separated. Taras stepped inside.

Elena called out. "When shall I say you'll be back?"

The doors rumbled closed. The elevator descended to the main floor.

From behind the lobby window Taras surveyed the street

No sign of the shadow team or the Mercedes.

He stepped out of the building onto the sidewalk. A Yellow Cab was parked across the street. Verenich flagged the driver. The roof light turned on. The driver made a quick U-turn and pulled up to the curb. Verenich jumped in.

"Where to?" the cabbie asked.

"Caridad's," Taras answered. "You know the place?"

"Sure do."

The driver spun around. Taras watched the gleaming building disappear behind him. He knew he would probably never set eyes on it again.

As he lifted the briefcase from the seat beside him it slipped out of his hands and fell hard on the floor of the cab. The cabbie glanced in the rearview mirror.

"Sorry," Taras said. "Butterfingers."

The cabbie returned his attention the road.

Taras picked up the briefcase.

Try as he might, he couldn't stop his hands from shaking.

37

JORDAN'S PHONE RANG as she inspected the Porsche. Agent Hawkins was calling back.

"Go ahead, Hawk," Jordan said. "You're on speaker with Chris."

"Cyber got back to me with more info on the flash drive," Hawkins said. "The account numbers do, in fact, belong to Bitcoin accounts."

"The Internet-based currency you talked about," Chris said.

"Precisely," Hawkins said. "We've expedited a warrant. These guys don't exactly have a stellar reputation when it comes to cooperating with the authorities."

"So we have names?"

"Yes," Hawkins replied. "Remember how each of the account numbers was preceded by two letters? Those were identifiers; the first initial of the last name, followed by the first initial of the first name. One of the files belongs to Dr. Rosenfeld – '*RI*,' aka Rosenfeld, Itzhak."

"And the others?" Jordan asked.

"DM belongs to Dowd, Michael; 'HJ' to Harper, Julie..."

She turned to Chris, "The victims in the El Segundo murders: Michael Dowd and Julie Harper. The strip club owner and his manager.

"Somehow they're all connected," Chris said.

"There are three more names," Hawkins said. "Taras Verenich, who we already know has a relationship of some kind with Rosenfeld. The other accounts belong to Ashley Granger and Marina Puzanova for a total of six."

"But no account for Zahava Rosenfeld," Chris said.

"No," Hawkins said. "Which means one of two things. Either she was collateral damage or she's neck-deep in this with her husband."

"We need to find Verenich," Jordan said. "He's the only one on the list whom we know for sure is still alive."

"So far, anyway," Chris said.

"I'm willing to bet he knows who killed the Rosenfeld's," Jordan said. "Probably Dowd and Harper, too. What about the file name, Hawk? Any idea what 'AWP' means?"

"Not yet."

"First Dowd and Harper, then Rosenfeld," Chris said. "If Verenich has been targeted we need to find him and get him into protective custody right away."

"The other names, Granger and Puzanova," Jordan asked. "What do we know about them?"

"No record for either name came up in the NCIC database search," Hawk replied. "There are half a million Ashley Granger's living in the United States. Far fewer Puzanova's. Cyber is also checking social media for any links to our victims."

"Besides Verenich, Granger and Puzanova, all the account holders listed on the drive are dead," Jordan said. "And the jury's still out as to whether or not Granger and Puzanova are still alive."

"Let's hope neither of them catches a bullet before we find them," Chris said.

Jordan thought about the crime scene behind her and the liquefied remains of Jenkin's victim.

"Or worse," she said.

38

TWO FIRE TRUCKS and an ambulance followed closely behind Laguna Beach police units as they arrived at the accident scene. On the beach, the driver of the first car to have lost control crawled out the window of his wrecked vehicle. Behind him, the engine compartment of the second car erupted into flames. Inside the vehicle, two small children screamed and beat their tiny fists against the passenger windows while their unconscious parents lay slumped in their seats, oblivious to the imminent danger facing their precious family.

Although the arrival of the emergency services had successfully diverted police attention away from the Suburban, access to the vehicle remained impossible. Entry and exit from the parking lot was blocked by fire trucks. Merrick watched a team of firefighters deploy a water hose from their truck and run down the embankment to the burning car, dousing the flames, breaking out the windows and pulling the children to safety, then wrench open the car doors to allow paramedics access to the trapped parents. On the driver's side of the vehicle the children's father was being cautiously extricated from the car and eased onto a backboard, his neck and body immobilized for safe transport up the hill to the waiting ambulance. On the passenger side of the car, a paramedic squeezed her way into the crushed compartment and pressed her fingers against the woman's neck, checked for a pulse, then moved her stethoscope across her chest, listening for a cardiac or respiratory response, found none. The paramedic looked at the police officers and firemen standing beside the car and shook her head.

Ellie stood with her hand clasped over her mouth, then broke into tears. "Those poor, poor people," she said.

"Yeah," Merrick replied. "Shame."

Long Beach.

Merrick walked around the corner of the shop. A footpath paralleled the road below the view of oncoming traffic. Egan had received his instructions and would be on his way. He would meet him there. There was no time to waste.

The police had found the contractor's truck. Which meant they had probably also found his remains at the back of the shopping center in Corona. Merrick assumed that by now all hell had broken out at Dynamic Life Sciences. DARPA was looking for him, as too was probably every other police agency in the country.

He picked up his pace, ran up the footpath to the sidewalk, rounded the bend, and crossed the road. The traffic behind him had come to a complete stop. Ahead, he heard the excited sound of children splashing in a pool.

The Acadia Motor Inn's neon-orange sign flashed NO VACANCY above the entrance to the main office and swayed lazily in rhythm with the gentle ocean breeze.

Merrick opened the door and stepped inside. The manager glanced up from his crossword puzzle book and set down his pen. He pointed to the outside sign.

"Sorry, mister," the manager said. "Like the sign says, we're full up."

"You use a pen," Merrick said. "I'm impressed!"

Confused, the manager looked up. "Say what?"

Merrick qualified his remark. "The crossword you're working on. Very few people are confident enough in their puzzle-solving ability to use a pen. Most use a pencil. It's so much easier. You make a mistake, erase it, make the correction, and move on. But using a pen exemplifies an entirely different level of commitment. We pen-users allow no provision for error. We're 'all-in', as the younger crowd is fond of saying. You can learn a lot about an individual by the approach he or she takes to solving such minor challenges as the completion of a crossword puzzle. I too have always loved them. They are an insignificant distraction, of course. But nonetheless a test of one's intellectual mettle." Merrick stepped around the counter. "I've always found crosswords to be incredibly stimulating and so much more enjoyable when completed with a friend. You've piqued my curiosity. Mind if I have a look?"

"Uh, sure... I guess so," the manager said, disarmed by the charm and confidence of the stranger. "This one clue does have me a little stumped."

Merrick laughed. "Isn't that always the case? There's always one clue that's a nuisance. But that's part of the fun, isn't it?" Merrick picked up the pen from the counter. "Which one is it that's tripping you up? I'm sure we can figure it out together."

"24 across," the manager said. The desk phone rang. He

disregarded the call, drawn back into the puzzle by Merrick's offer of assistance. "Seven letters: *'Serve as evidence or proof.'* Been stuck on that for the last twenty minutes. You got any idea what that is?"

"I may," Merrick said. "Mind if I borrow your pen?"

"Sure," the manager said. He placed the pen on the desk. The phone rang once, twice, three times. Frustrated that his work responsibility was getting in the way of puzzle-solving he finally said, "I better get that."

"Yes, of course. Go ahead," Merrick said. He picked up the pen. "No, wait. Yes, I've got it!" He laughed. He turned to the manager. "Isn't it funny? Sometimes the answer is so blatantly obvious it might as well be staring you in the face."

The managers let the phone ring. He turned his attention back to the puzzle.

"You figured it out?" he said. "What is it?"

Merrick plunged the pen deep into the man's neck. The manager's eyes widened. Merrick covered his mouth as he began to gag, then lowered him to the floor beneath the reception desk.

"Witness," Merrick whispered into the dying man's ear. He peered out the window and watched as the children played in the pool under the warm California sun. "W-I-T-N-E-S-S," he spelled out. "Something I can't afford to have."

The manager's eyes fluttered. His body fell slack.

A roll of paper towels and other housekeeping items sat on a shelf below the manager's desk. Merrick tore off several sheets, wiped the blood off the counter, and cleaned his hands. The keys to a late model Volvo lay in a glass bowl under the desk. Merrick scooped them out of the bowl and exited the office. On the key ring was the key to the front door. He locked it behind him as he left. A sign affixed to the wall in front of the Volvo read MANAGER.

Merrick started the dead man's car, backed out of his parking space, put the vehicle into gear, and left the Acadia Motor Inn.

Long Beach awaited, as did Commander Egan.

And payback.

39

"SO THAT'S IT?" Deputy Poole said. "We're shut
down... just like that?"

"It's not our game anymore, Jack," Chief Jenkins
said. "Tell the boys to box up everything they've processed
so far and hand it over to Colonel Hallier."

"You mean Mr. Green Suit?"

"I don't like it any more than you do," Jenkins replied.
"But we're done here. Hallier claims we're not equipped to
handle it, that it's too dangerous for Corona P.D., and that
we're to consider it a matter of national security."

"Bullshit," Poole replied. "I could say the same thing
about my wife's meatloaf."

"A Department of Defense team is on the way. Tell the
men to provide them with whatever assistance they need
when they arrive."

"Whatever you say, Chief."

"And Jack?"

"Yeah, Chief?"

"Your wife's meatloaf..."

"What about it?"

"Give Hallier the recipe. Tell him to lock it away some place no one will ever find it."

"Good idea," Poole said. "How about Nevada. Area 51."

Jenkins smiled. "That should be secure enough."

Poole shook his head and turned away. "I'll tell the boys to clean up."

"Good man."

"And don't forget about Friday," Poole called out.

"Friday?"

"Nora invited you to our place for dinner, remember?"

Jenkins put his hands on his hips. "You wouldn't."

Poole waved over his shoulder as he walked away. "Damn straight I would. I'll let her know it's your favorite."

CHIEF JENKINS SAT in his Jeep outside the barricade and reviewed his officer's incident reports prior to handing the case over to the Department of Defense.

Earl Kent walked over and leaned against the door. "I hear the feds are taking it from here," he said.

Jenkins kept reading. "Looks that way, doc." He held up Kent's paperwork. "Anything you want to add?"

Kent shook his head. "It's all there. Best I can give you, anyway. I'm just a simple medical examiner."

"A simple, Johns Hopkins-educated medical examiner," Jenkins added. "Tell me the truth, doc. What do you make out of all this? Last night I dealt with the first homicide Corona has seen in a decade and today you're scraping human paste off the ground. Next thing I know, the government shows up at our investigation and tells us thanks for keeping dinner warm, now kindly piss off."

Dr. Kent shrugged his shoulders. "Right place, wrong

time, Chief. Nothing more to it than that." The coroner's phone rang. He stepped away and took the call.

Jenkins returned to his paperwork. Two military vehicles pulled up to the entrance to the shopping plaza. He watched Deputy Poole point them in the direction of the crime scene and wave them through.

Dr. Kent pocketed his phone as he walked back to the Jeep. "That was forensics. Odontology confirmed the dental implant belonged to Dan Labrada."

"At least now we know who our vic is," Jenkins said. "The only remaining questions are who killed him and why. Maybe Poole's right."

"That it could be drug-related?"

"Yeah."

Kent shook his head. "I doubt it."

"Why?"

"The manner of death for starters" Kent said. "Unless Labrada was a drug kingpin or organized crime boss it's highly unlikely he would come to that kind of an end. And if he was a drug lord or Mafia, he probably would have come up on your radar a long time ago."

"True."

"Second, if he was a high-value player, DEA, FBI, or DHS would have advised you that they were conducting an op in your jurisdiction."

"You ever consider trading in your scalpel for a badge?" Jenkins asked.

Kent smiled. "Third... the Department of Defense took over your investigation, not the DEA, FBI, or DHS. DARPA doesn't deal with narcotics or organized crime. What about the wife in Norco? Did your officers check her out?"

Jenkins nodded. "She hadn't heard from Labrada since yesterday. and from what I understand didn't care if she ever did again. Apparently the two of them are on the ropes. She was planning to ask him for a divorce as soon as she worked up the nerve. She gave us everything we asked for. Labrada was clean."

"Too bad. It could have made life a little easier."

"Yeah."

The military vehicles accelerated through the parking lot and rolled to a stop in front of Chief Jenkins and Dr. Kent. Colonel Hallier greeted the soldiers.

Jenkins stepped out of the Jeep. "I guess it's time I get this over with."

"I suppose so," Kent replied.

The men watched as Hallier's soldiers removed several cases marked HAZMAT from their vehicles and carried them into the crime scene.

"Think Hallier would keep you updated on the case if you asked him nicely?" Kent asked.

Chief Jenkins shook his head. "I'd have a better chance of winning the lottery."

40

THE HOUR WAS late, and Terminal D at Sheremetyevo International Airport was quiet. Marina Puzanova sat in the Aeroflot departure lounge waiting to board the final flight of the night leaving from Moscow for Los Angeles.

She removed her cell phone and listened again to the call: *'I know who you are... I know what you are... I know what you did... Is Ilya enjoying his studies at Cal State?'*

Bastard!

She removed a notebook from her handbag and listed the details of the call: American accent, middle-aged. The sound of waves. The cry of seagulls. Dammit! So little to go on. Frustrated, she shoved the notepad back into her purse.

He seemed to know exactly who she was, what type of business she was involved in, and specific details about The Company.

Only one possible explanation made sense. Verenich had been compromised.

Whoever the caller was, he had gained access to her through Taras. From the moment they had first met Marina knew the American attorney could not be trusted. If her superiors had listened to her and taken her concerns about him more seriously, she wouldn't be sitting in the airport lounge right now, waiting to fly halfway around the world to take care of a problem that could have been dealt with long ago with a bullet to the lawyer's head.

Marina's phone rang. The code number '000' appeared on the screen. It was Kastonov, chairman of The Company. She answered the call.

"Good evening, Mr. Kastonov."

"Marina, my dear," Kastonov said joyfully. "How are you?"

She tried to suppress the anxiety in her voice. "Very well, sir."

"Splendid. First, let me apologize for calling you at this late hour," Kastonov said. "I'm sorry for the intrusion. I'm sure you've had a very long day."

"It's no intrusion whatsoever, sir. How can I help you?"

"I promise I won't take more than a minute of your time."

"Of course, sir."

"Very good. A quick question for you, if I may."

"Yes, sir."

The warm tone melted from Kastonov's voice. "My colleagues and I would like to know why you're leaving for America without permission."

Marina's throat felt dry. She had been under surveillance by Company operatives and did not know it. But why?

She swallowed hard. "Sir?"

"Now Marina," Kastonov said, "you know as well as I do we have rules in place for a reason. I would encourage you to look at this situation from my perspective. When a respected member of my organization, and one of my best people I might add, arbitrarily decides to leave the country, without warning or any upline communication with her handlers...well, what am I to think?"

"Sir, it's just that..."

"What do you suppose would be the first thought to go through my mind in a situation like that?"

"Mr. Kastonov, if I may be permitted to explain..."

"It's that someone has made a *deal*. I'm not saying for a minute this is the case with you, my dear. I wouldn't want you to think that that would be my first thought where you are concerned. Because if it were, I can assure you I wouldn't have given you the courtesy of this phone call."

Marina was quiet.

"Are you still there, my dear?"

She paused. "I am."

"Good. Now do us both a favor. Go home. Get a good night's rest. We'll talk about this in the morning. I'm quite sure we can put this little misunderstanding behind us."

"I'm afraid I can't do that, sir."

Kastonov was silent.

The Aeroflot-hostess announced the business passengers pre-boarding call over the public address system. Marina stood from her seat and extended the pull-up handle on her carry-on case.

"My business in the United States is personal, Mr. Kastonov. It has nothing to do with The Company. We will discuss it on my return."

"Marina. I strongly suggest you cancel your travel plans and leave the airport immediately," Kastonov replied.

"This does not concern you or The Company."

"You're making a grave mistake, Ms. Puzanova."

"Goodbye, Mr. Kastonov." Marina terminated the call. She let out a long deep breath. Good God, she thought.

What have I done? By hanging up on Kastonov she had stepped way over the line. They would make her accountable for her actions upon her return to Moscow. But none of that mattered right now.

Her only concern was protecting Ilya from danger.

As she walked down the gangway and entered the aircraft the stranger's words played in her mind: '*I'm going to take it all apart... in ways you can't even begin to imagine.*'

We'll see about that, she thought.

She had already established her priorities. First, secure Ilya. Second, terminate Verenich.

Marina stored her case in the overhead compartment and took her seat. She looked out the window of the aircraft and thought about her call with Kastonov. Insubordination of any kind was not tolerated. There would be consequences.

Maybe it was time for a new start. In a new country. With a new identity. Perhaps making a deal with the Americans in exchange for her knowledge of The Company might not be such a bad idea after all.

Marina fastened her seat belt and selected a magazine from the front seatback pocket. The cover read, "America's 100 Safest Cities." She opened the magazine and skimmed through the article:

Sunnyvale, California. The home of Silicon Valley offered plenty of companies in which she could invest her wealth and live very comfortably for the rest of her life.

Honolulu, Hawaii. The year-round warmth of Hawaii would indeed be a welcome change to the cold of Moscow.

Alexandria, Virginia. Some of the richest and most powerful men and women in the country lived there. She would have no trouble moving in such circles.

So many choices.

Kastonov's call had been the tipping point. She made up her mind. The time had come for her to leave The Company and get out of the business.

After she had settled her personal affairs she would meet with the FBI.

She laid the magazine in her lap and closed her eyes.

White sand, hot sun, ocean breeze.

Hawaii it would be.

Before long, the stress of the day overpowered her. She fell asleep. In her dream, she was walking along a secluded stretch of sandy beach. She could feel the heat of the sun on her face and the waves lapping at her feet. She had also found love on this island paradise. He put his arm around her, pulled her close and whispered in her ear: "I know who you are... I know what you are... I know what you did."

Marina woke with a start.

The engines revved and receded. The aircraft taxied for takeoff.

41

JORDAN RECEIVED A second call from Agent Hawkins. "Go ahead, Hawk. You're on speaker."

"Ever heard of a guy by the name of Alexi Vasiliev?" Agent Hawkins asked.

"The name doesn't ring a bell," Jordan said. Chris shook his head. "Not for Chris either."

"Vasiliev used to be a high-ranking member of the Russian mafia. I think Rosenfeld may have been acquiring his art and antiquities through him."

"Are you saying Rosenfeld was connected to the Russian mob?" Jordan asked.

"I can't confirm that yet. Our guys lifted several sets of prints from the back of the Pont Neuf and the Codex Leicester in Rosenfeld's bedroom. IAFIS came back with three hits. Rosenfeld's, of course, but also prints belonging to Alexi Vasiliev and another Russian, Vyacheslav Usoyan."

"Head of the Solntsevskaya Bratva," Chris said. "Russia's largest crime organization."

"That's right," Hawkins said. "Vasiliev is Usoyan's

brother-in-law. According to our intelligence Usoyan brought him into the family business a few years back. Seems he took to it pretty fast and received a number of rapid promotions within the Bratva, mostly due to his reputation for having an eye for art. Pretty soon he became the Bratva's go-to guy for stolen art and artifacts. They've placed hundreds of stolen pieces into the hands of the elite over the years, primarily with collectors in the United States, Canada, France, Spain and Portugal."

"Wasn't Usoyan on the Bureau's Top Ten Most Wanted a couple of years back?" Chris asked.

"Indeed. He was arrested in Russia for tax fraud, of all things, related to a financial institution of which he was the principal. It seems having access to all that money was a little too tempting. Usoyan ripped off the company for millions. Thousands of investors here in the States and abroad got burned. Many lost everything they had. We tried to arrest him when he was in the country but missed our window of opportunity by a matter of hours. By the time we received his arrest warrant he was already on a flight back to Russia. Since they have no extradition treaty with the United States it was over for us. Usoyan suspected law enforcement was on to him back home and he was right. Russian authorities took him into custody the second he stepped off the plane in Moscow. He handed the reins over to Vasiliev until he was released on bail. Since then he's gone underground. No one has seen or heard from him in years."

"Why would Rosenfeld buy his art from mobsters?" Jordan asked. "He could easily afford to pay whatever price the market was asking."

"Not in this case," Hawkins said. "These pieces have historical significance. They're not for sale. They're meant to be appreciated by the world, not just one man. But individuals like Rosenfeld with unlimited financial resources know who to connect with to make such acquisitions happen. And that kind of money buys silence."

"What I don't understand is why Rosenfeld would even want to be associated with Vasiliev or Usoyan," Jordan asked.

"I have an idea," Hawkins said. "But it's probably a long shot."

"Let's hear it," Chris said.

"Remember the files I found on the computer in Rosenfeld's panic room? The ones labeled Account 1 and Account 2? We clicked on the hidden link at the bottom of Verenich' website, entered one of the Account 1 codes into the search box and got a full profile of the girl: name, description, how much she billed out, even her purchase price. Here's my theory: What if Rosenfeld acquired the Pont Neuf and the Codex Leicester from the Bratva through Verenich?"

"That would connect Verenich to the Russian mob," Jordan said.

"Exactly."

"It might also mean that Rosenfeld's murder was a mob hit," Chris added.

"That's what I'm thinking," Hawkins said. "Maybe he tried to double-cross them. Like I said, it's just a theory."

"Verenich did tell us his clientele was primarily Russian," Jordan said.

"We need to get Ridgeway's permission to go back to Verenich' office and press him for answers," Chris said. "See if he breaks."

"He'll spout off about his rights, throw the Constitution at us, then toss us out on our asses," Jordan said.

"Wouldn't be a first for me," Chris said. "And I'm pretty sure my ass can take the fall."

"Mine too," Jordan replied.

42

MERRICK PULLED INTO the main entrance of California State University Long Beach campus behind the stolen motorcycle.

Egan stepped off the bike. "It's been a while," he said, shaking his handler's hand.

"So it has," Merrick replied. "Ready?"

Egan nodded. "Let's do it."

The two men entered the grounds and walked past the Visitor Information Center. A university police officer stepped out of the booth. The cop called out. "Can I help you, gentlemen?"

Merrick and Egan ignored the policeman.

The officer spoke again. "Hold up a second, fellas."

The men turned around.

"What's your business here at Cal State?" The cop smiled. "I hope you don't mind me saying so, but you both look a little old to be students."

Merrick laughed. "To be sure. I'm afraid our days of taking notes in the classroom have been over for quite some time. And I don't mind telling you it's much more enjoyable being on the other side of the lectern."

The cop leaned against the wall of the Visitor Booth. "What brings you here today?" he asked.

"My name is Professor Kincaid," Merrick lied. "This is my colleague, Professor Dawson. We're looking for a colleague, Dr. Ashley Granger. Would you happen to know where we might find her?"

The cop pointed down the road. "Molecular and Life Sciences Center, just off East Campus Drive. Is Dr. Granger expecting you?"

"No. In fact, we were hoping to surprise her," Merrick replied.

"Sorry professors," the cop replied. "University rules are cut and dry when it comes to visitors. No guests are permitted on campus without a pass." He picked up the phone. "Let me call Dr. Granger. I'll arrange that for you right now."

"I understand, Officer," Merrick replied. "I assure you we won't be long." The men turned and walked away.

The guard spoke into his radio. "You'll have to wait here until I contact Dr. Granger."

Merrick and Egan ignored him, kept walking in the direction of East Campus Drive.

The officer called out. "Professors?"

No reply.

The university cop issued a final warning. "Both of you stop right there!"

Merrick turned to Egan. "Connect with me when you locate Granger. Bring her to me. I'll find the boy."

"Yes, sir," Egan replied.

Lights flashed. A Cal State University Police car sped around the corner from West Campus Drive and braked to a hard stop in front of Egan. The officer stepped out of the vehicle, removed his baton, and opened the back door of the cruiser.

The cop walked up to Egan. He was solid, all muscle, and towered over him. He pressed the tip of the club against the soldier's chest. "Get in," he said.

Egan looked down at the weapon then up at the officer. He shook his head. "Trust me, Kong," he said. "You really don't want to do this."

"This is going to go down one of two ways," the cop said. "Either you get your ass into the back seat willingly or I'll cuff you and shove you in there myself. Your choice."

Egan looked up at the cop and smiled. "I'll bet you say the same thing to your wife. What do you call that in your house? Foreplay?"

"I won't ask a third time."

"You won't have to," Egan said. "I'll give you five seconds."

"For what?"

"To get out of my way."

The officer pushed the baton harder into his Egan's solar plexus. "That's it," he said. "Turn around and place your hands behind your back. You're under arrest."

"Three seconds, Kong," Egan said. "Tick-tock."

"Screw you."

Egan grabbed the shaft of the baton and held it tight. Shocked at Egan's strength, the officer struggled to pull the weapon free from his grasp, couldn't. The band around Egan's wrist began to glow.

"What the hell," the officer said.

"What is it with you guys?" Egan said, "You *never* learn." A pulse of blue light shot along the shaft of the baton, straight into the cop. The officer dropped to his knees, then fell against the crash bumper of his patrol car. He lay on the ground, semi-conscious, dazed. Egan tossed the baton aside.

A group of students had gathered at the intersection and watched the campus police attempt to arrest the strangers to no avail. Concerned for the welfare of the injured officers, four young men threw down their backpacks, walked across the street, and confronted Egan while their girlfriends recorded the event on their cell phones.

"Hey, asshole," one of the kids yelled out. "They told you to leave."

Another student stepped forward. "Yeah," he said. "Get the fuck out of here!"

The fallen officer warned the students. "Get back!" He yelled into his microphone. "Front gates. Officer down. I repeat, officer down!"

The students heeded the cops warning and stepped back. Egan walked past the police car and headed down the road in the direction of East Campus Drive.

Three additional police cars screamed to the scene, lights flashing, sirens blaring, taking up tactical positions on the road. The officers emerged from their vehicles; weapons drawn.

The sudden realization that gunfire might erupt at any second charged the already panicked crowd. The young men ran back to their girlfriends and snatched their backpacks up off the ground. Together they ran out of the University grounds and past the Visitors Information Centre, waving frantically at the passing traffic. An LAPD squad car took notice of the commotion, turned on its service lights, executed a U-turn, and accelerated back toward the students.

One of the officers screamed at Egan: "On the ground! Do it now!"

Egan looked at the police, then at Merrick. "Your orders, sir?"

"It's time," Merrick said. "Light it up."

"Yes, sir."

The men activated their devices. The bands around their wrists glowed bright red.

Egan raised his hand and directed Channeler's powerful energy at the police. Their squad cars began to shudder and shake. Tires hissed, blew out. The smell of burning rubber mixed with the putrid odor of scorched metal, melting vinyl and polystyrene as the cars burst into flames. Windshields shattered. Headlights popped. Police and onlookers watched in awe as Egan raised the burned-out shells off the ground, higher and higher into the air, lifting them by an unseen force, until they stopped and hovered in midair. With a swipe of his hand Egan caused the vehicles to take flight. Hurtling through the air, they crashed with tremendous force into the front entrance of the Nursing building.

Merrick pointed his fist in the direction of the parking garage and engaged Channeler. From inside the structure came a series of massive explosions – *boom! boom! boom!* He had caused the vehicles inside the structure to burst into flame. The intensity of the heat within the confine of the structure continued to build until it reached its flashpoint. The building started to rumble, then shake. Thick black smoke climbed over the waist-high walls of the parking levels and billowed skyward. Students staggered out of the building and collapsed to their knees, coughing, vomiting, trying desperately to suck life-giving oxygen back into their seared lungs.

The thunderous explosions brought students and faculty out of every building. The University's Emergency Warning System siren activated and blared a rising wail across the campus. Terrified students crashed out of the exit doors of the buildings and ran for cover, their screams barely audible above the deafening wail of the EWS.

Merrick turned his attention to the lecture halls, dining area and administrative facilities. The buildings began to tremble as though the Long Beach campus sat atop a treacherous geological fault line which was about to be ripped apart by the mother of all earthquakes. Glass exploded out of window frames, impaling the fleeing students with white hot shards. No longer able to withstand the violent assault the buildings creaked, moaned, sighed, and fell. From within the cloud of dust and debris pleas for help could be heard. While the injured begged for help the dying fell silent.

Hell had found the University.

On the streets, in buildings, even on rooftops, students and faculty sought refuge from the attack.

Merrick could feel the presence of Ilya Puzanova. Channeler confirmed it.

He set out in search of his target.

43

FBI ASSISTANT DIRECTOR Ann Ridgeway's incoming text from Special Agent Cobb simply read, "911." She called him immediately.

"We have a situation underway in Long Beach," Cobb said. "Numerous reports of massive explosions at Cal State University. LAPD's getting hammered with calls from students, faculty and residents, all reporting what they believe to be bomb explosions."

"Have we liaised with LAPD?"

"They're en route as we speak. Could be a terrorist attack."

"I'm on my way. Forward all intelligence updates to me the second they come in."

"Yes ma'am," Cobb said.

Ridgeway scrolled through her phone contacts, found "HRT," and pressed the call button.

"HRT. This is Chainer."

"David, it's Ann. Bring me up to speed on Long Beach."

The intensity of the conversation caught Hallier's attention. He walked over to the Assistant Director. Ridgeway opened the speaker on her phone.

"Hostage Rescue Team One is on the way. Team Two's gearing up. Two unfriendlies reported so far, could be more. Multiple casualties."

"Means and motive?"

"Unknown at this time."

Hallier motioned to speak to the Assistant Director privately. "Hang on, Sergeant." Ridgeway muted the call.

"What's going on?" Hallier asked.

"California State University at Long Beach is under attack. Two men on campus. You thinking what I'm thinking?"

"Merrick and Egan."

Ridgeway nodded.

"Put your man back on."

Ridgeway took Chainer off hold.

"Sergeant," she said, "you're on speaker with Colonel Quentin Hallier, United States Army, Department of Defense, DARPA."

"Colonel," Sergeant Chainer said.

"Sergeant," Hallier said, "I'm sending a tactical team to Cal State. Your men will liaise with mine. Tell your teams not to engage until we arrive. Set up a staging area outside the university. We'll work out an infiltration plan when I get there. Until then you and your men need to stand down."

"With all due respect, Colonel," Chainer replied, "We're not about to stand around and wait for the body count to rise. We need boots on the ground now."

"I understand," Hallier said. "Just get your men ready. I'll explain more when I get there. Do not engage with these men. Air support will be there within minutes."

"My guys are already in the air."

"That's fine. Just give us room to land."

"Copy that, Colonel. Ma'am?"

Ridgeway replied. "Go ahead, Sergeant."

"Word just came in. LAPD SWAT has been deployed."

Hallier shook his head. "They need to be recalled, Ann. They're walking into a death trap. Merrick and Egan will rip them apart."

Ridgeway nodded. "Sergeant, call SWAT. Tell them we have reliable intelligence that confirms this could be a military assault, not a terrorist attack. They're not trained for an engagement like this."

Hallier jumped in. "Sergeant, you need to make their Commander understand that unless he wants to see every one of his men wearing toe-tags within the hour they need to stand down and wait for DARPA commandos to arrive. We're equipped to deal with this. SWAT isn't. We're taking point on this operation."

Sergeant Chainer replied. "Copy that. I'll make the call." He hung up.

ADC Ridgeway turned to Hallier. "This just got real serious, real fast."

"You have no idea just how serious," Hallier said. He placed a call.

"Joint Forces Training Base Los Alamitos. Commander Aikens."

"It's Hallier. Tell Tactical they're green to go. Get them in the air now. Infiltration point is Cal State University at Long Beach. LAPD SWAT is on the scene. FBI Hostage Rescue Teams are en route."

"Copy that, sir."

"And advise them to expect to be met with advanced weaponry."

"Sir?"

GARY WINSTON BROWN

"You heard what I said, *advanced weaponry*. They're clear to engage using any means necessary to minimize further casualties."

"Understood, sir."

"Make sure you do, Commander. I want these bastards wiped off the planet. Tell your team to make that happen."

"Copy that, sir."

Ridgeway and Hallier rallied with Jordan and Chris. "It's going down now," the Assistant Director told her agents.

"Where," Chris asked.

"Long Beach."

44

THE CAB RIDE to Caridad's provided Taras Verenich with time to think.

Badly in need of a drink, he brushed past the maître d' and walked straight into the bar lounge. Ashley Granger would be arriving for their meeting at any moment.

The barkeep invited Taras to sit. "What can I get you?"

"Glenfiddich 18. Make it a double," Taras replied.

"Coming up."

He checked his watch. 6:01 P.M. Granger was already one minute late. Taras had absolutely no tolerance for tardiness, if even for sixty seconds. His time was too valuable to be violated. Had it been anyone else he would have tossed the drink back, thrown a twenty on the bar and walked out. But this meeting was important. The circumstances surrounding it called for a reluctant extension of his patience.

The barkeep placed a coaster under his drink. "Cheers," he said.

Where the hell was Granger?

A commotion outside the lounge caught Tara's attention.

The head chef, a no-nonsense Jamaican named Henry Hutchinson, was shouting and calling for the staff to join him in the kitchen. Henry's mother, Caridad, the restaurants namesake, as well as several of the wait staff, hurried through the steel doors. Taras soon heard crying, unintelligible murmurs, gasps of disbelief and muted conversation coming from the room. The steel doors crashed open. A young waitress walked out, blotting tears from her eyes. She walked into the lounge, sat in a corner booth, and played with the tissue she held in her hands.

Eric Cantor, the barkeep, stepped out from behind his station and walked to her table.

"What's wrong, Gabby?" Eric asked. He put his hand on her shoulder. "Did someone say something to upset you?"

Gabby shook her head. "You haven't heard?"

"Heard what?"

Taras nursed his scotch. He checked his watch. 6:15 P.M. Damn it, Granger!

"Cal State University," Gabby said. "The Long Beach campus."

"What about it?"

"Police have shut it down. Multiple explosions. They're saying it's a terrorist attack. No one knows for sure exactly what's going on."

"Anyone hurt?" Eric asked.

Gabby nodded. "Many. My nephew goes there. My sister can't reach him on his cell. Neither can I. Brian's only eighteen, Eric. That's too young to die." She began to weep.

The barkeep walked to the bar, snatched up the remote control and pointed it at the large screen television on the wall. TSN was broadcasting a basketball game. He switched to a local news channel.

"I was watching that, Taras snapped.

"One second," Eric replied.

"You always change channels on customers in the middle of the game?"

"This is important."

"Nothing is more important than watching the Lakers kick the crap out of the Hawks."

The customer was beginning to test Eric's patience. "Have you heard what's going down at Cal State?" the barkeep asked.

"Should I care?"

"Terrorists."

Taras set down his glass. "What are you talking about?"

"Long Beach campus is under siege. It's happening right now." He pointed at the screen. "Look."

The KTLA news report was streaming live from behind the police barricade. In the corner of the screen, video footage shot earlier from the stations *Skywatch* helicopter played in a continuous loop. The buildings closest to the entrance of the campus had been demolished, utterly decimated. Flames licked at the ground. The powerful thrust of the chopper's blades drew plumes of smoke up from the rubble and churned them high into the air. On the ground men and women ran for their lives. Others lay still.

Granger was at the campus!

Ashley Granger was an asset Taras couldn't afford to lose. She had been brought into The Company personally by Marina Puzanova. Friends since childhood, Marina would surely want to meet with her during her visit. Though Taras believed he had surpassed Granger in terms of his importance to the organization, the services she provided were irreplaceable. For years she had managed to keep her double-life as an ultra-high-priced call girl and madam a secret from the University. Through an excruciatingly careful selection process, she had introduced some of the women on campus to The Company with promises of student loans paid off in months rather than years. Over time, Grangers network had grown into the hundreds. She now supplied the largest number of recruits to The Company in the western United States. Most of the women had chosen to leave their educational pursuits behind in favor of traveling the world and servicing the needs of The Company's most discerning clientele.

It suddenly occurred to Taras why the Long Beach mathematics professor was late for their meeting. Could she have been caught up in the terror attack happening at the University? Or worse, be among the dead?

Taras tried to reach Ashley Granger on her cell phone.

Voicemail.

"When did this start?" Taras asked the barkeep.

"Half an hour ago. The details are still sketchy."

Taras shifted uncomfortably on his bar stool. The semi-automatic pistol in his waistband pressed into his back and served to remind him of the gravity of his situation.

Marina Puzanova was inbound from Russia and probably intended to kill him.

The mysterious silver sedan that had been parked on the upper level of the parking garage across the street from his office had resumed its tail on the Ferrari as soon as Avel had driven it out of the building, confirming his suspicion that he was under surveillance. But by whom? He had assumed it was The Company. Could it have been the FBI? He remembered the earlier visit from the two agents who had tried to press him for details about his relationship with Rosenfeld. Were they building a case against him? Was it just a matter of time before they stormed his office and arrested him? Exactly how much did they know about his involvement with The Company and his relationship with Rosenfeld?

Taras suddenly felt like his entire world was about to collapse. The panic attack he experienced on the drive to the restaurant returned with a vengeance.

He made a decision. Leave now. Stay ahead of them all. The Company. The FBI. Marina Puzanova.

Eric Cantor cleaned and polished the bar as he watched the news, then returned to Gabby's table.

Taras slid off the stool, picked up his briefcase, fished a twenty out of his wallet and slipped it under the glass. "Thanks for the drink."

The bartender nodded.

Taras walked out of the bar and left the restaurant.

Screw Granger. Screw Puzanova. Screw them all. Let them fend for themselves.

A taxicab was parked in Caridad's VIP parking area. Verenich opened the back door and jumped in.

"Take me to the private hangars at LAX," he ordered the driver. "Elite Air."

"That might take a while," the cabbie answered. "Have you heard about...?"

"...the problem at the University," Taras finished. "Who hasn't?"

"It's more than just a *problem*," the cabbie said. "The whole place is..."

"Are we talking or driving?" Taras snapped.

The cabbie turned around. "Mister, as long as the meter keeps running, I'll take you wherever you want to go. I'm just telling you traffic's a mess."

Taras pressed two one-hundred-dollar bills against the Plexiglas security window. "Get me there in half an hour and the money's yours."

The driver smiled. "Works for me." The cab pulled away from the curb.

Taras opened his briefcase, removed his passport, and placed it in his jacket pocket.

Tonight, he would leave Taras Verenich behind in the United States. *Taras Antipov* would start a new life in Central America.

The anxiety he had felt in the bar began to ease, pent–up tension to leave his body.

Soon he would be in the air.

He felt pleased with himself. He had had the foresight to pay attention to his instincts and it had paid off.

On the radio, a talk show host blathered on about the situation at Cal State and *'how I would handle these terrorist bastards if it were up to me.'*

Taras tapped on the divider. The driver glanced in the rearview mirror.

"Does that thing play music?" Taras quipped.

The cabbie didn't respond. He leaned forward and selected a soft rock music station.

Journey played *'Don't Stop Believin'.*

Taras laid back, closed his eyes, and fantasized about better days ahead.

He could feel the warm Costa Rican sun on his face.

45

TERROR REIGNED ON the university campus as Merrick went in search of his target.

For months he had watched the youth, knew everything about him; his daily schedule, the buildings in which he attended class, local hangouts, extra-curricular activities. Ilya Puzanova attended Cal State University as a mathematics prodigy. He was also one of the most talented players on the Long Beach men's basketball team, the 49ers. In the university sports complex, known as The Pyramid, a championship game was underway.

LAPD had cordoned off all roads leading into and out of the campus. Beyond the police barricade, an emergency triage station had been set up. Teams of paramedics busily attended to the wounded. On the road a cue of ambulances idled, waiting to transport the seriously injured to hospital.

Merrick walked calmly through the panicked crowd in the direction of the Pyramid. On his wrist, Channeler glowed. He could feel the energy of the device pulsing through his body. Incredible, he thought, this feeling of invincibility. Never in his life had he felt so fueled by hatred and motivated by revenge. He hungered for vengeance. Ahead, a student watched him approach. The girl froze mid-step and stared at Merrick, her pupils wide with fear. As Merrick walked closer, she began to tremble. Terrified of the stranger who had come into her life and proven himself to be capable of committing the most heinous acts, she lost her grip on her leather knapsack. The satchel slipped out of her fingers and dropped to the ground. A stream of urine ran down her legs and pooled at her feet. Her pretty face was gray, expressionless. The young woman's legs gave out from under her. She fell to her knees.

Merrick walked up to the coed and placed his hand against the side of her face. Through Channeler, he sensed her thoughts. Her mind was busy processing her circumstances, helping her to rationalize the inevitable and accept her fate. Merrick experienced the rush of her blood as it drew away from her extremities and pooled in the center of her body; a physiological process to protect her vital organs in preparation for death.

Merrick picked up the woman's knapsack and placed it in her hand. "I'm not here for you," he said. He took her by the elbow, helped her to her feet and held her until she regained her balance and could stand on her own without assistance. The light began to return to her eyes. She refocused, took a shallow breath. Her body shuddered. A second, deeper breath followed the first.

"Can you walk?" Merrick asked.

The woman said nothing.

"Try."

Merrick slowly released his grip on her arm. The student took a tentative first step, then a second.

"You'll be fine," Merrick said. "Go. Live your life."

The woman watched in stunned silence as Merrick walked away.

The Pyramid.

Above Merrick, a LAPD helicopter approached. The pilot angled the craft toward him, then descended and drifted closer, narrowing the distance between them. A sharpshooter readied himself in the open doorway and settled into position. As the officer steadied his rifle to fire, Merrick responded. A stream of energy left Channeler and struck the aircraft, tossing it wildly in the air. From the ground Merrick heard the steady *meep-meep-meep* of its operational warning system announcing the malfunction. Its tail rotor began to turn out of sync with the main rotor. The helicopter began to spin wildly in the air. Merrick watched as the pilot struggled with the joystick, fighting unsuccessfully to regain control of the falling aircraft. The bird plummeted from the sky and crashed on State University Drive, its shattered blades slicing through the air and lodging into the walls of the surrounding buildings. Thick gray smoke poured from the wreckage as Merrick approached the downed chopper. Its unconscious occupants made no sounds or displayed signs of life. An eerie silence settled over the crash site.

News of the attack had not yet reached the ravenous basketball fans inside the Pyramid. Merrick crossed the grounds. Around him lay the remains of the structures which had been decimated by Channeler together with the bodies of the fallen and the dead. Inside the Pyramid, the boisterous crowd chanted *Long Beach! Long Beach! Long Beach!* as they counted down the last seconds of play.

"9!... 8!... 7!"

From behind Merrick came a massive *boom* as the

doomed police helicopter exploded, its death cry sending a plume of fire high into the evening sky.

"*6!... 5!... 4!*"

Merrick engaged Channeler and pointed it at the ground. The ground beneath his feet began to rumble.

"*3!... 2!... 1!*"

The blare of the game-ending siren marginally drowned out the roaring crowd.

Inside the Pyramid, the concrete floor of the sports complex began to vibrate and shake. Ceiling lights flickered. The eighteen story angular aluminum walls buckled, then split.

The congratulatory fanfare ceased.

Elation gave way to confusion.

Had an earthquake struck the campus?

Fearing the worse, the anxious crowd made their way to the exits and began pouring out the doors.

Nothing could have prepared them for what they saw.

Before the game, their campus had looked pristine, perfect, proud. Now the grounds were now covered in rubble. The smell of death hung in the air, and they found themselves facing a phalanx of police and emergency vehicles.

Sometime between tip-off and dropping the game-winning basket, California State University at Long Beach had become a war zone with the Pyramid Ground Zero.

The response was immediate.

Confusion morphed into panic.

Panic escalated into hysteria.

Hysteria gave birth to chaos.

The students fled the Pyramid and ran for cover wherever they could find it.

Merrick forced his way through the screaming crowd

into the building. The coaches had gathered both teams at center court.

One player stood away from the rest of the team. He was looking up, examining the crumpled metal walls of the structure. The nameplate on the back of his jersey read PUZANOVA.

Merrick walked across the hardwood floor and grabbed Ilya.

Ilya struggled to break free as his coach and teammates ran to his aid. Merrick responded with Channeler. With a sweep of his hand, he threw the men off the court and onto the sidelines.

Coach Wallerston yelled to his players, "Get out! Run!" The shaken athletes scrambled to their feet and bolted for the exits.

Ilya Puzanova fought to break free of Merrick.

Merrick wheeled the frightened teen around, grabbed him by his throat and lifted him off the ground. Ilya gasped, choked, tried to kick and strike back, couldn't. Merrick tightened his grip. The fight soon left him. The teen's body relaxed.

Merrick dropped him. Ilya fell to his knees, grabbed his throat.

"Who are you," Ilya gasped. "What do you want?"

"What I've wanted for years," Merrick replied. "For your slut mother to watch you die."

46

B EN EGAN STOOD on the front steps of the Molecular and Life Sciences Center and watched as the police helicopter spun out of control, fell from the sky, and crashed to the ground.

Students and faculty broke through the doors of MLSC and streamed past him, flooding the campus, screaming, and fleeing at the sight of the carnage.

Granger was here. Egan reviewed the download of the objective in his mind, saw the woman clearly, then turned and entered the building.

The halls were filled with faint whispers and hushed cries. Doors slammed around him as those too frightened to venture outside barricaded themselves inside classrooms, labs, offices, and meeting rooms.

Egan tested several door handles. All locked.

Wall signs provided direction to the Department of Mathematics and Statistics. At the end of the hall a reader plate read 'Prof. Ashley Granger, Director.'

Egan turned the handle. The door opened freely.

The office was dark. Egan flipped the wall switch. Fluorescent ceiling lights flickered to life.

He stopped and listened. All quiet.

A mug of coffee sat on Granger's secretary's desk, still warm to the touch.

A second office door ahead: Granger's private office.

Egan called out. "Dr. Granger?"

No reply.

He tried the door. Locked.

Egan stepped back. "I know you're in there, Dr. Granger," he said. "Please come out."

Inside the room something fell to the floor, followed by the sound of scattering papers. A woman gasped.

"My colleague would like a word with you, Doctor."

Egan tried the door handle again.

A woman's voice called out. "Go away!"

The target Granger was inside.

"I'm afraid I can't do that," Egan replied.

"I have a gun!" Ashley Granger yelled. Her voice shook. Fear challenged rage.

"And I'm sure you'll use it," Egan said. "But for your sake I'd prefer you didn't."

The bullet tore through the door and missed Egan's head by inches.

Channeler glowed. Egan placed his palm against the door.

"I wanted to make this easy for you," Egan said. "I guess that's not going to be possible."

The steel door to the professor's office blew out from its frame. Egan stepped into the room. From beneath the safe cover of her desk Ashley Granger screamed, then sprang to her feet, leveled the weapon at Egan and pulled the trigger.

The gun failed to fire.

She pulled the trigger again and again and again yet was

unable to execute a single shot. Finally, she stood frozen in fear, hands shaking, her body wholly incapacitated.

Egan walked up to the terrified woman, pried the weapon out of her hands and took her by the arm. "Come with me."

Ashley Granger tried to resist. "I never wanted any part of this," she said. She began to cry.

"Let's go," Egan said.

"Where are you taking me?"

"Be quiet."

"I have money," Granger pleaded, "Plenty of money. You can have it all. Just let me go. *Please!*"

"Not my concern."

"Wait. Wait!" the mathematics professor begged. "I know things. Important things. About important people."

"I'm just the courier lady," Egan replied. He pulled the professor down the hallway.

"They call themselves 'The Company!'"

"Stop."

"I can take them down."

"Quiet!" Egan said. He clasped his hand over her mouth.

A parabolic mirror, mounted on the wall at the end of the corridor, revealed the approach of a

six-man assault team. LAPD SWAT had begun a floor-by-floor sweep of the building.

Textbook, Egan thought.

The police officers rounded the corner, moving slowly, weapons at the ready.

Ashley Granger looked up, saw the advancing heavily armed tactical team.

She pulled away from Egan and used the only weapon available to her.

She screamed.

47

ILYA PUZANOVA SAT on the basketball court massaging his bruised throat. He looked up at Merrick. "What the hell are you talking about?" he said.

"Your whore mother murdered my daughter."

"My mother... a *murderer*?" The teen scrambled to his feet. "You're out of your damn mind, mister. My mother is a real estate broker." Ilya leaned over, caught his breath. "The only thing she's ever killed is a bottle of wine."

"Ten years ago," Merrick said.

Ilya regained his composure. He looked past Merrick. The Pyramid's emergency exit doors were open. Clouds of dust billowed into the entranceway from outside the building. Loudspeakers announced unintelligible commands to the fleeing crowd.

"Ten years ago... *what?*"

"Her name was Paige," Merrick said. "She was a student here. She'd just started to live her life."

"Here?" Ilya said, "At Cal State?"

Merrick didn't reply.

Shadows ran past the emergency doors, silhouetted against the streaming sunlight.

"She was beautiful," Merrick continued, "just like her mother. She had the most incredible eyes. Blue as sapphires. No one could say no to Paige. She could have been a fashion model. But she wanted more. She was a gifted mathematician, just like you. Which brought her here. To Cal State. She wanted to study under Granger."

"Dr. Granger?"

"The *bitch* Ashley Granger. She recruited Paige and introduced her to your mother."

Ilya looked confused. "My mother doesn't even know Dr. Granger. She would have told me if she did. And what do you mean, recruited?"

"To The Company."

"The *what?*"

"Granger and your mother run the biggest prostitution recruitment ring on the West Coast out of this campus. They have for years. My daughter was one of their girls."

Ilya stepped forward. "You know you are one-hundred-percent psycho, right?"

Merrick raised his hand. Channeler glowed.

Ilya stared at the strange bracelet around the man's wrist. He would not be intimidated. "Fuck you," he said. "You're lying."

"Your mother's a broker all right. But she sure as hell doesn't sell real estate."

"You're insane," Ilya yelled.

"What do you know about her?"

"Who?"

"Granger. Her lifestyle, how she lives."

"What do I care? She's my professor."

"Do you know her personal net worth is ten-million dollars? And that she owns three homes in Malibu and four in Florida, plus a villa in Tuscany? That she drives a Maserati *and* a Porsche? You think she can afford all of that on a professor's salary?"

"So she's rich," Ilya replied. "Big deal. This is the Gold Coast, pal. She probably comes from money like ninety-percent of the people who go here do."

"The only reason Granger has what she has is because of The Company and her relationship with your mother. And don't expect Blaire to stick around much longer. Granger's been priming her for weeks."

Ilya was angry. "How do you know about my girlfriend?"

"Let's just say you've been under surveillance for months."

"Surveillance? What are you, a spook? CIA? NSA?"

"It doesn't matter who or what I am. All that matters is what I plan to do."

"Why me?" Ilya said. "I've got nothing to do with any of this."

Merrick's anger flared. He grabbed the teen by his jersey. He thought of Paige and the pain of her loss. He held in his hands the filthy spawn of Marina Puzanova, living, breathing, *alive*. The unfairness of it all was almost too much to bear. It took all his resolve not to activate Channeler and drain the life out of the bastard right then and there.

Merrick threw him to the ground. "Sit there and wait," he warned.

Ilya saw the hatred in his attacker's eyes. This was not the time to challenge him.

"For what?" Ilya asked.

Merrick connected with Egan's brain neural interface:

Do you have Granger?
Confirmed.
The Pyramid.
On my way.

Merrick answered the youth. "Payback."

48

A T THE REQUEST of the FBI, California Highway Patrol motorcycle cops sped ahead of the motorcade, stopping traffic at all major intersections en route to California State University in order to facilitate the team's statewide emergency passage.

Hallier, Ridgeway, Jordan and Chris arrived at the Long Beach campus to sheer pandemonium. Most of the students had fled the grounds. Those who obeyed the emergency loudspeaker warnings yet remained on campus had locked themselves inside classrooms. Parents who had heard the news of the unfolding events had rushed to the grounds. Attempts by police to hold them back had failed. In a collective act of desperation, they forced their way through the barricades and ran into the University in search of their children.

The CHiP motorcycles slowed at the outer perimeter security checkpoint and were directed to a tactical staging area. Heavily armed FBI SWAT and Hostage Rescue Team members were gearing up, preparing to be deployed. Above the University, a throaty *shwoop-shwoop-shwoop* sound filled the air. The military helicopter sighted a position within infiltration distance of the Pyramid and descended. DARPA soldiers jumped from the chopper as it touched down, weapons at the ready. The eight-man black ops team dropped to one knee, claiming a perimeter around the bird. As the chopper lifted off the soldiers maintained a tight ground formation, then slowly backed away to join the assault contingency and receive their instructions.

Jordan and Chris quickly exited their car, opened the trunk, and slipped into their bulletproof vests.

Hallier and Ridgeway rallied their command personnel. FBI Hostage Rescue Team Leader Special Agent David Chainer and DARPA Team One Commander Blaine Aikens met them as they exited their cars.

Chainer provided the agents with a status update. "LAPD's already inside," Chainer told Assistant Director Ridgeway as they walked to the staging area. "SWAT's started their first sweep." He pointed to the Molecular and Life Science building.

"Damn it!" Ridgeway said. "How long ago did they breach?"

"Two minutes."

LAPD SWAT commander Sergeant Wayne Cowell joined the group.

"Did you authorize those men to proceed?" Hallier snapped.

Cowell held his assault rifle against his chest. "I did."

"Goddamn brilliant, Sergeant!" Hallier yelled. "Your men are as good as dead! Why the hell didn't you wait? You have no idea who to look for in there. And you sure as shit don't have a clue what you're up against!"

"What I'm up against?" Cowell pointed to the smoldering wreckage of the downed LAPD helicopter. "Are you kidding me? Look around you, Colonel. It looks like goddamn Syria. This is Long Beach, for Christ sake, not Aleppo. My guys got shot out of the sky by who-the-hell-knows-what. I can't raise them on comms. I don't know if they're alive or dead. I've got a whole city full of terrified citizens and mounds of rubble where less than an hour ago buildings stood. Even the goddamn media is wearing flak jackets. And you want to know why I didn't wait for you."

Hallier pressed. "Recall your men, Sergeant. Do it now. You don't want to lose another team. Let us handle this."

"I think we can manage to deal with a couple of terrorists, Colonel."

"Not these two. They're not terrorists. Do you even have a fix on their location?"

"We're sweeping the grounds."

Hallier shook his head. "In other words, you don't. Dammit Sergeant, don't be a fool. Tell your men to stand down before…"

A massive explosion erupted from the Molecular and Life Sciences building so concussive in its intensity Jordan felt the pressure of the blast right through her vest and into her chest. An entire wall of the MLS building had blown out. Shards of glass and metal debris rained down on the grounds. Sergeant Cowell watched in horror as two members of his breach team fell out of the building.

"Jesus Christ," Cowell said. The SWAT leader yelled into his microphone.

"*Traynor, status report!*"

No reply from the breach team leader.

"*Sterling!*"

Only silence.

"*Kwan!*"

Dead air.

"Daniels... Augustine... do you copy?"

"Forget it, Sergeant," Hallier said with disgust. "They're gone."

Cowell stared at the burning building.

"I tried to warn you," Hallier said angrily. "That's right, Sergeant. Take a good long look. The deaths of those men are on you. Get used to living with that."

Obscured by rolling dust clouds, two distant figures exited the building and raced across the campus: a man and a woman.

Jordan focused on the man's psychic signature as he ran. "It's Egan," she said, then picked up on a second signature, similar yet different; the same one she had felt in Corona. It had to be Merrick. "There," Jordan said, pointing across the campus. "That's where they're headed. Merrick's in the Pyramid."

Hallier turned to DARPA Team One leader Blaine Aikens. "They have hostages. Commander, equip your men with Thermite launchers and dispatch them to the Pyramid. Tell them to hold fire until we have a lock on both targets. I say again, *both targets*. Do you understand?"

"Copy that, Colonel."

"Thermite?" Ridgeway asked.

"A chemical incendiary. Bullets are useless against Channeler. By just activating the device Merrick and Egan are protected. A bullet wouldn't be able to hold its trajectory. It would skip off Channeler's energy field like a stone across a pond. We'll have to launch a dozen or more Thermite grenades at the field to try and weaken it. All we need is for one to get through and detonate. If it does it'll be game over. Merrick and Egan will be incinerated right where they stand."

"What about the woman, Egan's hostage?"

"If she can get to safety she'll live."

"And if she can't?"

"Then she won't."

Chris Hanover stepped forward. "Colonel, I might know how your men can take out Merrick and Egan and still keep the woman alive."

"I'm listening," Hallier said.

"I know this campus," Chris said. "I studied here. There is a service entrance at the back of the Pyramid. Agent Quest and I can get inside and take up a secondary position. We'll try to secure the hostage while your men press the attack from the front."

"It's worth a shot, Colonel," Ridgeway said.

"All right," Hallier agreed. "But you just saw what happened to SWAT. You're not going in there alone. Lieutenant Bestow will cover you."

The DARPA commando stepped forward.

"I'm good with that," Jordan said. Chris nodded. "Me too."

"All right," Hallier agreed. "You've got five minutes to gain entry and get into position before Commander Aiken and his team move in. After that, all bets are off. Hostage or no hostage this ends tonight."

Across the campus the Pyramid loomed, enveloped in a smoky haze.

"You ready?" Lieutenant Bestow asked the agents.

"As I'll ever be," Chris said.

"Let's do this," Jordan said.

They ran.

49

"MOVE!" EGAN YELLED. He shoved Ashley Granger through the main entrance doors into the Pyramid. The mathematics professor stumbled but caught herself before she fell.

The structure's foundation, weakened by the tremendous energy exerted upon it by Channeler, moaned and sighed under the enormous weight of its triangular walls. The building leaned at a precarious angle. Its compromised aluminum skeleton creaked, threatened collapse.

Ilya called out to his professor. "Dr. Granger!"

Ashley Granger heard the teen's voice.

Ilya tried to run to her. Merrick grabbed him by his jersey, pulled him back. "Not so fast," he said.

Ilya yelled at Egan. "Don't you dare touch her!"

Granger called out. "Ilya! Are you okay?"

"I'm fine, professor," he replied. "What's going on here? Who are these guys?"

"I don't know. Don't worry. The police are here now."

Keeping watch on the professor and her student, Egan walked over to Merrick. "Nice work with the chopper."

Merrick smiled. "It made for one hell of an introduction."

Egan nodded. "Military's here. A Blackhawk just touched down."

"Then they've already made their first mistake," Merrick said.

"What's that?"

"They showed up."

Egan pointed to their prisoners. "What about those two?"

"Kill them."

Egan raised his hand to carry out the order.

Ilya stepped in front of Granger. "If you want the professor," he said, "you're going to have to go through me."

Egan stared at the teen. "Seriously? You did not just say that, right. That is so Hollywood, kid."

Ilya refused to move. "You heard me, asshole."

Egan raised his hand. "You'd think a smart kid like you would know it's never a good idea to piss off the guy with the superweapon."

"Fuck you."

Darkness filled the entranceway. A metal canister clattered across the floor.

Egan recognized the ordinance. "Grenade!" he yelled. "Get down!"

As the Thermite grenade rolled toward them Egan waved his hand. The device flew back toward the breach team. Upon detonation, the incinerated remains of two soldiers marred the floor of the Pyramid where seconds earlier they had stood.

Egan turned to Merrick. "Next time they come at us it'll be harder and faster."

Merrick pointed to their hostages and the metal

bleachers surrounding the basketball court. "Get them down between the seats and out of sight," he said. "We'll take care of this first and deal with them later."

Ilya lunged at Egan.

Egan saw the attack coming and thrust the heel of his palm into the teen's solar plexus. Ilya felt the air escape his lungs. He fell to his knees. "Stay down kid," Egan said. "I'm in no mood for heroics." He pointed his finger at Ashley Granger. "Get that little pain in the ass on his feet. Both of you get between the bleachers and lay down."

The professor helped Ilya across the basketball court and into the seating area. The injured student lay on his side. Granger knelt beside him.

"You're going to be okay, Ilya," Ashley said.

The teen's breathing was heavy, labored. He shook his head. "It hurts really bad."

"Relax. You'll feel better in a few minutes."

"You don't understand. My chest guard. I think he broke it."

"Your what?"

"Chest guard. I have to wear it when I play. To protect my heart."

Granger lifted Ilya's jersey. Egan had struck the teen with such force that the nylon protector had shattered inside its harness.

"Lay still," the professor said. "I'll be right back."

"No!" Ilya said. He grabbed Granger's arm. "You heard what he said. He'll kill you!"

"No, he won't. We're hostages now. Which means we're the only bargaining chip they have if they want to get out of here alive."

"I don't think leaving here alive was ever part of their plan."

"I do. Now sit tight."

Ashley Granger walked back across the basketball court and faced Merrick and Egan. "The boy has a heart condition," she said. "You hurt him badly. He needs a doctor."

Egan walked up to the professor. "Get back there and lay down."

"What do you need him for?" Granger said. "Keep me. Let him go."

Channeler glowed.

"Don't press me," Egan said. "I'll drain the life out of you right here, right now."

Ashley stepped closer to Egan and stared him down. "Then do what you have to do."

"Bitch," Egan muttered.

Merrick walked over. "There's movement outside, Commander."

"You want me to take care of her first?" Egan asked.

"That won't be necessary," Merrick said. He struck Granger in the face with such force the woman collapsed at his feet, then dragged her unconscious body back to the bleachers and dropped her beside Ilya. The teen had passed out. His breathing had become shallow. Merrick checked his pulse. It was faint, but he was alive.

The two men walked into the middle of the Pyramid.

The aluminum walls of the structure vibrated from the blade churn of an inbound chopper.

"If they want in," Merrick said, "they're going to have to work for it."

He raised his hand.

Channeler glowed.

The Pyramid shook.

Around them the foundation of the massive structure started to buckle, its architectural design and masterful engineering now pushed beyond its limit, no longer able to withstand the supernatural assault of Channeler.

The Pyramid fell.

50

O N BREACHING THE rear door of the Pyramid, Jordan, Chris and Lieutenant Bestow felt the ground tremble. Jordan felt an enormous rush of psychic energy begin to build. Cracks rippled along the concrete walls of the receiving area. Suspended ceiling tiles shook loose from their aluminum grids and fell to the ground. Fluorescent lights grew brighter, then exploded in their fixtures. Janitorial chemicals shuddered and danced on metal shelves, then fell and broke, their contents spilling across the floor. The air in the structure had become thin, hard to breathe, as if every last oxygen molecule was being pulled out of it.

Under Bestow's feet the floor groaned, growled, and started to crack. "Take cover!" he yelled. He pushed the agents to safety under a heavy gridiron archway. The terrified soldier looked down. The ground beneath his feet began to rip apart. He was slipping down into the darkness.

"*No!*" Jordan ran forward and threw herself onto the edge of the ever-widening gap, grabbing blindly for the disappearing DARPA operative. Too late, she caught the barrel of his weapon as it slipped from his grasp.

Bestow was gone. The chasm had swallowed him alive.

Hanover grabbed Jordan's legs and pulled her back. Not satisfied with taking just one life, the crack in the floor kept advancing toward them, anxious to claim its next victim.

Chris yelled over the thunderous sound of the destructive force. "He's gone, Jordan. Come on! We have to get out of here!"

Jordan pulled Bestow's Thermite grenade launcher out of the hole, slung it over her shoulder, and ran behind Hanover out of the receiving area. Behind them, the building started to collapse.

"Get down!" Jordan yelled. She pushed Chris to the ground and fell over him, covering him with her body.

The Pyramid emitted a horrific screech as its tubular support beams fatigued and bent under the power of Channeler. The foundation had begun to consume itself.

"We need to get inside," Chris said as Jordan helped him to his feet. "We'll be safe there. There's almost no chance the entire Pyramid will fall. It was designed to withstand earthquakes and structural compromises much greater than this."

"Like this isn't enough of a structural compromise for you?" Jordan said. "Maybe you'd prefer an earthquake on steroids?"

Chris pointed to a set of doors just ahead.

"When we get through those doors, we'll hit a ramp that leads into the sports arena. Cover will be minimal. Which means that for a few seconds we're going to be completely in the open, fully exposed. There are metal bleachers around the basketball court. We'll need to get to cover fast and get eyes on Merrick and Egan and the hostages. There's an announcer's booth above the court. Assuming it's still there, that's where I'll be headed. I'll have a clear view of the court. I can take them out from there. But I'm gonna need that gun."

Jordan examined the weapon. "I assume you've never fired one of these before?"

"Of course, I have," Chris replied. "Took a class at Quantico. Incendiary Weapons 101. Right after light saber training. You know for an old guy Yoda's pretty damn fast."

"From Star Trek to Star Wars. Funny."

"Relax, Jordan," Chris said, "I know the lay of the land here, remember? That gives me home court advantage. Plus, I'm a trained sniper. If there's a decent vantage point inside, I'll find it. When I do, I'll launch every damn grenade in that thing until those bastards have been vaporized."

Jordan handed him the weapon. "You sure you can do this?"

"I am."

"Positive?"

"Positive."

"How positive?"

"*Seriously?*"

"I need to know."

"Okay.   One-hundred-and-twenty-three-percent positive."

"That's a mathematical impossibility. You can't be more than one-hundred-percent positive."

"We're quibbling over math?"

"Hey, it took me a long time to break you in," Jordan said. "I'm not too keen on going through that again with a new partner."

"Excuse me? Did you just say you broke *me* in?"

"Now who's quibbling?"

"Pass me the damn grenade launcher."

Jordan handed him the weapon. "You know you're only going to get one shot at this. If Merrick or Egan see you, they'll kill you."

"Thanks. I already figured that out. Didn't even have to do the math."

"I'm serious."

"Me too. I hate math. Avoid it as much as possible."

Jordan shook her head. "For the record, you're not fooling me."

"How's that?"

"I know you just want to fire the really cool gun."

Chris smiled. "Busted."

"Try not to blow yourself up."

"I'll do my best."

"I'm serious, Chris." Jordan held tight to the shoulder strap of the gun.

Hanover saw the look of concern in her eyes. His voice was calm. "I'll be fine, J," he said.

"You'd better be," Jordan replied.

Chris peered through the crack in the double doors leading into the sports arena. "Looks clear," he said. "Stay on my six. Move fast and quiet. As soon as you're inside, tack left. The bleachers are double step in height. They should provide perfect cover. You ready?"

Jordan nodded.

The man-made earthquake suddenly knocked out the electrical system. The facility plunged into darkness. Sunlight streamed in through slits in the damaging aluminum walls. Chris and Jordan waited for their eyes to adjust to the dim light.

"All right," Chris said. "Here we go." He grabbed the door handle, eased it open, slipped inside, leveled the weapon straight ahead, peered down the sight, hugged the wall, reached the arena entrance, waved his partner through, then broke to the right and headed for the announcer's booth.

Jordan took cover in the bleachers.

51

ASHLEY GRANGER WOKE up on the floor of the Pyramid with a broken jaw. She had passed out twice on her return trip to consciousness. She struggled to regain a foothold on her senses.

The building was dark. Scant ribbons of sunlight bled in through deep slashes in its wounded, triangular roof. The massive sports facility had toppled. One of the four corners of its base rested on a bed of crushed concrete and twisted metal.

Ilya! Ashley dragged herself to her knees. Blood dripped from her mouth and nose and pooled on the hardwood floor. Her eyesight was impaired, no doubt a result of the powerful blow delivered by Merrick. She turned her head, searched for Ilya, and saw his sneakers jutting out from the end of the metal bleacher. She crawled to her student. He was alive. Thank God.

Merrick walked over to her, grabbed her by the jaw, and twisted her head to get a better look at the injuries he had inflicted. "Welcome back," he said. Ashley wanted to scream, couldn't. A tsunami of pain rushed over her and threatened to drag her back down into the depths of unconsciousness. She resisted.

"How much did they pay you?" Merrick said.

"Wha... uuu... tockkking... abwwt?" The professor tried to push the words out through her spittle.

Merrick squeezed the woman's crushed jaw. The riptide of pain pulled harder this time.

"Tell me everything," Merrick demanded.

"Nuthnggg... to... tell," Granger spat out. Even in the scarce light, Merrick could see the left side of the woman's face had turned black, a mass of broken blood vessels.

"Can't or won't?"

Granger didn't answer. Bubbles of blood formed in the corners of her mouth, on her lips.

Merrick wrapped his hand around the woman's neck. Channeler glowed. Ashley gagged.

"Tell you what," Merrick said. Granger felt her body begin to grow cold. She shivered. "I'll make you a deal. Answer my questions and I won't kill your young friend."

Merrick placed his free hand on Ilya's ankle. The teen moaned. His leg began to spasm.

"Dnnn't... hrrrrt hm," Granger pleaded.

"How much I hurt him will depend entirely on what you have to say," Merrick replied. He squeezed Ilya's ankle tighter. The teen groaned, tried to move. Merrick held him firmly in place.

"Paige Merrick," Merrick said. He released his grip on her jaw. "When did you approach her?"

"Who?" Granger asked.

Merrick increased Channeler's energy stream through their bodies. Ashley felt her body temperature plummet.

GARY WINSTON BROWN

She shook uncontrollably. Ilya screamed. Merrick slowly let up on the intensity level. The professor's body temperature returned to normal. Ilya moaned.

"You heard me," Merrick said. "When?"

Even in her physiologically depleted state, Ashley knew she needed to buy time. The assault team had tried to rescue her twice so far; first when she was being dragged out of her office in the Molecular Life Sciences building, and a few minutes ago, when they attempted to breach the Pyramid. They won't let me die, she thought. They'll try again soon. Tell him the truth. It won't matter. They won't let him walk away from this. How could they?

"I dnnnt," Ashley said. "She apprcched me."

"That's a lie."

The professor battled against the horrendous pain, formed the words, then enunciated them as slowly and clearly as she could. "You wanted to know everything," Granger began. "My top girls did the recruiting. It was invitation only. Recruiters earned a percentage of the annual earnings of every new girl they brought in. Paige jumped at it. Said she was bored with her life, that school was too easy. She was looking for an adventure, something daring, risky. I wasn't going to say no to her. She was perfect. From her first date she was in demand. She could have worked twenty-four hours a day if she wanted to. The Company has a bonus program. When a girl bills out her first million in revenue, they buy her a Maserati. For most it takes them a year. Paige earned hers in nine months. No one had ever done that before, not even me. But I did not kill her." Ashley freed herself from Merrick's grip. "I had nothing to do with Paige's death."

"Liar."

"Believe what you want," she said. "You're going to kill me anyway."

"Then who did?"

"I don't know. One day she was working, the next she wasn't. She just disappeared. I thought one of her clients bought her from The Company. Paige's buyout was ten million, which was nothing to the men she dated. They could drop that playing Blackjack in Monaco every night of the week if they wanted to. I found out later that a complication arose which affected her ability to earn for The Company."

"What kind of a complication? Who told you this?"

Granger looked down. Merrick tried to grab her jaw. She pulled back. "My boss," she said. "Marina Puzanova."

"What did Puzanova tell you?" Merrick pressed. "What happened to Paige?"

"A bad date with some Japanese billionaire. He drugged her in his room, then cut her up. It was bad. He slashed her face so many times she was no longer marketable."

The news stunned Merrick. He let go of them and stood.

"*Marketable*?"

"Marina's words, not mine." Granger looked down. "That's how she put it. I'm sorry."

Merrick stared at the woman in disbelief. "You're sorry?"

"There was nothing anyone could do for Paige, not even Marina. It was Kastonov's call. His word is final."

"This man, Kastonov. Did he kill her?"

Ashley Granger shook her head. "Not personally. He arranged for her transfer to Argentina."

"Argentina?"

"You don't want to hear this."

The news of the horrific assault his daughter had

endured at the hands of the deranged billionaire crushed Merrick. The fight inside him was dying. His chest ached.

"All I want to hear, once and for all, is the truth."

Granger glimpsed movement in the bleachers below the announcer's booth. A figure crouched in the shadows.

"The Company has a contingency plan. Which they put into effect when a girl like Paige is no longer marketable."

"What kind of plan?"

Ashley hesitated. He would kill her when she told him. "I can't."

Merrick threatened to grab her throat.

Granger leaned back. "They rent out their womb, then sell the baby. Two-hundred-thousand per child."

Merrick couldn't believe what he was hearing.

Granger continued. "Only three pregnancies are permitted, then the girl is harvested. Her viable organs are sold on the red market."

Merrick stared at the beautiful, Ivy-league educated monster.

"All of this started with you," Merrick said. "You fucking slut."

Granger elbowed herself backwards along the metal seat away from Merrick. The look in his eyes confirmed their conversation had not just taken him to the brink of insanity; it had sent him toppling over its edge.

Merrick stepped forward with renewed rage. Channeler glowed. "If Paige had never heard of you, never come here to study under the great Dr. Ashley Granger, she'd still be alive today."

"Please," Ashley begged. "No more."

. . .

THREE THUNDEROUS DETONATIONS rocked the fallen Pyramid. Chunks of concrete and plumes of dust blew across the basketball court.

The breach had been successful.

DARPA commandos and FBI SWAT stormed inside, followed by the Hostage Rescue Team.

DARPA Team One Commander Blaine Aikens called out. "Drop your weapons! Do it now!"

52

CHRIS TOOK ADVANTAGE of the diversion offered by the massive explosion. As FBI agents and DARPA commandos breached the structure, he hurried down the steps from the top of the bleachers. Jordan lay crouched between the floorboards in the seating structure, her weapon trained on the two men standing in the center of the sports arena. Hanover provided cover as she rose to her feet. Together they advanced toward Merrick, Egan, and their hostages.

Jordan felt the remarkable intensity of Commander Egan's cybernetically-enhanced mind as he became aware of their presence behind him.

Egan turned and walked toward her. "It's you," he said.

From their cover positions inside the crumbling building the operatives and agents waited for permission to engage the two men.

Chris stepped in front of Jordan. "Not one more step you son of a bitch," he warned.

"It's okay, Chris. I've got this," Jordan said.

Hanover slowly moved aside, his weapon leveled at Egan, keeping him squarely in his sights.

"I'm glad we could meet," Egan said. "I thought I felt someone probing around in my head earlier. To be honest, I didn't think that was possible. It was you, wasn't it?" He smiled and wagged his finger. "Naughty girl. Not even dinner and drinks first. Just a straight slide into home plate."

Jordan motioned at the bloodied woman sitting beside the injured teen. "Looks like they could use a little help. What do you say we let them leave so medical can take a look at them?"

Merrick grabbed Ashley Granger by her hair, yanked her head back. The woman cried out.

"No one leaves!" Merrick screamed at Jordan. "No one!"

Egan screwed up his face. "Now you did it," he said. "You pissed off the doc. Bad idea. You guys might want to think about ordering in, 'cause this is gonna be a long night. I'm good with Chinese. You?"

Jordan ignored Egan's smart remark and holstered her weapon. "Dr. Merrick, my name is Jordan Quest. I'm with the FBI. I'd like to talk with you if I may. Would that be all right?"

Chris warned. "Jordan... don't."

Jordan stepped forward. To her left a team of DARPA commandos began to advance. She raised her hand, then heard Hallier's order in her ear bud communication system: *"All teams hold."*

Commander Aikens raised his fist. The breach team stopped.

In the dimly lit structure, laser beams from dozens of assault rifles crisscrossed one another in the dusty air. Red dots danced on the chests of the two men, pinpointing their targets.

Jordan continued. "We know what happened at Dynamic Life Sciences, Dr Merrick."

Merrick threw Granger aside. The woman fell to the floor and began to sob. Merrick's voice cracked when he spoke. "They had to die," he said. "I had no choice. I needed Channeler."

"We also found the flash drive and the information on Dr. Rosenfeld's computer. We know all about the accounts and the money transfers."

"They murdered my Paige!" Merrick screamed. His wounded words echoed off the walls of the crippled Pyramid. "Do you have any idea what that did to me? To my wife? It killed us. Do you know how Paige died?" He pointed to Ashley Granger. "What this *bitch* admitted that the people she works for did to her? How they abused my baby girl and farmed her out, desecrated her body, then rendered her, like an animal, and sold her piece by piece? She was only twenty-four-years old. She had her whole life ahead of her. And they took it all away."

The Rosenfeld mansion, Jordan thought. *The roses on the floor. She had counted them: twenty-four. A rose for every year of his daughter's life? The flowers were a memorial.*

"I made a promise to my wife that anyone who had anything to do with Paige's death would die," Merrick said. "That all of them would pay. Every last one."

Hearing the words, Hallier removed the photograph from his pocket which Merrick had left in his personal property box at Dynamic Life Sciences. The family picture, taken in Paris, at the foot of the Eiffel Tower. He read the words on the back: *ALL WILL PAY.*

Merrick turned away and communicated with Egan. Egan nodded, the psychic command received.

On the wrists of both men, Channeler glowed.

"Now these two will die."

Jordan yelled. "Dr. Merrick, no!"

Hanover looked up. The metal walls of the Pyramid started to shake and split. What was left of the great building was about to come down on them all. Chris ran forward, grabbed Jordan by her tactical vest, pulled her back. "We need to get to cover, now!" he yelled.

Hallier issued the order to the DARPA commandos: *"All teams engage!"*

Ridgeway gave the GO order to her team.

DARPA and FBI SWAT advanced on the men and their hostages.

53

M ERRICK RAISED HIS hand and leveled it at the ceiling. "Bring it down," he said. "Every last piece of it!"

Egan opened his arms as the DARPA commandos and SWAT teams opened fire.

The slugs ricocheted harmlessly off the wall of energy produced by Channeler. The two men and their hostages remained unharmed.

With a sweep of Egan's hand, the advance teams left the ground and flew backwards through the air, slamming into what was left of the Pyramid's concrete foundation.

As the second wave made their move the ground beneath them started to tremble. The men fell, struggled to their feet, stumbled once more, tried to push ahead, couldn't. Jagged metal panels from the Pyramid's ceiling tore loose and rained down, slicing through the air like dozens of guillotine blades, burying their razor-sharp edges deep into the hardwood floor.

Ashley Granger watched as a SWAT team member was cleaved in half by the falling debris. She screamed as the upper and lower sections of the dead man's torso separated and drifted apart on the quaking floor.

With Merrick and Egan's attention diverted to maintaining their defense, Ashley Granger helped Ilya to his feet. "You have to get out of here," she said, talking through the excruciating pain in her broken face. She pointed to the service entrance beyond the two agents that led out of the Pyramid; the same route Jordan and Chris had used to gain access to the building. "Run, while you can."

Ilya shook his head. "I don't think I can stand, much less run."

"You have to try," Ashley said.

Merrick drew upon Channeler's immense power. The tubular framework of the Pyramid's skeleton began to break apart. Sections of steel pipe rained down from the ceiling like javelins hurled by an army of invisible assailants. The metal rods pierced deep into the floor. The deadly projectiles found four members of the breach team as they moved in, impaling them, pinning their bodies to the ground.

"Come with me," Ilya said.

"I can't," Granger replied.

"I'm not leaving without you. They'll kill you."

"I know."

Ilya looked confused. "Why would you say that?"

Granger took the teen's face in her hands. "I don't have time to explain. Perhaps one day you'll get your answer. But for me, this is how it must be. It's my time."

As Jordan and Chris advanced on the men from behind, Channeler emitted an aurora of incredible power, illuminating the interior of the Pyramid in a shimmering wall of pure energy as awe-inspiring to observe as it was terrifying to experience.

Jordan motioned to Granger to send Ilya to her. The

woman nodded, helped the teen to his feet, and pointed to the two agents.

"Get to safety. Hurry!"

"But professor!"

"*Hurry, Ilya!*"

Ilya shuffled his wounded body across the floor to Jordan.

The ground on which Merrick and Egan stood remained steady, unaffected by the power of the device.

Jordan and Chris advanced to meet Ilya. Jordan placed one arm around his neck, the other around his waist. "Let's get you out of here," she said.

Hanover stayed ahead of his partner as they backed away, then stopped. He trained the Thermite grenade launcher on the two men.

"I have a shot," Chris said.

"Not yet," Jordan said. "The woman's not clear."

"I'm holding this position."

"Chris, don't!"

Hanover dropped to one knee, steadied himself.

"Go, Jordan! Get the boy out of here!"

Ilya shuffle-stepped with Jordan to the service ramp at the back of the Pyramid.

"How's the leg?" Jordan asked. "Can you walk?"

Ilya weight-tested his leg. The pain had abated. He nodded. "It feels pretty solid. I think I'm good."

"All right," Jordan said. "Listen to me carefully. Go down that hall and through the doors. There's a gap in the floor. Hug the side of the wall and you'll be able to pass it. You're home free after that. Think you can manage it?"

"Yes, ma'am."

"Good." Jordan turned to head back into the Pyramid.

Ilya grabbed her arm. "You're not coming with me?"

Jordan shook her head. "My partners in there. I'm not leaving without him. Now go!"

Jordan waited until she watched Ilya Puzanova disappear behind the door then headed back up the service ramp and into the Pyramid.

Chris was crouched on one knee. She crept up behind him, tapped him on his shoulder.

"Is the kid safe?" Chris asked.

"He's on his way out."

"Good." He sighted Merrick and Egan in the crosshair of the weapon's scope. "Let's see what this baby can do."

Hanover slipped his finger off the stock of the grenade launcher and placed it on the laser trigger, marking the ground between the two men. He took aim. "Come to Papa, motherf--"

Ashley Granger made her move.

Intent on taking her own life, she ran toward the deadly wall of energy that was Channeler.

Chris lowered the weapon. "What the hell?" he said.

Egan caught up to her and threw her to the ground.

Merrick turned on the woman.

But in that split-second Ashley Granger accomplished exactly what she had hoped to do. She had diverted the men's attention away from their defense to pursue her.

Instantly, Channeler's force field fell.

The two men stood the middle of the Pyramid.

Relieved of its last ounce of structural integrity, the entire building collapsed. The assault teams ran for cover.

Merrick, Egan, and Ashley Granger lay buried beneath a mountain of twisted metal and concrete debris.

54

JORDAN AND CHRIS watched as the fractured ceiling of the eighteen-story Pyramid shook violently. Chunks fell from the foundation walls as it cracked and crumbled.

"It's coming down!" Chris yelled. "Fall back!"

The fatally wounded Pyramid let out a dying breath in the form of a thunderous *boom!* then succumbed to its injuries. The two agents raced for the safety of the service entrance's reinforced archway. Structural steel supports fell from the ceiling, clanging on the ground behind them. Panels of the Pyramid's aluminum walls ripped apart, soared through the air, and smashed into the metal bleachers like a symphony of cymbal crashes. Industrial diffuser lights mounted high up in the ceiling exploded, raining white-hot metal and glass down upon the agents.

The once impressive sports facility had collapsed and lay in ruins atop the crushed metal bleachers. The air, redolent with the smell of burning electrical wires, crackled, hissed, and smoked beneath the wreckage. Thick black smoke snaked through the debris, found the surface, struck out and coiled skyward. Clouds of dust floated up from the ground, stirred by the arrival of an ocean breeze. The orange hue of the setting sun provided light.

Under the twisted wreckage of the fallen structure lay Dr. Jason Merrick, Commander Ben Egan, and Ashley Granger.

Jordan coughed, brushed away the dust and smoke, and looked for Chris. She found him a few feet away, partly covered by a sheet of the aluminum ceiling. He was unconscious. Blood poured freely from a gash in his forehead.

"Chris!" Jordan pushed away the fallen debris, scrambled to her partner and examined his wound. He would need stitches, but the injury was not life-threatening. She lifted his head and applied pressure to the gash. He began to come around.

"You okay?" Jordan asked.

Chris opened his eyes.

"Thank God," Jordan said. "I thought you were dead."

He groaned. "You run like a girl, you know that?"

"That's probably because I *am* a girl."

Chris nodded, touched his forehead, winced. "Next time we're trapped in a building with a couple of psychopaths and the place starts to fall apart, do me a huge favor?"

"What's that?"

"Wear running shoes. Those heels aren't cutting it."

Jordan smiled. "You know I can outrun you on my worst day, Hanover. Heels or no heels."

Chris tried to push himself up, felt lightheaded, lay back down. "Fat chance. I pushed your ass out of the way, you fell, and I became a ceiling sandwich. That's how it went down."

"Pardon me," Jordan replied. "You did not push my ass out of the way. I had three easy strides on you."

"Doesn't matter," Chris replied. "That's how my report's

going to read: 'Building falling. Ran for cover. Agent Quest's ass in the way. Pushed it, I mean her, to safety. Injured by falling debris. Saved the day.'"

"You're a real American hero, Hanover."

"I prefer *super*hero."

"I'm sure you do."

"I think I deserve a parade."

"Now you're hallucinating."

"No doubt the result of my near-critical injury," Chris said. He touched his forehead.

"Oh, so now it's *near critical*."

"Which I sustained in the line of duty..."

"Apparently."

Chris smiled. "...while pushing your ass out of the way."

Jordan shook her head. "What am I going to do with you?"

"Admit it. You love it."

"Yes, as a matter of fact, I do."

Chris sat up. The pressure Jordan had applied to his wound had worked. The bleeding had stopped. A mountain of rubble occupied the center of the Pyramid.

"Merrick and Egan," he asked, "They're dead?"

"They just had a building fall on top of them," Jordan replied. "What do you think?"

She helped Chris to his feet.

The agents looked around them. The entire facility had fallen. In the dusty haze, DARPA commandos and FBI HRT teams slowly began to make their way toward the middle of the fallen Pyramid, ground zero of the destruction.

Suddenly there was movement. A blue light began to throb beneath the debris.

"God, no!" Jordan said.

Channeler had been activated.

55

WHEN THE BUILDING fell, Egan tried unsuccessfully to protect his handler from the cascade of metal that had been the Pyramid. Trapped beneath the wreckage, Jason Merrick struggled to move his body, then became acutely aware of the reason for his immobility. He was anchored to the floor, his legs impaled by mangled tentacles of reinforcing steel bars. His effort to scream met with little more than a whisper: "My legs!"

In his attempt to control Granger, Egan had turned his attention away from the energy vortex. The field, which had shielded them from the falling debris, had collapsed. Panels of serrated metal and steel beams were piled high around them.

"Dr. Merrick!" Egan yelled. He slid across the floor and began prying the steel rods out of Merrick's legs. Merrick screamed in agony.

Egan cradled the scientist in his arms, then rose to his feet. "I'm going to get you out of here," he said.

Merrick's head lolled to one side. Ashley Granger's lifeless eyes stared up at him from the rubble. She had been decapitated, her head the only part of her crushed body recognizable beneath the mass of concrete, steel, and broken glass.

Merrick drifted in and out of consciousness. "Stay with me, Doc," Egan yelled. "You hear me? Stay with me!"

A familiar voice spoke to Merrick, soft, gentle, and comforting: *It's all right, Jason*, the woman said. *Everything is going to be fine.*

Merrick spoke. "Alma?"

Voices rose outside the wall of twisted debris. The assault team was coming.

Merrick touched Egan's arm. "Put me down," he said.

The metal band on the Commander's wrist glowed bright blue.

"I can hold them off as long as I need to," Egan said.

Merrick shook his head. "No."

"Don't worry, Dr. Merrick. I've got you."

"Put me down."

"But..."

"Please, Commander."

Egan hesitated. He could still protect them. He could summon a tremendous burst of energy and send it across the entire campus killing every soldier, FBI agent and SWAT cop around them, decimating the place and every other building around it for miles.

Merrick spoke, his voice weak. "There's one last assignment I need you to complete."

His words brought Egan back to reality. He dropped to the ground and lay Merrick on the floor.

"There is a metal tube in my pocket," Merrick said. "Take it out."

Egan opened Merrick's jacket and retrieved the cigar-shaped cylinder.

"Open it."

Egan unscrewed the end cap, dropped it on the ground.

"Take it out... slowly."

Egan turned the tube on its side. The thumb press of a syringe slid into his hand. He removed the injection device from the tube.

"It's the second phase of GENESIS," Merrick whispered, "the LEEDA project. You're ready, Commander. You've earned it."

Egan examined the injection device in the pale light. A rose-colored liquid fluoresced within its clear barrel. The syringe vibrated against the palm of his hand.

"Inject yourself," Merrick said, "Your thigh."

From outside the walls of their self-made tomb, loud voices accompanied the sound of chunks of concrete and sheets of metal being thrown across the floor. They were coming for them, getting closer.

Egan inverted the needle and watched as a tiny air bubble drifted to the surface of the strange liquid. He removed the needle's protective plastic sheath and tossed it aside. Holding the syringe firmly in his hand, he pressed the plunger and freed the trapped air. A single drop of the precious solution rested atop the bevel of the primed needle. He placed the tip of the syringe against his pant leg.

Merrick watched as he prepared the injection. "You should feel a rush at first," the scientist said. His breathing had become more difficult, labored. "That will be adrenaline," he continued. "It will be followed by a brief sensation of euphoria. Are you ready?"

Egan nodded. "Yes, sir."

"Good."

Merrick closed his eyes, concentrated, connected with Egan's brain neural interface, and sent the operative his final assignment.

Egan acknowledged the download. "I understand."

Merrick winced as a wave of pain hammered his chest. "After the injection there will be no turning back. Know that your body will follow your mind, Commander. Do you understand this?"

Egan nodded.

"Good," Merrick said. "This will be your final assignment. When it has been completed, I want you to start a new life. LEEDA is my gift to you. You will become wholly integrated; the human embodiment of a lifetime of my research, all that I have worked for. I can't think of anyone more deserving."

"Thank you, sir."

"Remember the importance of what I said, Commander. *Your body will follow your mind.*"

Commotion outside the twisted metal walls.

Mere feet away now.

Egan jammed the needle deep into his thigh, pushed down on the plunger, and injected himself. He fell on his side, his body shocked into submission by the rush of the LEEDA formula as it coursed through his bloodstream. Within seconds the primary effect of the injection subsided. The secondary wave spread through his body and brought with it a feeling of mental strength, power, and exhilaration unlike anything he had ever experienced in his life.

Channeler unlocked from his wrist.

The device fell to the floor.

"It's done," Merrick said. "The transition is complete. Now concentrate. Follow the target. Finish the assignment. Go where LEEDA takes you."

"Yes, sir."

Inside the metal fortress, a rose-red light glittered and encompassed Egan.

Merrick smiled. "Goodbye, Commander," he said.

The walls fell.

The scientist felt a crushing pain in his chest, took his last breath, and closed his eyes.

The DARPA commandos pushed aside the last of the debris. "Hands!" they yelled. "Show me your hands!"

Merrick offered no response. Commander Aikens knelt and checked his pulse. Hallier stood beside him. He shook his head. "He's gone, Colonel."

"Secure the body immediately," Hallier ordered. "Get it back to Los Alamitos. Keep a guard on it."

"Yes, sir," Aikens replied. He motioned to the corpse of Ashley Granger. "And the woman?"

"Not our concern. Leave her for the coroner."

"Yes, sir."

Hallier looked down. The Channeler device lay at his feet. Beside the metallic band lay a spent syringe and metal tube, marked LEEDA. The Colonel pocketed the items. "Jesus," he muttered.

Hallier warned Commander Aikens. "No one but DARPA gets near this body, understand? Secure it for transport."

"Copy that, Colonel."

"Good," Hallier said. He turned to leave.

Aikens stared at Merrick's body and Grangers mutilated corpse. "Colonel?"

Hallier stopped. "What is it?"

"Where the hell is Egan?"

Hallier walked back. "Listen carefully. No questions.

Maintain your post. Under no circumstances does that body leave your sight. Think you can manage that?"

Aikens soldiered up. "Yes, sir."

HALLIER WALKED AWAY from the dead man and placed a call to his superior at DARPA.

"This is Ford."

"It's Hallier, Brigadier General."

"Situation report."

"Merrick is dead, sir. Egan is gone."

"What do you mean... gone?"

"Precisely that, sir. We were too late. LEEDA is active."

56

JORDAN, CHRIS, AND Assistant Director Ridgeway found Ashley Granger's decapitated corpse in the debris pile, then watched as DARPA commandos transferred Merrick's body into a field transport bag and zipped it shut.

Ridgeway presented her credentials to the Special Operations team leader. "Open it up," she said. "I want to see who was responsible for this."

The soldier shook his head. "Sorry, ma'am," he said. "No can do." The commando motioned to his men. They stepped forward, lifted the body bag, prepared to leave.

"Where's the second body?" Ridgeway asked.

"Ma'am?"

"Soldier, you know as well as I do that there were two men standing here, not just one," Ridgeway said. "So I'll ask you again. Where's the second body?"

The commando ignored the Assistant Director and addressed his men: "Transfer the package to Los Alamitos. Full protection detail." He turned to leave. Chris blocked his way.

"Sir, you need to step aside," the DARPA commando said.

Hanover ignored the warning. "The lady asked you to open the bag."

The commando waved his men on. "I'll catch up," he said. He turned to Chris. "First things first. I'll take back that weapon."

Hanover handed him the Thermite grenade launcher. The soldier pointed to the gash on Chris' forehead. "That looks painful."

"Nasty shaving accident," Chris said. "I've had worse."

"Not from me," the soldier replied, "but the nights still young."

Chris stepped closer. "Don't let me stop you from trying."

Ridgeway spoke. "That will be enough, Agent Hanover."

Chris held the soldier's stare.

"Agent Hanover," Ridgeway said, "Stand down."

Chris slowly stepped aside. The soldier nudged his shoulder as he walked past, glanced at Ridgeway, then whispered in his ear. "Have mommy put a Band-Aid on your boo-boo," he said. "If you ask real nice maybe she'll kiss it better for you too."

"The offer's still open," Chris replied. "Anytime, anywhere."

The agents watched the DARPA commandos leave the crumbled Pyramid carrying Merrick's body.

Jordan looked at her partner. She shook her head. "Really?" she said. "Of all the guys in the world to pick a fight with you want to tangle with that guy?"

"He doesn't look so tough."

"He's trained to *kill*."

"I can handle myself."

"Chris, the man has forgotten more about self-defence than you'll ever know."

"I've learned a few moves over the years, you know."

"News flash," Jordan said. "Watching Ultimate Fighting on pay-per-view with a beer in one hand and a slice of pizza in the other does not qualify as expert instruction."

Ridgeway interrupted. "Are you two just about done?"

Jordan said nothing.

Chris smirked. "She started it."

"Very mature, Agent Hanover," ADC Ridgeway replied.

"Sorry, ma'am. Yes, we're good."

"All right. It looks like we're wrapped up here. I'll liaise with Colonel Hallier later. In the meantime, have another look around the scene. Grab whatever evidence you can find."

"Yes, ma'am," Jordan answered.

"And meet me in my office tomorrow afternoon for debriefing. After all the craziness that's gone on here today it might be wise if we collaborate our reports on this one."

"We'll be there," Chris said.

Jordan knelt and inspected the area where the commandos had recovered Merrick's body. A few yards away, a Los Angeles city coroner tended to the body of a dead FBI SWAT agent.

"That could have been you or me," Jordan said.

"Yeah, I know," Chris replied.

Blood-soaked steel rods lay on the ground where Merrick's body had been retrieved. Under one of the metal shafts lay a small plastic object.

"Got a glove on you?" Jordan asked.

Chris fished a latex medical glove out of his jacket pocket.

"Thanks."

"No problem," Chris said. "I always make it a point to carry protection."

Jordan rolled her eyes. "I'm sure you do."

"Find something?"

"Maybe." Jordan slipped her hand into the glove. "I don't suppose you have a pair of tweezers with you as well?"

"Sorry, I'm all out of medical supplies," Chris said. "Try this." He removed a twenty-dollar bill from his pocket, folded it lengthwise twice, then again in half. "Presto! Tweezers."

"That should work."

"I'm gonna need it back when you're finished with it."

"The glove?"

"*The twenty.*"

Jordan smiled. She picked up the item.

"What did you find?" Chris asked.

"Looks like a needle sheath."

Chris winced. "I hate needles. Suture needles in particular."

"How old are you?"

"Very funny. I've been stitched up too many times to count. Take it from me, needles were designed with a singular purpose in mind: to inflict as much torture on human beings as possible."

"Then it's probably a good thing you didn't take on Mr. DARPA back there. It would have been suture

city for you."

"Ha-ha," Chris said. He watched Jordan extricate the item from beneath the bloody steel rod. "Did you know that the Egyptians were the first to come up with the idea of suturing? They made needles out of bone and used a rough cord to close the incisions."

THE SIN KEEPER

"You're a wealth of knowledge, Hanover," Jordan replied. "Let me guess. National Geographic Channel?"

Chris ignored the barb. "They used them in the process of preparing a body for mummification."

"Thank you, Tutankhamen," Jordan said. "I feel so much more informed. Got an evidence bag handy?"

"Hang on. I'll grab one from the Coroner."

Jordan held the plastic sleeve up to the light and rolled it between her fingertips. Trace material from the contents of the syringe sparkled inside the cover. Suddenly the sleeve began to vibrate. "What the hell?" she said.

Chris returned holding a small evidence bag. "Will this do?"

"Perfect," Jordan said.

He opened the mouth of the bag. "Drop it in."

Jordan didn't reply.

"You okay, J?"

"Me? Yeah, sure. I'm fine."

The needle sheath clipped the edge of the evidence bag as Jordan dropped it. She caught it in her ungloved hand. A tiny drop of the rose-colored solution escaped the plastic cover. It glimmered on the palm of her hand.

"Hold on," Chris said. "I'll get a wash kit."

"No... time..." Jordan said. She collapsed.

"Jordan?" Chris yelled as he watched her fall. "Jordan!" His partner lay on the ground, unconscious. "Agent down!" Chris yelled. "I need medical! Get me medical!"

JORDAN RACED through a spinning tunnel of brilliant light. A kaleidoscopic vortex of color exploded around her: rose reds, bright yellows, blinding whites. She felt as though she had fallen into a wormhole and was traveling through space at the speed of light. As fast as her journey had begun it came to an abrupt halt. The connection, or whatever it was, had been broken. Jordan didn't just come around. She was thrust back to consciousness. She sat up, gasping for air.

Chris steadied her as FBI paramedics rushed to her side. "What the hell just happened?" he asked.

"I don't know," Jordan said. She stared at her hand. Her palm was dry. No trace of the solution was visible. "Oh, God!"

"What's wrong?" Chris asked.

"Whatever was in that needle absorbed into my skin. It's in me now."

"What is?"

"I don't know. Something... bad."

57

FBI SWAT CONTINUED their building-by-building sweep of the campus, escorting the terrified students and faculty to safety. For some, the horror of the attack had left them so incapacitated they could not walk. Members of the tactical team were forced to carry them from the buildings in their arms.

The site swarmed with emergency services personnel. Firefighters cut through the wreckage of the downed FBI helicopter to gain access to the unconscious officers trapped inside. Students from the university's School of Nursing worked beside police and medical teams tending to the injured, assessing the dying, and pronouncing the dead.

On the sports track and baseball fields adjacent to the fallen Pyramid, two military evacuation choppers approached in trail pattern. The second bird maintained its position in the air while the first descended, its makeshift landing zone marked by four flashlights placed on the ground in "T" formation. Hallier covered his face, waited for the dust cloud kicked up by the rotor wash to settle, then walked to the helicopter to meet the medical team as they deployed.

"Inside," he yelled over the deafening roar of the chopper engine. He pointed to the Pyramid. "Multiple casualties, plus a DB requiring armed transfer to JFTB Los Alamitos."

The medic looked confused. "Sorry, sir," he said. "Did you say you want us to provide armed transport for a *dead* body?"

"Did I stutter?" Hallier yelled.

"No, sir," the pilot replied.

"Then you heard me correctly. And don't let it out of your sight."

The medic saluted. "Copy that, Colonel."

Throughout the campus, Cal State University facilities management had erected a network of portable lighting stations. The generators switched on. The halogen lamps glared. Within minutes Long Beach campus was illuminated in harsh white light.

Hovering news helicopters kept their distance from the emergency airspace that had been claimed by the military. News crews returned to the police barricades and resumed their live-to-air report on the aftermath of the attack.

Having been cleared by medical and recovered from the ill-effects of the strange liquid, Jordan and Chris sat on the steps outside the Pyramid.

"You sure you're all right?" Chris asked.

"I think so," Jordan replied. "Still a little lightheaded, but I'm okay."

"What happened back there?"

"I don't know."

"Do you remember passing out?"

"Sort of. It felt more like I was falling. I didn't realize I'd lost consciousness."

"Do you remember what you said when you came around?"

"That's a little fuzzy."

"You said something bad was in your body."

Jordan opened her hand. A tiny dot, no larger than a pinprick, marked the point where her body had absorbed the solution.

"Let me have a look."

"Really, Chris. I'm fine."

"Humor me."

Chris took her hand, opened her fingers, found the red mark, and massaged her palm. "You scared the hell out of me back there," he said. His touch was gentle.

"Sorry."

"Look, Jordan," Chris said, "I know you can handle pretty much anything that this job could ever throw at you. And I'll probably never fully understand your gift. It's just that..."

"Just what?"

"I'd never forgive myself if something happened to you."

Jordan stood. "Don't go there, Chris," she said. "I don't want you taking responsibility for me. We're partners. It's natural for you to want me to be safe. Same here. We protect each other."

Chris nodded. There was more he wanted to say but this was not the time or the place. "Fair enough," he said.

"We should get back inside. Ridgeway wanted us to have a look around. Maybe we can turn up more on Merrick."

"Agreed," Chris replied. "Speaking of bad guys, I had Egan dead to rights in my scope before all hell broke loose and the building started to collapse. But then this pink glow appeared inside the wall of debris. He was there and then he... wasn't."

"I know."

"The mark on your hand," Chris said. "Does what happened to him have anything to do with why you passed out after you touched the needle sheath?"

Jordan nodded. "I think so."

"You think after the building fell Egan went... somewhere?" Chris said. "You know... Back to the Future, flying DeLorean, flux capacitor kind of stuff?"

"Something definitely happened to him."

Chris stared at his partner. "I don't know about you, but in my world, people don't just suddenly vanish into thin air."

Jordan was quiet, her silence telling.

"Wait a minute," Chris said. "The liquid from the needle cap was the same color as the light I saw coming from the debris pile. It shimmered on your skin. I saw it when you collapsed. Did you go somewhere?"

Jordan hesitated. "Yes. Not physically, of course, but mentally. Something happened that I can't explain. Maybe because my exposure was minimal so too was the effect."

"So if Egan had injected himself with a syringe full of that stuff..."

"His exposure would have been massive," Jordan finished. "There's no telling what effect it would have had on his body."

58

MARINA PUZANOVA CLEARED airport customs at LAX at 6:00 A.M. after an exhausting thirteen-hour flight from Moscow. Any desire for sleep that her body demanded had been rendered impossible by the frequent intrusion of nightmares. Marina sensed the dark dreams were, in fact, premonitions; portents of the danger facing Ilya. In their phone conversation, the stranger said he had been keeping close tabs on her son, knew his whereabouts at all times, his daily schedule, the classes he attended at Long Beach, even when he spent time with his girlfriend. He was also aware of her involvement with The Company. The how and why of it all was unimportant. This person, whoever he was, had proven himself to be a viable threat, not just to her professionally, but to her family. This could not be allowed. She thought of Kastonov. No doubt he would demand that she answer for her insubordinate act of leaving the country without Company permission, but she didn't care. As much as The Company had saved her from the streets and provided her with a life better than anything she could have imagined, her first and foremost duty was to protect Ilya. If The Company found it unacceptable that she would choose protecting her own son over the 'greater good' then they could go straight to hell. Marina knew how valuable her secrets were to the international police intelligence community. There wasn't a country in the world that wouldn't roll out the red carpet and make a place for her should she decide to turn. She knew there would be no welcome mat waiting for her in Russia when her business in the U.S.A. had been concluded. America might be just as good a place as any to a start new life, under a new name, with a new identity.

Marina handed her inspection card to the customs officer and exited the arrivals gate. Beyond the automatic doors, well-wishers gathered in eager anticipation of the arrival of friends and family. Two toddlers stood in front of an attractive young couple, their handmade sign reading *Dobro pozhalovat' v Ameriku!* - Welcome to America! As their grandparents walked through the doors the children threw down the sign, squealed with delight, ran under the steel handrail, and flung themselves into their open arms. The heartwarming reunion drew a quiet round of applause from the crowd.

Marina walked down the exit ramp, turned on her cell phone and tried to call Ilya. The call went straight to voice-mail. Like so many teenagers who lived on their phones, it was unlike Ilya to have the device turned off. Concerned, she decided the best course of action was to go directly from the airport to Ilya's condominium.

A group of travelers stood outside a Starbuck's coffee kiosk watching several banks of television monitors. The look of concern on their faces drew Marina's attention. Several Los Angeles television stations were reporting on the catastrophic events that had taken place at Long Beach campus while Marina was still in the air.

A man stood with his arm around his wife. She cried quietly.

"What's going on?" Marina asked.

She woman caught her breath. "It's the University," she replied. "They think it was a terrorist attack."

The video loop refreshed: a police helicopter falling from the sky, crashing, and bursting into flames... students fleeing the grounds... buildings turned to rubble... dozens of police, fire and medical vehicles on the scene, their flashing service lights lighting up the night... the fallen Pyramid.

"My daughter goes to Long Beach," the woman said. "We flew in to spend a couple of days with her. I can't reach her. The police have shut down all cellular communication in the area in case more bombs are hidden on the campus. They're afraid they could be detonated remotely by cellular transmission. What in God's name is happening in this country?" She wept.

A ticker scrolled across the bottom of the screen beneath the graphic images:

BREAKING NEWS... Twenty dead in suspected terrorist attack at California State University Long Beach Campus... 4 FBI SWAT agents... 16 students... Dr. Ashley Granger, Professor of Mathematics, found dead at scene... Names of additional deceased withheld pending family notification... No groups have yet claimed responsibility for the attack.

.   .   .

ASHLEY! Marina recognized the name of her friend and business associate. Was Ilya dead too? She had to get to the University right away.

No sooner had she left the crowd and walked toward a taxi stand when two men stopped her.

"Marina Puzanova?"

"Yes."

"Mother of Ilya Puzanova?"

"I am. What's going on? Has something happened to my son? Oh, God!"

The men presented their credentials. "FBI, Ms. Puzanova. Are you aware of the incident that occurred last night at California State University?"

Marina nodded. "I just saw it on the news."

"Your son is fine, ma'am," one of the agents said. "He was on campus at the time of the event and was slightly injured during the attack, but it's nothing serious. We're speaking with him, as well as other students we think might be able to assist us in identifying the individuals responsible for the attack. We're holding him and the others in protective custody until we've taken their statements. We can take you to him now."

"Yes, of course," Marina said. "Where is he?"

"Bureau headquarters, downtown L.A. Do you have all your bags, ma'am?"

"Yes."

The agent put his hand on Marina's shoulder. "Try not to worry, Ms. Puzanova. We'll have you downtown in no time."

"I want to call him," Marina said. "I want to speak with Ilya."

"I'm sorry," the second agent replied. "That won't be possible. Not until our agents have completed the debrief. I assure you there's no cause for concern. It's just protocol.

Right now, we need to gather as much intelligence about the event as we can."

"Wait," Marina said. She stopped. "You don't believe he's a suspect, do you?"

"Not at all, ma'am" the agent replied. "Like I said, it's just routine."

Together they walked through the arrival's terminal, past the taxi stand, up the ramp to the parking garage and took the elevator to the fourth floor.

Marina couldn't stop thinking about her son. "How long have you been holding him?"

"Since last night."

A black sedan was parked in the back corner of the garage. The agent clicked the remote, started the car and lowered the windows. He took Marina's travel case from her and placed it in the trunk of the car.

The second agent opened the rear passenger door. "Make yourself comfortable," he said. "We'll get you to your son as fast as we can."

"Thank you," Marina said. She sat in the back seat and placed her purse beside her.

The agents stepped to the back of the car, conferred quietly, then closed the trunk lid.

A thought occurred to Marina. Why had the agents parked here? Surely they could have parked in the Police parking zone, located immediately outside the terminal entrance. After all, they were here on official business. Marina suddenly realized that she had become so focused on Ilya and the situation at California State University that she had let logic evade her. She was not thinking straight. She refocused. How did the FBI know she was on this flight? Her visit to the U.S.A. was to have been a surprise to Ilya. She had not told him she was coming. The only person who was aware of her travel plans was Taras Verenich. Suddenly something felt very wrong.

Marina reached for the door handle. The electronic locks engaged.

"What's going on?" she said.

The agents walked to either side of the car and stood at the open windows. Each of the men wore latex gloves on their hands. From their jackets they retrieved their Company issued Tokarev pistols, each fitted with a sound suppressor, and unloaded their clips into the Russian madam. Marina's body flailed in the back seat of the car as the bullets tore through her body. Having emptied the rounds from their weapons into their target, the assassin's lowered their guns. One of the gunmen raised the windows, then shut off the engine and remote-locked the doors.

Walking to the opposite end of the parking garage, one of the killers dropped the key fob to the death car down an open drainpipe, then opened the doors to the silver Mercedes. The two men got in the car and left the airport.

Clear of the exit gate, the passenger placed a phone call.

"Yes?"

"Your package arrived, sir."

"When?"

"Twenty minutes ago."

"What condition is it in?"

"Damaged."

"How bad?"

"Irreparably."

"And the second package?"

"We're tracking it now."

"Let me know when you've got it."

"Yes, sir."

"One more thing."

"Sir?"

"The Los Angeles office is to be closed. Please inform the staff."

"Understood."

The call disconnected.

The driver accelerated and headed for the freeway.

Traffic into downtown Los Angeles was lighter than usual.

59

THE TWO MEN entered the office of Verenich Law and presented their identification to the receptionist. Elena greeted them.

"FBI," the first man said. "Taras Verenich, please."

Elena smiled. "Two visits from the FBI in as many days," Elena said. "I hope no one here is in trouble!"

"Ma'am?"

"Just kidding," Elena said. "Two of your colleagues dropped by yesterday."

"When was this?"

"Late afternoon."

"What time?"

"4:00 P.M., I think."

"Who did they ask for?"

"Mr. Verenich."

"Did he meet with them?"

"Briefly, yes."

"What did they talk about?"

Elena shifted uncomfortably in her chair at the odd

question. "Why would Mr. Verenich share that information with me?"

The second man spoke. "Who were they? What were their names?"

"I'm sorry. I don't recall."

"You keep track of visitors, right?" the second man said. "Show me your log."

The tone of the conversation had changed, become interrogative. Elena was accustomed to dealing with the occasional upset client and had been instructed never to tolerate rude behavior for a second.

"Perhaps you could tell me the purpose of your visit," she said.

"Where's Verenich?"

"Excuse me?"

"Your boss," the first man pressed. "Where is he?"

Elena nervously arranged the file folders on her desk. "I'm afraid Mr. Verenich is not in the office today."

"When will he be back?" the man said.

Elena felt her blood pressure start to rise. "It's not my job to keep tabs on my boss," she said.

The man leaned over the counter and put his hand on top of the files. "Don't get smart with me lady."

"With *you*?" Elena replied. "Trust me, if I were to get smart with you it would be an unfair contest." She pushed the man's hand aside. "Mr. Verenich left the office yesterday afternoon, right after talking with two of your associates. He said he would be out of the office today on personal business and that he would be unreachable. I have no idea when he will be returning."

"We'd like to see his office," the second man said.

"I'm sorry," Elena said, "I can't permit that."

The man smiled. "We're not asking for your permission."

Elena leaned back in her chair. "Don't get me wrong," she said. "You're very charming and all, and much better looking than your friend. But I'm sure you read the sign on the door on your way in. This is a law office. You may find this a little hard to believe, but around here we actually *know* a thing or two about the law. So unless you have a court order to search the premises, this counter is as far as you go." Elena's phone rang. "I'll be sure to tell Mr. Verenich you stopped by." She reached for the receiver.

The second man leaned over the desk, placed his finger on the button and disconnected the call.

"What do you think you're doing?" Elena snapped.

The man picked up the receiver. "Call Verenich."

Elena crossed her arms. "Your visit is over gentlemen," she said. "Enjoy the rest of your day."

"I won't ask a third time."

"That's it," Elena said. She held out her hand. "Give me your credentials. I'm calling your office."

"No problem," the man replied. He opened his jacket, removed his silencer-fitted pistol, and shot Elena twice; one bullet between her eyes, the second through her heart. *Thwup... thwup.*

Elena's head jerked back with the first shot, fell forward with the second. The shooter walked around the reception desk, lifted the dead woman's body out of her chair, rolled it under the desk and slid the chair back into place. Cast-off blood and brain matter speckled the floor behind her.

The assassins moved through the office quickly and efficiently.

Seated at a conference table, Verenich's support team became their first victims. *Thwup! thwup! thwup! thwup!*

thwup! thwup! thwup! Less than five seconds. Seven staff members, all wiped out.

In the supplies room, one of the clerks was busy making photocopies while a second filed the printed documents into white three-ring binders. They looked up as the strangers entered the room and fired their weapons. Both men fell dead.

In the vault, Verenich's admin staff were pulling files to be sent out for digital imaging. Two bullets ended their conversation and their lives.

A male voice called out from the office on the opposite end of the floor. "Elena?"

The men stopped, listened, and determined the man's location.

Corner office.

Verenich?

They raised their weapons and advanced down the corridor in the direction of the voice.

The man called out again. "Elena, you there?"

Footsteps coming toward them. The assassins waited.

The man stepped out of the office, saw the strangers and their guns, and turned to run. *Thwup!* The first bullet ripped through his leg. *Thwup!* The second round found its mark in the small of his back. He fell across the threshold of Taras' office, tried to crawl inside. The shooter walked up to him and pushed his foot into the bullet hole in his leg. The clerk screamed.

The first man opened his cell phone, looked at the picture he had been emailed of their second target, showed it to his partner and shook his head. "It's not him," he said. The shooter pressed the hot muzzle of the silencer into the base of the fallen man's neck.

"Verenich. Where is he?"

The man tried to move, couldn't. The second bullet had left him paralyzed. He struggled to speak. "I don't know!"

"Who are you?"

"Holt... J-James Holt. I'm just a clerk," he said.

"Bullshit. The burn box. Where is it?"

"The *what*?" The shooter pressed the tip of the silencer against Holt's temple. "I swear to God I don't know anything about a burn box!" Holt cried. "All I know is Mr. Verenich has a safe."

"Where?"

The man tried to point. "On the wall. Behind the picture."

"What's the code?"

"I don't know."

Thwup! A third bullet tore through Holt's shoulder. He screamed. The gunman pressed the silencer against the back of his head. "You sure about that?" he said.

"*4-9-2-8!*"

To his partner, the gunman indicated the Rockwell painting mounted on the wall behind Taras' desk. "Try it."

The man walked into the office, ripped the painting off its wall track and exposed the safe. Verenich's burn box, the repository in which he was required to keep all files about Company matters, would be locked safely inside it.

His partner entered the code. The door clicked open. The burn box sat on the bottom shelf.

"Got it."

"Get the files."

The man pulled out the box, opened it. Empty. "No joy," he said.

"Verenich, you prick," the shooter said. He stood up, pulled the trigger, and blew a hole in the back of Holt's skull. He stepped over the dead man's body, inspected the empty box, then threw it across the room.

"Shit," he said, "He's not going to like this." He took out his cell phone and placed a call.

"Yes?"

"Sir, the Los Angeles office has been closed as requested."

"And the second package?"

"Not on the premises."

"Need I remind you how important it is that it be found?"

"No, sir."

"Get back to me when you have it."

"Yes, sir."

The caller hung up.

The two men walked to the reception area, rummaged through Elena's purse, found her keys to the office, turned off the lights, locked the door and took the elevator to the main lobby.

Holt's killer dropped the office key into a garbage container outside the entrance to the building.

They walked across the street, took the elevator to the upper deck of the parking garage and resumed their surveillance.

Yesterday they had lost the Ferrari when it sped through the lights ahead of them.

They would continue to watch the building.

Sooner or later Verenich would return to his office.

When he did, they would kill him.

60

"**L**ONG BEACH IS going to remember last night for a very long time," Ann Ridgeway said.

The Assistant Director had requested the agent's presence in the boardroom. Their discussion centered on the bizarre and unusual events that had occurred over the past week. Jordan and Chris sat at the front of the room. Agent Hawkins presented his findings to the team.

"I spent the better part of yesterday with my team digging through the Rosenfeld's computers," Hawkins said. "We concluded that all the murders, to one degree or another, are related to this man."

Behind him, Jason Merrick's picture filled the wall monitor.

"Hallier's target," Ann Ridgeway said. "Dr. Jason Merrick."

"Correct," Hawkins replied. "Dr. Merrick - or more specifically what happened to him - has been the key to this case. And we might not have made the connection if DARPA hadn't asked for our help."

The picture on the screen changed. It showed an evidence photo taken of the flash drive found at the Rosenfeld crime scene.

"It came together for us with the flash drive you retrieved from Dr. Rosenfeld's mouth," Hawkins said. "At first we thought the 'AWP' file contents were strings of code. Turns out they are account numbers; one for each victim. You may recall the first letter refers to the victim's surname, the second letter to their given name. In other words, "DA" represents Dowd, Aaron, RI for Rosenfeld, Itzhak. GA is Granger, Ashley, HJ is Harper, Julie. The remaining two files, VT and PM, stand for Verenich, Taras, and Puzanova, Marina."

"Chris and I met with Verenich yesterday," Jordan said.

"You believe he's a target too?" Chris asked.

"I'd bet on it," Hawkins replied. "And after what happened yesterday there's a chance he's already dead."

Ann Ridgeway interjected. "For now, let's proceed on the basis that he's still alive. As soon as we locate Mr. Verenich, we'll offer him protective custody until we can determine the degree of danger he's in."

"What's the connection between Merrick, Rosenfeld and the other vics?" Jordan asked.

"That goes back ten years to the murder of Paige, Dr. Merrick's daughter," Hawkins said. "Her body was found in South America. Merrick and his wife thought she was still attending class at Cal State. Turns out she had left the University in favor of a new career as a high-priced escort. That's where these three come in."

The photos of Ashley Granger, Taras Verenich and Marina Puzanova stared back from the screen.

"Granger, on the left, was Paige's mathematics professor at Cal State. The two were close, perhaps even pursuing more than a student/teacher relationship judging by their social media posts. But what the University didn't know about Professor Granger was that she was leading a double life as an executive escort. The working theory is that Granger encouraged Paige to join her in the business. This is where Marina Puzanova comes in. These two go way back. Puzanova's a key player in a Russian crime outfit that calls itself The Company. She controls the prostitution side of their business. Their center of operations is Moscow, but they conduct business globally, catering exclusively to the uber-wealthy, primarily providing women, luxury automobiles, fine art, illegal adoptions... even harvesting human organs for private surgery transplantation. We think Granger was being paid by Puzanova to recruit new girls into the operation."

"How do they acquire the children for adoption?" Chris asked.

"Conception farms," Hawkins replied. "Babies conceived specifically for the purpose of sale to the wealthy."

"Jesus," Chris said. "And the body parts?"

"Remember when I searched Rosenfeld's laptop? We found a fake link at the bottom of the Verenich Law homepage. Clicking on that link opened a search box. The files labeled *Account 1* and *Account 2* contained the profiles of hundreds of girls. When we traced them, we found they all had two things in common. First, they were highly educated or academically gifted. Second, they all came from affluent families. The girls in Account 1, the younger group, were all high school seniors and honor students. Most of them had been offered scholarships to major universities. The women in Account 2 were either attending university or alumni."

Jordan said, "So the girls were *targeted*?"

Hawkins nodded. "We think that was Granger's job. We also believe she's just one of many such recruiters working for Puzanova and The Company that have been placed in educational institutions around the world. But that's only part of it. We think they were selected because of their genetic superiority. Professor Granger and operatives like her lured them in with the promise of big money, which they paid out handsomely. Later the girls were used to meet supply and demand on the other side of the business. If one of the girls met the genetic profile a particular client couple was looking for, she'd be "rewarded" by The Company with a fully-paid luxury vacation. What the girl didn't know was that this was a one-way ticket to a Company conception farm where she would be impregnated with the client's sperm. Girls sent to the farm served two final purposes for The Company. The first was to produce babies. When she was no longer considered valuable, she'd be killed, and her organs sold to Company red market brokers."

"The luxury vacation was a death sentence," Jordan said.

"Correct," Hawkins replied.

"What about Marina Puzanova?" Chris asked. "Any idea where she is?"

Hawkins shook his head. "No. And even if she set foot on American soil tomorrow, we couldn't detain her. We've got nothing substantial on her. She's only one cog in the wheel of an organization whose influence stretches across continents. Taking down The Company requires assembling a multi-agency operation on a global scale. We've reached out to the Russian government. As usual, their policy on matters like this is to handle them on their own. Interpol has agreed to assist, but without Russia's direct cooperation it could take years."

Chris asked, "Why was Rosenfeld targeted in the first place?"

"They found his Achilles heel," Hawkins replied. "His weakness for fine art and antiquities. Which he found a way to get more of through Verenich. Dr. Rosenfeld was a good man, but he let greed get the better of him. He met Verenich at a FreeSurge fundraising auction to which Verenich had contributed a very expensive piece of French art, no doubt for the express purpose of getting his attention. He probably told the doctor he had unlimited access to such one-of-a-kind priceless pieces."

"Like the Codex Leicester and the Pont Neuf displayed in the anteroom outside the bedroom," Jordan said.

"Exactly. Both were stolen. Our forensic search of Rosenfeld's computer proved he was laundering money through FreeSurge and several of his other enterprises for Verenich. We think he was doing this in exchange for acquiring new pieces for his private collection that no one else in the world would ever have access to. What he didn't know was that the pieces he was receiving from Verenich were coming through Alexi Vasiliev and Vyachlov Usoyan – two high-placed leaders in the Solntsevskaya Bratva who report directly to the head of The Company, Anton Kastonov. The Russian mob has a nickname for Kastonov. They call him 'Grekh Khranitel' or 'The Sin Keeper,' so named because of his reputation for using his top girls to extract detailed and often secret information from highly-placed Company clients, then using that information to blackmail and extort huge sums of money from them later in exchange for his silence and protection."

"So Rosenfeld was in bed with the Russian mob and didn't even know it," Jordan said.

Hawkins nodded. "We also think Dr. Merrick used his

Department of Defense privileges to access the supercomputers at Dynamic Life Sciences and launch his own private investigation into what happened to his daughter. He probably started by looking into Granger, connected her to Puzanova and Verenich, and finally Verenich to Rosenfeld. That's how he found out about The Company."

"I'm quite sure the Department of Defense isn't about to confirm your suspicions anytime soon," Ridgeway said.

Hawkins agreed. "Not likely."

Agent Cobb knocked on the meeting room door.

"Yes?" Ridgeway said.

"Sorry to intrude, ma'am. Colonel Hallier from DARPA is on the line. He says he'd like a word with you."

Ridgeway motioned to the conference phone in the center of the table. "Put him through."

"Right away." Cobb closed the door. The phone rang.

"Good afternoon, Colonel," Ridgeway answered.

"Thanks for taking my call, Ann."

"My pleasure." The agents stood to leave the room. Ridgeway gestured for them to stay. "My team and I are recapping the case right now, Colonel. Agents Quest and Hanover are with me, as well as our head of Cyber Support, Agent Hawkins. Do you mind if they listen in?"

"Not at all," Hallier replied. "I want to thank you and your team for your assistance. You all did a fine job under exceedingly difficult circumstances. It would be my pleasure to work with you again, anytime."

"Thank you, Colonel. The feeling is mutual."

"I also wanted to let you know about a development in the case as it pertains to Dr. Merrick."

"Oh?"

"I received a call this morning from Sergeant Cowell, LAPD SWAT. He told me the uniforms who took eyewitness statements at the scene connected a car and motorcycle parked outside the main entrance of the university to Merrick and Egan. Fingerprints confirmed it. Both were stolen."

"Has LAPD interviewed the owners of the vehicles?" Ridgeway asked.

"One's dead, the manager of the Acadia Motor Inn in Laguna Beach who owned the car. Uniforms interviewed his wife. She had noticed that the car was gone and assumed her husband had stepped out to run a few errands. But then she found the front office door locked and no one on duty. She looked through the window and saw him lying beneath the counter in a pool of blood. A pen was stuck in the side of his neck. The prints on it matched Merrick's."

"Murderous bastard," Ridgeway replied. "And the owner of the bike?"

"Dr. Brian Harvey," Hallier replied, "an emergency room physician at Mercy General Hospital. He's fine. Apparently, the doc had just bought the motorcycle. Only had it for a couple of days. He stepped out on his break to check on it, saw it was missing and called the police right away. The prints on the bike were Egan's. Responding officers also found a missing squad car from a neighboring jurisdiction in Mercy General's parking lot. Turns out it was one of three missing units."

"What do you mean, missing?"

"They haven't been able to reach five of their officers since yesterday," Hallier said. "Total loss of radio contact. No one knows what's going on. Their department is in a complete panic."

"Have they announced a General Alert?"

"Yes, within an hour of their disappearance. All off-duty

emergency services personnel have been called in to assist in the search. Fire and rescue too."

"I'll put in a call. If they want our help, they've got it."

"I'm sure they'd appreciate that, Ann. Again, thank you."

"Anytime, Colonel. Keep in touch."

"Will do."

ADC Ridgeway disconnected the call. "Anything else Agent Hawkins?"

"No, ma'am," Hawkins replied. "That's everything we've been able to ascertain thus far."

Chris stood. "If that's that case then I'd like to make a suggestion. Lunch is on me. Massey's Steak House. Ten minutes."

"I'll cover the beers," Hawkins said.

ADC Ridgeway laughed. "Massey's it is. But make it in thirty. I need to speak with both of you in my office. It's urgent."

"Take a seat," Ridgeway said. She handed Jordan a file folder. "Your next case," she continued. "Serial killings in New York City. Ritualistic by the looks of it. NYPD has asked for our help."

From the file, Chris retrieved a copy of a handwritten letter and read the note. "He's daring the police commissioner to catch him. That takes a pair."

Jordan asked, "Has New York been informed that we'll be joining their investigation?"

"They know you're on your way," Ridgeway replied. "You'll be liaising with Special Agent Max Penner and his team. They'll provide you with whatever support you'll need."

"When do we leave?" Chris asked.

"9:00 A.M. tomorrow morning," Ridgeway said.

"Thank you, ma'am," Jordan said. She and Chris stood to leave.

ADC Ridgeway shook their hands. "Be safe, agents."

"Always," Chris said.

61

COLONEL QUENTIN HALLIER returned the guard's salute, pushed open the stainless-steel doors leading into the morgue and flipped the wall switch. The fluorescent ceiling fixtures crackled, flickered, and flashed to life. The black bag lay on the autopsy table.

Hallier opened his cell phone and placed a call.

"Ford."

"It's Hallier, General. I'm at Los Alamitos. Merrick's body has arrived."

"And Channeler?"

Hallier unzipped the bag. The top-secret device remained attached to the dead man's wrist.

"Intact, sir."

"Remove it and keep it safe. Escort the body back here for destruction."

"Yes, sir."

Hallier removed the spent syringe from his pocket. We have a further complication, sir," he said, "LEEDA has been compromised. I have the injection device. It's empty."

"Merrick injected himself?" Ford asked.

"No, sir. Egan did."

"Tell me you have him in custody."

"I'm afraid not, sir."

"What is his status?"

"Unknown at this time."

"What does that mean, Colonel?" Ford snapped. "Either the Commander is in custody or he isn't."

"We were unable to reach Commander Egan before he injected himself, sir. He's... missing."

"Jesus Christ."

"What are your orders, sir?"

Ford was furious. "My orders, Colonel? What in God's name do you think my orders are? We have a one-of-a-kind, multi-million-dollar military asset somewhere out there that we can't find because we've turned off every goddamn means of tracking it. My orders are that you fly back here with the body and Channeler, put together a recovery team, and find Egan. I don't care how you do it. Just track him down, wherever the hell he is."

"And when we do, sir?"

"Deal with him... with extreme prejudice."

"Understood, General."

"You bloody-well better," Ford said. "Either your team brings Egan in alive or you retire him permanently. I'll be damned if I'm going to have an asset with his abilities out of our control and running rogue."

"Copy that sir. Egan will be handled appropriately."

Ford was right, Hallier thought. Merrick, Egan, the Channeler and LEEDA projects, the scientific team at Dynamic Life Sciences... all of it had been under his direction. The fact that Merrick had been able to figure out a way to steal the project right out from under them was inex-cusable.

Ford continued. "What about project records?"

"Unsalvageable, sir."

"How the hell is that possible?"

Hallier recalled a text he had received less than an hour ago from Dr. Han informing him of a security breach at Dynamic Life Sciences. He relayed the update to Ford.

"Last night, DLS's computer system was the target of a time-delayed electromagnetic pulse bomb. It detonated at 9:00 P.M. The facility is offline, sir. They're completely in the dark."

"Surely they backed up their data?"

"The attack was thorough, sir. There's nothing left. The entire server farm dedicated to the GENESIS project is six-feet under."

"Let me guess. No backup, for reasons of national security."

"I'm afraid not. No one except DLS computer staff and Dr. Merrick had access to the room."

"What about outside of DLS?" Ford asked. "Could Merrick have backed up the data externally?"

"We're checking into that, sir."

"Hardcopy?"

"No physical files. Just a notepad in Merrick's desk drawer containing a list of names. All but three had been stroked out. There was a number for a cell phone in Moscow which matched a name on the list: Marina Puzanova."

"You think Merrick planned to sell Channeler and LEEDA to the Russians? To this Puzanova?"

"It's possible, sir," Hallier replied. "If that's the case,

perhaps what happened at Long Beach was an orchestrated event."

"Meaning?"

"That it could have been a demonstration. Using Egan... attacking the University... maybe someone wanted to see first-hand that the technology worked before they bought it. Long Beach would be all the proof a buyer would need to confirm Channeler's capability. Merrick would have been paid billions. Any country with deep pockets and a non-extradition treaty would grant him asylum in a heartbeat, assuming he lived to collect the money after the transaction was completed."

"Close it," Ford said.

"Sir?"

"Shut it down. Bolt the goddamn doors. Bring every piece of equipment back to DARPA for examination, right down to the last computer chip. Have data forensics determine if anything in those servers is salvageable."

"Copy that, sir."

Ford sighed. "I can't believe this. Hundreds of millions of dollars and a decade of defense research... all gone, possibly in Russian hands. Do you have any idea how far back this will set our defense initiatives if this turns out to be true? There'll be hell to pay, Colonel. And I'll be damned if I'm going to take the heat."

"I understand, sir."

A voice came over the intercom on Ford's desk. "General?"

"What is it?" Ford barked.

"An urgent call for you sir," Ford's assistant said. "The White House is on line one."

"Thank you, Connie."

To Hallier, Ford said, "Get on this, Colonel. Get me answers. And bloody-well get me Egan!"

"Yes, sir."

The line went dead.

FORD TOOK a deep breath then pressed the flashing button. "This is Brigadier General Ford speaking."

The White House operator spoke: "Please hold for the President."

62

TARAS VERENICH, NOW *Taras Antipov,* floated on his pool lounger, sipping a scotch on the rocks, and enjoying the warmth of the Costa Rican sun on his face. Beads of coconut-scented perspiration trickled across his brow and crept into the corners of his eyes. He unrolled the terry towel neck support, blotted away the stinging sweat, and looked out over the edge of the saltwater infinity pool. Mist drifted lazily over the jungle treetops below his mountainside estate.

He had paid three million in cash for the place, but in terms of the seclusion it offered the property was priceless. A single-gated road led into the property, manned around the clock by six armed guards whom he rarely saw yet grossly overpaid to ensure his safety. Taras seldom had a requirement to leave the estate. Whenever he needed supplies or food or women he simply flew into town and used a driver. His helicopter sat on a landing pad at the edge of the property.

The location of the estate was its key attribute, so ensconced into the rugged hillside that it was practically unreachable from the hillside below, and as impenetrable as any mountain fortress. The landscaping of the grounds had been designed with Taras' personal safety in mind and featured a state-of-the-art underground security system consisting of military-grade improvised explosive devices which would prove fatal to any trespasser unfortunate enough to set foot on any of the twenty pressure-plates strategically buried under the grass. A discrete pathway provided Taras with safe passage off the grounds and into the surrounding jungle if ever the requirement for a quick escape should prove necessary.

His thoughts turned to Marina and how she would react when she arrived in Los Angeles and found him gone. She would be furious. But did she really think he would be stupid enough to wait for her to put a bullet in his head? And what was this bullshit excuse she had given him that the reason for her trip to America was because she believed her son was in danger? He shook his head. Arrogant bitch. He was far more intelligent than she gave him credit for. He was sure The Company knew it too. They would never have been able to gain the financial foothold they now enjoyed on the West Coast had it not been for him turning Rosenfeld by taking advantage of his weakness for fine art and using him to launder millions through his many companies.

The Company owed him his freedom and he was taking it, whether they liked it or not. He had just decided to move his retirement date up by a decade or so.

Granger was dead, or so he presumed, and the FBI had come sniffing around his office asking questions about Rosenfeld. Both were good reasons to get out unscathed while he could.

All signs pointed in the same direction. The Company's American operations had come under scrutiny. Which meant now was the time to disappear. The Company had made him rich, but he had done the same for them. As far as he was concerned, they were even. Living here in his mansion-in-the-mist for the rest of his days would be his reward, one he had planned for and dreamed about for many years. Finally, it was here.

Taras spun the last mouthful of scotch around in his glass and gulped it down. In need of a refill, he hand-paddled over to the edge of the pool, raised himself out of the floating chair and stood on the ladder.

A tremor ran through the handrail and step. An earthquake? He quickly stepped out of the pool and onto the deck.

On the opposite side of the pool, the water level suddenly dropped. Taras watched as a series of small waves radiated across its surface, gained momentum as they flowed toward him, then broke over the edge of the concrete deck and splashed at his feet. Inside the mansion, a heavy ceramic vase fell from its pedestal in the main hall. Taras heard it shatter on the marble floor.

The crash of the vessel was followed by a dazzling burst of brilliant pink light. Taras shielded his eyes. "What the hell?" he said.

Although confident he was perfectly safe in his hilltop hideaway, Taras nevertheless carried a fully loaded Colt semi-automatic pistol with him at all times. He lifted his towel off the chaise lounge, grabbed the weapon and chambered a round.

Footsteps on the marble floor. Inside the mansion.

Coming closer.

A man he had never seen before suddenly stood on the open terrace.

"Well, that was pretty damn cool," the stranger said, walking toward Taras. He looked strong, tough, military.

"Who the hell are you?" Taras asked. "How did you get in here?"

"Actually, I'm still trying to figure that out for myself," Ben Egan answered. "But you have to admit it's one hell of a way to make an entrance."

Too shocked to speak, Taras raised the weapon and pointed it at the Commander.

"I really wish you wouldn't do that," Egan said.

The man's physical appearance began to change right before Taras' eyes. His skin turned gray and thick and looked as tough as a rhinoceros.

Terrified, Taras fired round after round at Egan. He continued to squeeze the trigger even after the last bullet had been fired and the clip was empty. *Click-click-click...*

The slugs bounced harmlessly off Egan's skin and fell to the ground. Egan knelt, gathered up the spent rounds and threw them into the pool. Taras watched as his skin instantly returned to normal.

"Who are you?" Taras said. His arm fell to his side. The gun slipped from his fingers and fell. It clattered on the pool deck.

Ben Egan stepped to the edge of the pool. "I have a message for you from Dr. Jason Merrick."

Taras shook his head. "I don't know who you're talking about."

Egan began to walk around the edge of the pool. Taras backed up.

Egan stopped at the bar cart. "You mind?" He poured himself a Scotch, tossed in a few ice cubes, took a sip. "Single malt," he said. "Personally, I'm more of a blended man. But back to business. Does the name Paige Merrick ring a bell?"

Taras said nothing. He appeared to be in shock. He supported himself by holding fast to a pool chair.

"Okay, okay," Egan continued. "I can see you're a little weirded-out, what with the whole appearing out of nowhere and bulletproof thing I've got going on. Let me throw out a few more names you might recognize. Ashley Granger. How about Aaron Dowd? Marina Puzanova? Itzhak Rosenfeld? Tell me when I'm getting warm."

Taras nodded.

"Ah, Itzhak Rosenfeld!" Egan said. The Commander set down the glass on the bar cart and clapped his hands. "All right. We're going to play a game. I hope you like *Jeopardy*! Your category is '21st Century Seriously Fucked-Up Homicidal Psychopath's.' Ready? Here's the answer: 'This organization, of which you are a member, murdered Dr. Merrick's only daughter, Paige.'"

Taras looked over his shoulder.

"You have ten seconds to answer and your time starts... *now*."

The escape route, Taras thought. He could make a run for it, navigate his way around the strategically buried IED's. Not knowing their locations, the son-of-a-bitch would be blown to pieces when he tried to follow.

Egan hummed the theme music from the iconic television show: "Ding, di-ding-ding-ding... ding... ding... boom-boom. Time's up. So, what's the clue?"

"Fuck you," Taras said.

The helicopter.

"No, that's definitely not it," Egan said. "It's 'Who is The Company.'" But in light of your current predicament, I can appreciate how you might consider 'fuck you' to be a reasonable answer."

Taras gathered his nerve. He tried to run.

Egan raised his hand. Pink light shimmered on the pool deck. Taras' feet locked in place. He looked down, then up at Egan. "Jesus Christ," he said.

"Yeah, I know," Egan responded. "Pretty cool, huh? The military always gets the best toys."

The look on Taras' face revealed the sheer terror he felt inside. "This can't be possible," Taras replied. "*You* can't be possible."

Egan walked around the pool and faced him. "Trust me," the Commander said. "I'm *quite* possible and this is *very* real. You never answered my question about Paige Merrick. You remember her, don't you?"

"Why would I?"

"Because you and the people you work for murdered her."

Taras struggled to free his feet, couldn't.

"I didn't kill anyone."

"Maybe not personally. But you arranged for her to be transferred out of the country."

"That was Granger, not me."

"But you knew what would happen to her."

"That's not the same thing."

"It was to Dr. Merrick."

Taras smiled at Egan. "Paige Merrick," he said. "Now I remember her. She was one sweet piece of ass. I'd heard of her dad but never knew him. Was he doing her too?"

Egan clenched his fist.

Verenich's feet left the ground as Egan lifted him high into the air. The attorney screamed as he floated high above the pool. Egan released him. He fell into the salt water.

"Motherfucker!" Taras yelled.

"I told you," Egan said, "the military always gets the best toys. If you thought that was neat, you're gonna love this." Stage three of the GENESIS project, *Integration,* was now complete. Ben Egan had become the physical embodiment of Channeler and LEEDA and was now the most technologically advanced biological weapon known to man. The only one of his kind in the world. The ultimate super-soldier.

He opened his hands and directed Channeler's energy into the pool.

Around Taras, the salt water began to conduct the strange pink light. Bubbles floated up from the bottom of the pool. Steam rose from its surface. The water was becoming warmer. Taras tried to swim but the pink light held him in place.

"Please, don't kill me!" Taras pleaded. "I don't want to die. Not like this!"

Frightened out of their treetop perches by Taras' cries, a flock of birds took flight. They glided above the mist momentarily, then descended into the jungle, out of sight.

The water temperature began to climb. Smaller bubbles gave way to larger ones. The water started to simmer.

Taras began to scream.

The pink-hued water began to boil.

As fast as they formed on Taras' body, blisters puffed, oozed and burst. A pungent scum spread across the surface of the water. Sinew separated from bone as Taras' body dismantled itself. What was left of the attorney fell apart and drifted down, forming a layer of human sediment on the bottom of the pool.

Taras Verenich, aka Taras Antipov, was no more.

Egan broke the connection. He stared in fascination at his hands. Dr. Merrick would have been proud. Integration had been a success. He looked down at Verenich' remains. "It's over, Doc," he said. "Rest in peace."

The view of the jungle valley was peaceful, serene. Egan walked to the bar cart and poured himself another Scotch.

The remote control for the satellite television in Taras' poolside bedroom lay on the bar cart. He turned it on.

Verenich had been watching KTLA News in Los Angeles. A reporter stood in front of the remains of the fallen Pyramid, commenting on the bizarre events that had taken place at the University. The anchor thanked her and moved on to the next story:

"Turning to local news, police are investigating a kidnapping of five of their own. After receiving what he stated as a credible tip from a protected source, retired Los Angeles Police Chief James Kenton requested the LAPD investigate an abandoned furniture factory located in Yorba Linda. The responding officers found several missing police vehicles inside the factory, in addition to a stolen van. But here is where the story takes a bizarre turn. Found within a locked room in the factory were the missing police officers, as well as several teenagers being held in their custody. Yorba Linda P.D. would not offer an explanation as to how the officers ended up locked in the room. Chief Kenton further advised that a knife, found in the factory, has been connected to a series of brutal murders dating back five years. A media blackout on the case has been ordered pending further investigation."

Egan smiled. Kevin and Lauren were safe. Eventually, the truth about Colin Thackery would also come out.

The news anchor continued his report:

"In further news, a woman was found shot to death, execution-style, in a parking garage at Los Angeles International Airport. LAPD homicide is investigating. The victim's name is being withheld. A downtown Los Angeles law office was the scene of a multiple homicide this morning. Police are investigating an

apparent mass murder that took the lives of thirteen staff members. The principal of the firm, immigration attorney Taras Verenich, is being sought for questioning. Authorities are quick to point out that Mr. Verenich is not considered to be a suspect at this time but is rather a person of interest in the case. Anyone with information on the whereabouts of Taras Verenich is urged to call local police or Crime Stoppers."

Egan switched off the television and walked into the bedroom. He opened Taras' closet, pulled a number of items from their hangers and threw them onto the bed, along with a backpack he found in the corner. Although Taras was slightly heavier than Egan, the two men were about the same height and physical build. The fit of the clothes was adequate, as too was a pair of hiking boots. Egan stuffed the clothes into the knapsack and threw it over his shoulder. He stared at the SIG P226 pistol, silencer and clip he had tossed on top of his old clothes. He would have no further use for the weapon.

Egan searched the room. Behind the mirror, he found Taras' wall safe, pulled the door cleanly off its hinges, removed several stacks of bills, and stuffed the money into the knapsack. On the shelf in the safe he placed the gun, silencer, spare ammo clip and the spent casings he had retrieved from the bedroom of the Rosenfeld assignment.

He walked into the kitchen, rummaged through the pantry, filled the knapsack with enough provisions to last him a few days, and walked back outside to the pool deck.

The surface of the pool reflected a passing cloud.

Egan looked up. The heat of the sun felt good on his face.

The successful completion of his mission felt good on his soul.

He thought of Merrick's last words to him: *start over.*

That had now become necessary. A DARPA tactical team was already being assembled. They would come looking for him. Of that he was certain. Perhaps one day they would find him. In the meantime, his training had taught him how to avoid capture and stay off the radar. He was now better equipped to do that than any other man on the planet.

The jungle seemed like a good place to disappear.

63

MARISSA DeSOLA POURED a thin glaze of sweet Thai sauce over four perfectly prepared salmon steaks, plated the fish with generous servings of fresh steamed vegetables, and carried the meals into the dining room.

"Thank you," Jordan said. She turned to Emma and Aiden. Her children were seated beside her on opposite sides of the table. "Hey, you two. Manners."

The children answered. "Thank you, Marissa."

"Better," Jordan said.

Marissa smiled. To Jordan, she said, "Wine?"

"Sure," Jordan said. "It's been a crazy day."

"In that case, I'll bring the bottle," Marissa said.

Jordan laughed.

Marissa returned to the kitchen, opened the wine cooler, selected a Cakebread Cellars Chardonnay Reserve, and poured two glasses.

The front gate intercom buzzed.

Marissa pressed the speaker button. "Hello?"

"I'm looking for an FBI agent by the name of Jordan

Quest," the visitor said. "She's about five-foot-five and pretty handy with a nine-millimeter. Anybody there fit that description?"

Jordan recognized Chris' voice over the intercom and called out to Marissa. "Ask him if he's got a warrant."

Chris heard Jordan's voice and answered. "Hilarious," he replied. "Don't make come back here with a SWAT team."

"What do you think, kids?" Jordan said. "Should we let him in?"

Emma and Aiden called out. "Yes!"

Marissa laughed. "One second, Agent Hanover. I'll buzz you in."

Chris waited for the iron gates to part then drove up to the front entrance of Quest Manor and parked under the portico. Marissa met him at the door.

"So nice to see you again, Agent Hanover."

Chris gave Jordan's housekeeper a hug. "You too, Marissa," he said. "And enough with the 'Agent Hanover'. It's Chris."

Marissa laughed. "Okay, Chris. Come on in."

Chris smiled. "So where are the little hellions?"

Marissa teased him with a stern look. "The *children* were just sitting down to dinner."

"And their mom?"

Marissa helped Chris off with his jacket and hung it in the hall closet. "In the dining room. Care to join us?"

Chris shook his head. "Thanks, but no. I just wanted to drop by, say hi to the kids, and have a quick chat with J."

Jordan walked around the corner into the vestibule. Emma and Aiden rushed past her. "Chris!" they cried.

Chris dropped to his knees. The children launched themselves into his arms. "Hey, monsters!"

Emma threw her arms around his neck and squeezed.

"Whoa," Chris said. "That's a killer choke hold you've got there!"

Emma let up on the pressure. "I've been practicing what you taught us."

"Apparently I'm an excellent instructor," Chris replied.

"Yeah," Aiden said, "except I'm the one she practices on." He put his hands around his neck, fake strangling himself.

Chris stage-whispered in Emma's ear. "Are you keeping your brother in line?"

"Yes!" Emma replied.

"Good," Chris said. "Hey, I've got a surprise for you guys. You ready?"

"Yes!" the children answered.

"What are you up to?" Jordan asked.

"No good, as usual," Chris said. To the children he said, "You two need to cover your eyes, real tight. No peeking. Got it?"

"Okay!"

"I'll be right back. Don't move."

"We won't," Emma said. She parted her fingers.

Chris pointed his finger at her. "Cheater!" he teased. "Close 'em up!"

Jordan snuck up behind her children and covered their eyes. Emma squealed with delight. Aiden laughed.

Chris ran down the front steps to his car, opened the passenger door and lifted the precious package into his arms. As he walked up the steps, Marissa gasped. Chris put his finger to his lips. *Shh!*

Jordan smiled.

"You guys ready?"

"Ready!"

"Okay. Open 'em!"

In his arms, Chris held Lucy, the Golden Retriever pup

he and Jordan had found hiding alone and afraid in the back of the closet at the Rosenfeld murder scene. Lucy wore a bright red bow around her neck. She let out a nervous cry followed by a big yawn.

"A puppy!" the kids yelled. "Is she for us?"

Chris looked at Jordan. "You said the kids would love a dog. And this little lady needs a good home, especially after all she's been through. Forensics has cleared her. They also ran her chip, contacted her veterinarian, and explained the situation. There is a bit of paperwork that needs to be completed but he's fine with transferring her medical records over to you. If you want to adopt Lucy, she's all yours."

The Retriever sniffed the air, recognized Jordan's scent, and cried happily. She struggled to be free of Chris and dog-paddled into Jordan's arms.

"Of course, we'll take her," Jordan laughed. It was hard for her to get the words out between Lucy's onslaught of wet kisses.

"Can we play with her, Mom?" Emma said. "Yeah, Mom," Aiden added, "Can we?"

Jordan put Lucy down on the ground. The dog sat quietly in front of the children as they fussed over her.

"Try this," Chris said. He removed a tennis ball from his pants pocket and handed it to Aiden.

"Lucy, you wanna play?" Aiden said. "Come on girl, fetch!" He rolled the ball across the floor.

Too nervous to move, Lucy watched the yellow ball roll across the vestibule and down the main hall.

"It's okay, girl," Emma said. "You can play. Go get your ball!"

As if realizing that this was her new home, that every-thing was going to be all right, and that the Quest's were her new family, Lucy let out a playful *'ruff!'* She raced after the tennis ball as fast as her little legs would carry her with Emma and Aiden in hot pursuit.

"You realize those two aren't going to get any sleep tonight," Jordan said.

"Yeah," Chris said. "But did you see the look on their faces? Priceless."

Jordan hugged her partner. "You're the best, Hanover."

"Yes, I am."

Jordan laughed. "At least stay for a glass of wine."

Chris put his arm around her. "That depends. Are we're drinking the good stuff?"

Jordan smiled. "Is there any other kind?"

Marissa stopped and smiled as Lucy raced past. She walked back toward the dining room. "I'll keep dinner warm," she said.

JORDAN AND CHRIS sat in the oak-walled study. Lucy ran in, greeted them with an ecstatic *woof!*, scampered in circles at Jordan's feet, rolled on the Persian rug, barked again, then raced off in search of Emma and Aiden.

Jordan laughed. "Someone's making herself right at home."

"She's going to love it here," Chris replied. "And the place could benefit from a little extra protection when you're away."

Jordan pointed to the Crestron panel on the wall. "Have you seen my security system?" she teased. "This place is better protected than Fort Knox."

"I'm glad," Chris said. He looked around the room at the shelves of books. "Don't you ever get lonely here, Jordan? I mean, forty-thousand square feet is a hell of a lot of space for four people. Don't get me wrong, I like to stretch out as much as the next guy, but geez!"

"It is," Jordan agreed. "But it's all I have left to remember my parents by."

"I get that," Chris said. He swirled his wine, seemed nervous, very *un*-Chris like.

"You didn't just come by to drop off Lucy, did you?" Jordan asked.

He shook his head. "No."

"Is everything okay?"

Chris looked up. "That's what I wanted to ask you."

"I don't understand."

Chris walked to the fireplace and set his glass on the mantle. "I've never seen you that physically affected before."

"You mean at the Rosenfeld's? What happened to my hands?"

"Yeah."

Jordan stood. She walked across the room and put her hand on his. "I'm fine. Transference comes with the territory."

"Maybe, but it's scary as hell to watch you go through it."

"I'm sure it is."

"How often does it happen?"

"Once in a while."

"Can you control it?"

"No. It just happens."

"Did you experience it when you were a kid, too?"

Jordan shook her head. "No. The episodes with transference started after the plane crash."

Chris took her hand in his. "Then I guess as long as you're not in any physical danger when it occurs, I'll just have to get used to it. It's just that, like I said, I worry about you."

Jordan smiled. "I know you do."

"Then do me a favor?"

"What's that?"

"Let me *keep* worrying about you." He leaned in to kiss her.

Jordan pulled back. "I don't think I'm ready for this, Chris. Not yet anyway."

Embarrassed, Chris said. "I'm sorry. I didn't mean to press."

"Don't be," Jordan said. "Really, it's me. I'm just not there yet. Things are still too fresh in my mind."

"I understand," Chris said. "I'm not going anywhere."

"Good," Jordan said. "Because I wouldn't want you to." She gave him a kiss on the cheek as Emma and Aiden ran into the room. The kids were in a panic.

"Mom! Mom!"

"What's wrong?"

"It's Lucy!" Emma said. "She did her business all over the kitchen floor. And her poop stinks worse than Aiden's!"

JORDAN SAW Chris to the door.

"Well, it looks like my work here is done," Chris said. "Enjoy the new puppy."

Jordan laughed. "Goodnight. I'll see you tomorrow."

Chris walked down the steps and called out over his shoulder. "New York, here we come!"

She laughed. "It'll never be the same again."

Chris opened his car door and looked up at Jordan. "You're beautiful, you know that?"

Jordan smiled. "See you tomorrow."

IN THE LIBRARY, Jordan refilled her wine glass. She thought about her late husband Keith, and Chris, and how privileged she was to have had two such strong and caring men come into her life.

As she sank back in her favorite chair, she felt something pinch her leg. She stood, placed her hand inside her pocket and removed the plastic needle sheath she had picked up from the floor of the Pyramid at the location where Egan had disappeared. A trace amount of the pink solution shimmered inside.

The last time the liquid had touched her skin her mind had been catapulted... somewhere. She was still at a loss to explain the experience.

Curious, Jordan held the needle cover in her hand. Once again it began to vibrate. She gripped the object tighter.

Then... she *traveled*.

———

SHE FOUND herself standing in the middle of a jungle path, surrounded by lush greenery. In the distance she heard the roar of a waterfall. Overhead, a flock of the most beautiful tropical birds she had ever seen soared gracefully under a canopy of fine mist. A man walked on the trail ahead. Sensing her presence, he stopped and turned around.

Jordan gasped.

She recognized the man.

She hoped he had not recognized her.

Egan spoke to her. "I know you're out there, Agent," he said. "I can feel you. Listen to me carefully because I'm only going to say this once. Do yourself a favor. Leave me alone."

Ben Egan raised his hand. The flash of pink light that followed was blinding. Jordan looked away.

When at last she opened her eyes, a light rain had begun to fall in the jungle.

The trail ahead was quiet.

The air felt electrified.

Ben Egan was gone.

Jordan dropped the needle cover and broke the connection.

There was nothing veiled about the Commander's threat. His powers and abilities were unlike anything she had ever seen and far superior to hers. Pursuing him would be extremely dangerous.

On top of the fireplace sat a wooden Chinese puzzle box. Jordan removed it from the mantle, disassembled the toy, placed the plastic sheath containing the mysterious solution in its hidden compartment and fitted it back together. Only she knew the secret sequence by which the box could be opened and closed.

She needed time to think.

Commander Egan's secret would keep for the time being.

Jordan returned the puzzle box to the mantle and left the library.

She locked the door behind her.

ABOUT THE AUTHOR

Gary Winston Brown is a retired practitioner of natural medicine and the author of the Jordan Quest FBI thriller series and other works of fiction. His books feature strong, independent characters pitted against insurmountable odds who are not afraid to stand up for those in need of protection.

On the Author-Reader Relationship

Getting to know my readers and building strong relationships with them is one of the best parts of being a writer. I put a great deal of effort into creating my books. My goal with every novel I write is to make it better than the last, earn your five-star review, and make your reading experience the best it can be.

I'd love to know what you thought of this book (or boxset). What did you like about it? Who was your favorite character? Did I keep you wanting to know what was going to happen next? What do you want to see in an upcoming novel?

Please subscribe to my monthly newsletter. I'll send you the series prequel, *Jordan Quest*, for free as a thank you. Be sure to follow me on Amazon for updates on forthcoming books and new releases.

Follow me on Amazon

Please Post a Review

May I ask for your honest opinion. Did you like this book?

Reviews are the lifeblood to my work as a novelist. They mean the world to me. Long and fancy isn't necessary. What matters is your honest opinion. Did you enjoy this book? Did I deliver a good story to you? Rate it five stars and say a few words about what you most enjoyed about it. Or choose another rating. Your feedback is what matters. It's what makes me a better writer. And the better I can get at writing my books the better the reading experience I'll be able to provide to you.

Why your review is so important

I am a relatively new writer. I don't have a huge marketing machine or advertising department behind me like mainstream authors do to help build a buzz around my books and get them out in front of millions of readers.

But I do have *you*.

I am very grateful to have a growing following of loyal, committed readers who take the time to let me know what they think of my books. If you liked this book (or boxset) I would be extremely grateful if you would take a few seconds to post a review. It can be as long or short as you like. All reviews are appreciated and helpful to me.

Thank you!

Gary

ALSO BY GARY WINSTON BROWN

The Jordan Quest Thriller Series (in order):

Intruders

The Sin Keeper

Mr. Grimm

Nine Lives

Live To Tell

Jordan's next adventure is coming soon!

Follow me on Amazon for the latest updates on new releases.

Coming in 2021:

The Matt Gamble thriller series

(vigilante justice, organized/international crime, assassination, spies, political).

The Vanishing (stand-alone thriller)

Made in the USA
Monee, IL
20 December 2024